pleasant COMPANY

A Novel by Mark Louis Mitchell

"Mack The Knife" English lyrics by Marc Blitzstein, used by permission
from ALBERT PUBLISHING CO., INC.

ISBN 978-1434879523

PLEASANT COMPANY

"The whip for the horse,

the bridle for the ass,

and the rod for the backs of fools."

--Proverbs 26

At The Top of His Game

Heat bore down on the graveled asphalt of the Club lot and the asphalt returned the heat in shimmering waves and a dust devil which rose from a mound of dirt near two large dumpsters. At the north end of the lot an agitated scrub jay left a line of eucalyptus to circle the swirling devil; when the cloud exhausted itself the jay targeted a calico tabby hunkered by the fender of a white Rolls Royce. He flew by twice squawking but the cat made no move; finally the bird backed up its challenge with a screeching, wing-flapping attack that found success, the tabby retreated to the cover of the Rolls undercarriage and the jay flew away.

The calico cat emerged moments later from beneath the wheel well of a red Porsche a few cars down the line. He poked his head out cautiously, and satisfied that the noisy jay had left, stepped out into the shade of the Porsche and sat down. He was a large, well-fed cat and the Club cooks had adopted him, hence there was no need to bother with catching and killing birds. He ate what bankers ate, dined with attorneys, supped with doctors. There wasn't much to do except sit quietly in a spot of shade and twitch his tail, for he was a cat and quite grateful of it.

A collective cry rose up from the tennis courts east of the parking lot that was punctuated by a tennis ball that bounced by the cat and away. Inside the stadium a score of spectators seated in the upper rows looked over the hedges separating the courts from the lot and watched the errant shot bounce and roll towards obscurity. They sighed and shifted and cursed, and the two players on the court left their positions and headed for the sidelines, to rest and gather strength for the final set of the Memorial Day Tennis Tournament.

It was oppressively hot. Intermittent breezes drifting over the nearby Arroyo rustled through the eucalyptus and died; the loose confederacy of spectators seated in the bleachers glanced wistfully towards the trees, which had so selfishly frolicked in the wind and consumed it. The fans perspired and squirmed and snapped their fingers at a handful of waiters running orders to the bar, and when they were bored they cursed. Cursed the Club and its lack of shaded bleachers, cursed the umpire in his chair, cursed the harried waiters, cursed the young players on the court. They faulted those who were eliminated in the early rounds for leaving them with two unpopular boys, one of whom would unfortunately claim the Tournament crown, and those who could no longer stand this thought gave up and left.

Match play began early in the day, with four contenders. These were players who, having battled it out in the most wretched of elimination rounds earlier in the week, found themselves alive and kicking in the Semi-Finals of the Arroyo Tennis and Country Club's annual Memorial Day Tournament. Two hundred fans filled the stands in the early morning to cheer their champions; by one o'clock p.m. only a hundred remained and now, at three-forty five, there were but thirty or so. Things were far less polite now, as these die-hards got drunk and vocal. Faced with another hour's worth of match play in the scorching afternoon sun they grew irritable and tossed nasty comments towards whomever and whatever displeased them. There was no shortage of targets.

At the moment it was the Umpire who incurred their wrath. Unfamiliar to the Club and its players, he was a sub brought in at the request of the Federation President after the Arroyo's regular umpire suffered a heart attack and died while vacationing in Palm Springs. Throughout the day he was the object of much scorn and derision and now was wary of any tough judgment; each ruling served only to provoke the spectators whose mutterings made him uneasy.

In the first match of the morning an older man was eliminated in sets of 6-0, 6-0... a blanket, shameful skunk. The vanquished man's bile rose in the Clubhouse bar; he returned to the courts and hissed to the crowd that the Tournament was rigged and the Umpire a fop, until finally his own churlish resentment exhausted itself. Truth being a variable the crowd picked up his banter and had a splendid time booing, yelling encouragement and insults to the players, and getting smashed. It was all in good fun which annoyed the man who'd started the trouble; had he stayed and not slunk off before the final match began he'd have witnessed the general regression of tennis etiquette and wallowed in the surliness.

The match in progress when the disorder began featured the returning Club champion, a seventeen-year-old lefty with a calculated style of play that dismantled his opponent's offense. The kid drummed the power out of rocket serves, chopped down volleys, and kept his opponent, a swift young lawyer, off balance and clumsy. Reducing the lawyer to a doormat in straight sets, the kid flipped off the crowd when the boos began. The introductions at the start of the Finals went unheard as the fans hooted while the two players were presented, one being Tory Lewis, the lefty who'd just won, and the other a twenty year old guest player named Peter Albright. Ringers were out of favor this day, the Umpire noted, though the fans didn't much like Lewis either.

The Umpire marveled at their quality of the play during the first sets for both young men played with a vengeance. Their knees and elbows bled from diving across the hard court and they were drenched in sweat. Tory Lewis changed his tactics from calculated surgeon to frenzied killer. Peter Albright played a successful game of baseline return and would not be drawn to the net; the second set he tried a variety of shots that failed him and he won only four of the ten games.

Though they were both quality athletes neither was the epitome of sportsmanship; they pointed derisively at each other after unforced errors and both complained about the other's style of play. The Umpire ruled against each impartially and the match went on, at the urgings of the crowd and one fat man in particular who stood up and yelled "Hurry this damn thing up!"

Seated courtside with a wet towel draped over his head, Tory Lewis scanned the crowd for the voice that had yelled to the umpire. It was the same voice that had taunted him during important points and it was only a matter of identification to mark the loudmouth for revenge, a brick through his windshield or a spree on his tab. He turned away from the boorish crowd and glanced over to the lot to see if the cat was still there, but he was not.

The Umpire called "time" and Tory reluctantly turned back to the court to focus through the glaring sun at his opponent, seated in a similar folding chair a few yards down the line. A cluster of sport bags surrounded the boy, the grips of numerous racquets jutting from them like punjie sticks. Peter Albright was groping through the bags trying to select a suitable weapon, and several times settled on a particular grip only to change his mind and move on to another. At last he pulled one from his quiver and after beating the strings against the palm of his hand, seemed satisfied.

"What a jerk," Tory sighed. He dropped the towel from his head and fumbled through his own bag for a fresh pair of wristbands. Finding a dry pair he pulled them on, picked up his racquet, and moved out to the baseline.

The fans began to murmur. Tory heard two women criticize his serving and he scratched his armpit at them. "Disgusting," he heard one of them say. "Come on Tory!" someone shouted, and another echoed the cheer. Tory waved his racquet in acknowledgement and the noisy fat man hollered "Serve the ball goddammit!" This time Tory saw him.

"Shut up fatty!" He leveled his racquet at the man. "You'd probably die of a coronary if you were out here!" The man flushed and glowered and rose halfway out of his seat until his embarrassed wife pulled him down. "First service!" demanded the Umpire.

Across the court Peter Albright crouched and swayed rhythmically. Tory put his first serve dead in the box and Peter Albright slashed it back to the baseline, where Tory picked it up with a slice backhand and sent it into the net. "Love fifteen," the Umpire announced.

Tory aced Peter Albright the next two serves with dazzling accuracy that placed the ball in the dead zone, at the edge of the alleys. Albright picked up Tory's next service and made a rare chip and charge offensive, but Tory forced him back with a lazy lob then volleyed Albright's return out of the air like a dead fly. Albright was visibly upset and fumbled his way through the next point, eventually losing it and the game after Tory rattled him with five forced backhand returns.

The next two games each player held serve. Peter Albright produced a new shot, a straight two-handed forehand that effectively controlled Tory's topspin, and Tory countered in the third game by repeatedly drop-shotting Albright and forcing him to come to the net, where they would trade insults as Tory smacked balls hard cross-court out of Albright's reach. The fans loved it, tossing cupfuls of ice onto the court, leaving the frustrated Umpire pleading for order. Order was not to be found however, and when Peter Albright served the fourth game each serve was called "Out!" by the fans, whether or not it was. The fifth game was similarly umpired from the gallery and the match seemed doomed but the intervention of the bartender (who threatened to cut off their drink supply) quieted the crowd. The players changed over without further incident and started the sixth game.

To the crowd's credit their scorn galvanized the players and the first point of this game took half a minute and involved some spectacular shots. When Tory Lewis finally won it on an overhead smash he received bona-fide applause and took it as his anointment. Albright arrested this when he stopped mid-toss, called a time-out, and headed for the sidelines leaving Tory waiting at the baseline with his hands on his hips. After Albright switched racquets once more then skipped back to his side Tory decided he'd had enough and headed for the Umpire's chair.

"This is the third time that jackass has changed racquets," he said. The Umpire looked down at him and pushed the droopy brim of his hat away but said nothing. Tory waited and the man finally shrugged "what can I do?!"

"Well look," Tory continued, "he didn't break any strings, so this is obviously a ploy of some kind to take away my momentum...there's got to be a rule against this kind of thing."

"There isn't, Mr. Lewis."

"Sure there is," Tory urged. "How 'bout rule twenty-one?"

"That doesn't apply here."

"Sure it does. He's deliberately hindering my victory."

The Umpire, who was tired, sweaty, sunburned, and frustrated with the collapse of civilized sport this day, rapped his pen against the splintery desktop and jabbed his finger at Tory. "Look here Lewis, you're in danger of default if you don't proceed with match play! Now get on out there!"

The whistles and jeers that erupted from the gallery deflated and humiliated the Umpire. He stared down at his score sheet and let the insults

of the rabble fall on his back. He had no recourse, no reprimand for them...
they were drunk and mean and his was a thankless task to try and keep these
last games playing and submit a winner to the Club, after which he could
collect his pay and leave the Arroyo forever. As he prepared to serve the
young player once more with the threat of disqualification Tory Lewis looked
over to the stands then turned away and headed back to his baseline to wait
for Albright's serve. The crowd quieted.

They had expected to see a penalty, an ejection, for it was routine that
Tory Lewis' approaches to the chair yielded some kind of scene. Normally
Tory would have indulged them, but he did not know this umpire and his
calls, unlike those of his recently deceased predecessor, were unprejudiced.
The umpire had done his best to keep order in spite of the crowd and was
undeserving of the abuse they heaped on him. At the start of the day Tory
had been full of pessimism; he was certain the chair had been chosen by
the Club brass for his ability to penalize at whim. When he shut the lawyer
out without incurring a single unfair call his suspicions waned though he
wondered whether this judge wasn't smart enough to trump up some penalty,
or if he was just biding his time. At the end of his first set of the finals he felt
even more encouraged and played Albright to win. So, at the moment the
crowd picked up their jeering, Tory decided to let the matter go and finish up
Albright; hopefully there would be no more racquets exchanged and he could
return as Arroyo's champion.

Having acquiesced, Tory waited for Albright to resume the game.
"Ready?!" Albright called.

"Serve!"

Albright did, a curving rocket that glanced off the line and thundered
back into the windscreen. Tory never saw it and looked expectantly to the
Chair, who was silent.

He crossed to the deuce half of the court and adjusted his grip. Albright
came down on the ball hard, serving it near the center line and Tory picked it
up with a decent forehand but Albright returned with a low groundstroke that
Tory came in on awkwardly. His shot flopped and died outside the line.

"Thirty-fifteen," proclaimed the Umpire.

"Thirty-fifteen," echoed Peter Albright.

The next two points were all Albright, with Tory slashing and twisting to intercept the short balls that flounced weakly over the net, then running back madly to return the high lobs that followed. Albright had switched tactics and was hitting light, well placed touch shots to keep his opponent running. Tory countered with as much topspin as he could but his transition game was slowed; he had played a match before this one and was tiring in the heat. Albright knew this and thusly mixed his repertoire to keep Tory running.

Albright was ecstatic about winning the sixth game and pumped his fist when Tory's miss-hit went long and out. Tory had stumbled and fallen after hitting the ball and lay on his side on the hot surface, hating Albright's celebration and his conquer-with-weakness game. As he picked himself up Peter Albright rapped the head of his racquet smartly against the baseline and waved him up. "Come on! Hurry up!"

Tory looked at the Umpire. The Umpire looked back. Tory shook his head in disbelief and gathered up the two balls that were bounced to him. He stood at the service line trying to control his anger. The crowd booed the delay and the boo's made him angrier still. He glared at them and when they quieted he tightened his grip, stared at the ground, and concentrated.

Tossing the ball high in the air he came down on it with a perfect smash. How Albright picked it up Tory could never begin to figure; the serve has so much spin it caromed wildly when it bounced, but Albright's return was a good one, a hard shot to Tory's backhand. Tory chopped it back, moved center court, and prepared to volley. He killed the return with a little wrist roll; the ball dropped flatly on the other side of the net as Peter ran up to it, too late. Tory grinned and rested his racquet head atop the net.

"All those racquets but no ability."

"Go to hell," Albright snapped.

"Hurry up!" someone from the stands chided, mimicking Albright's earlier exhortation perfectly. "Eat shit!" Peter screamed, whirling around and coming face-to-horde with the jeering Arroyo tennis fans. Tory snickered at Peter's fluster and the fans' enthusiasm for mockery, which was building to a catcalling crescendo.

"See, even they think you're a weenie."

Albright whirled around to face him. His face was contorted into a knot. "Fuck you Lewis. I'm wiping you out."

Tory stiffened and leaned closer. "What was that?!"

"Fuck you!"

Leaping over the net Tory punched Albright with a hard left hook; Albright staggered backwards and dropped his racquet and Tory snatched it up and flung it over the stands into the parking lot where it clattered and slid under a cream Mercedes. The Chair Umpire slid down from his perch and Club officials appeared from nowhere and ran to separate the two players, but not before Tory hammered Peter Albright with two more lefts, the second of which broke Albright's nose and sent blood cascading down his face. In the midst of the melee Tory heard the Umpire shout "Match canceled!" and the jubilant celebration of the spectators in the stands.

2

Justice

A regiment of ants marched back and forth across the concrete floor in front of his locker, and Tory Lewis watched them for a while until he tired of their diligence and drooled spit on them. The ants scattered frantically under each barrage, and a few unlucky insects caught in the target zone wriggled helplessly in the muck. Their lines quickly regrouped however, and Tory's mouth dried up before the ants were seriously inconvenienced.

Deep in the locker room a steel door yawned on its hinges. Tory quickly pulled off his sweat-soaked shirt before the footsteps found him.

"They want you in the Chairman's office Lewis."

Tory looked up at the man, some Club official he didn't know. "Yeah? What for?"

"You know what for. Come on."

"Well alright. But you're gonna have to wait. I haven't showered yet. I'm still in my tennis clothes. Can't go to see the Chairman in tennis clothes."

The official laughed sharply and scratched his chin. "I'm sure they'll bend the rules for you this time. Let's go."

Tory followed the man, wriggling into his warm-up jacket and cursing silently. By the time he had crossed the foyer, climbed the stairs, and arrived at the Chairman's office in the administrative section he had received no fewer than twelve dirty looks from passing members.

"Wait here!" the man growled when they reached the Chairman's reception area. Tory sank into a very nice blue and white couch and the man disappeared behind the large oak doors of the main office. The only other person in the reception area was the Chairman's secretary, a skinny humorless lady prone to flower print frocks and beehive hairdos, who was busy transcribing notes from a Dictaphone.

A clock ticked. The keyboard clicked. The Dictaphone whirred. A car drove by outside. Tory shifted uncomfortably and stared at the secretary, who had not looked up from her work to acknowledge either him or the Club official. Finally he stood up and went over to her desk.

"What would you do if I put my penis in your ear?"

The secretary whirled around and yanked off her headphones. "What?!"

"I asked whether you'd care if I had a piece of candy."

"Help yourself." She went back to her computer and Tory grinned and shook a Tootsie Roll from a glass jar perched atop a bookcase. He took his time unwrapping the candy, humming "The Stripper" as he did so. He had just returned to the couch when the large oak doors clicked open and the official reappeared. "Get in here," he said.

Tory stepped carefully around the man into the Chairman's dark, oak paneled office. A single window looked out on the upper level parking lot and the walls were dotted with old photographs charting the Club's history: a new building under construction in '59, four grinning men clutching Trophy cups from the 1979 Club Golf Tournament, tuxedoed men with their beautiful wives gathered 'round the tree at a Christmas party...

Seated in three leather clawfoot chairs were the Umpire and the two Club officials who'd broken up the fight; the Chairman, a thin bald man in a brown sport coat, sat behind a massive mahogany desk. No one was smiling and the Umpire looked very embarrassed. Tory eased himself slowly into an empty chair and the official who'd been his escort for the journey from the locker room went behind the Chairman and stood there.

"Well you're probably all wondering why I called you here," Tory began, but the escort-official barked "Shut up!"

The Chairman glowered and tapped a gold pen against his desk blotter. "Nice going."

The room sat mired in anger. Tory sighed and scratched his knee.

"Lewis, do you remember the last time you disrupted a match…? Remember the warnings you were issued?"

"No, I can't seem to recall. Maybe you'd better refresh my memory."

"You little fuck," the escort-official muttered.

The Chairman continued. "It was last fall, during the Halloween Doubles. I warned you that if you ever insulted anyone, flipped off anyone, argued with the umpire, threw your racquet…that I'd bust you. Well you were warned then, and today you've accomplished all those things in the most repulsive, unsportsmanlike exhibition of bad tennis behavior ever shown here." He leaned forward over his desktop. "Just what the hell did you think you were doing, hitting an opponent, a guest, during the middle of a Championship match?! You've put us smack in the middle of a lawsuit with your little tantrum! What kind of game do you think tennis is, anyway?!"

"You're a goddamn disgrace!" the escort-official shouted.

"Dickhead."

"What did you say?!" the man demanded, stepping out from behind the Chairman. "Look Chuck, we don't need another fight," the Chairman said firmly. Chuck reluctantly returned to his guard.

Tory stood up. "I don't have to take any more of this shit."

"Sit down!" the Chairman roared.

One of the Club officials seated nearby leaned over and gently pushed Tory back into his chair. Tory glared at him but complied.

"None of you were out there. Why don't you ask him how the whole thing started." He indicated the Umpire with a nod. "Too bad my grandfather wasn't there today. He'd be appalled at the people you're letting in here now. Fools. Drunks. Imbeciles. " He stared at Chuck.

"They didn't start the fight Tory," the Chairman said calmly. "You did. We know what happened out there and we regret it, but you should have kept your head. That's the trouble with you Lewis'. You can't keep your heads."

"Oh my folks would love to hear that, why don't you tell them that the next time you go begging for money for a new building."

"I wasn't referring to your parents," the Chairman said quickly. "I was referring to your siblings...Janelle burning down those cabanas, your brother Tim stealing from the liquor locker..."

"That was Mike, not Tim. And Janelle didn't 'burn down' the cabanas, that was an accident."

"...and there have been many other incidents at Cotillions, Christmas parties, swim meets, and tennis tournaments where the pleasures of other members have been ruined by the inconsiderate actions of the Lewis clan." The Chairman paused.

Tory glanced around the room. "C'mon guys, don't be shy, join in!"

"You're really asking for it Lewis!" Chuck seethed. Tory ignored him and pushed his hair back away from his forehead. "I think your kangaroo court is forgetting that I'm the reigning Club champion and that my family owns two thirds of this joint. We've done a lot of good around here, especially in sports."

"That's not the point," one of the officials said.

"Well get to it!"

There was an exchange of hesitation between the officials. The Chairman clasped his hands together across his desk and took a breath. "Tory Lewis you are suspended from Arroyo club tennis for the rest of the year, you are restricted in using the Club facilities. You can neither play tournaments here nor play under the Club affiliation, you can't use any of the lower courts, swim in the pool, charge food or drinks. An administrative panel will convene to review your case and make a decision whether or not to revoke your membership."

Time stood still in the office with the participants static in their chairs until the Chairman broke the spell by pulling his hands from the desk and placing them in his lap. "Your parents, of course, will be notified of today's incident."

Tory, who for his part had listened to his sentence with his head cocked slightly and his arms folded across his chest, suddenly unfolded them, grasped the arms of his chair, and stood up. "Is that all?"

The Chairman nodded.

There was silence in the room again. Outside the faint whir of the Dictaphone resumed. "Okay…" He took a step towards the door, stopped, and turned around to face the Umpire. "You were very fair today," he said.

The Umpire watched the boy go and felt worse. None of the Club officials said anything and neither did they move, so he stayed seated too. Chuck stood motionless behind the Chairman with his arms folded across his chest, and the Chairman rubbed his eyes and fiddled with a mechanical calendar shaped like a coin. After an eternity the Umpire glanced uncomfortably around the room, cleared his throat, and rose out of his chair. "Goodbye," he said, shaking the hand of each man seated near him, then the Chairman's. He did not shake Chuck's and neither did Chuck offer to shake his, but halfway out the door the Umpire stopped and turned to look at the men in the room. "You know, he's an excellent player."

None of the officials responded, but instead became interested in bits of stray lint in the carpet and flyspecks on the window. The Chairman finally tore his gaze from the mechanical coin and nodded to the Umpire. "Yes, we know."

"He's probably the best Junior player I've ever seen…other than a professional, I mean…" Encouraged, he looked at them but there was no reaction. "Well, goodbye."

"Goodbye," the Chairman offered. "Thank you for your help today."

The Umpire nodded his acceptance and shut the door behind him. He stood wearily in the reception area, feeling disoriented and disappointed. Disappointed he had not diffused the tensions on the court, disappointed the members had acted with such violent enthusiasm in the stands, disappointed he had not downplayed the whole incident when the officials had questioned him. "What kind of place is this?" he whispered to himself.

"What was that?" whined the secretary, who had turned and pulled her headphones off her ears.

"Oh nothing," said the Umpire.

"I have a check for you sir," the secretary sniffed, handing him an envelope across her desk. The Umpire took it, said "thank you" and headed out into the Club halls for the bar.

<u>3</u>

Champions Lost

During Tory's journey from the Chairman's office back to the locker room his perceptions of time and space were altered and a strange calm, a sense of total relief, settled on him after he emerged from the Chairman's wood paneled chambers. Instead of humiliation he felt victory; as he journeyed to the Hall of Champions (as the old locker room was named) he noticed things about he Club that he'd never noticed before: the grandeur of the brass staircase banister, ornate and gleaming as it held silent guard over its marble steps, the carved beam ceilings frescoed with paintings of unspoiled California landscapes, filigreed crown moldings and wainscotings, and the deep plush of carpets. Things that he and likely the entire body of membership took for granted, assimilating the splendor into common, everyday habitat.

Then the path took a different perspective, and in the trip to the Hall of Champions, deep and remote in the bowels of the Club, he was purged of Peter Albright and the rigors of the Tournament, and what had been his obsession seemed miles away. He followed the labyrinth of hallways and arrived at the locker room. Grasping the iron handle he yanked the huge steel door open, exposing the dark maw of the cavernous room. Still in the grip of this strange metaphysical awakening he paused and listened to the quiet.

The Hall of Champions, once the epicenter of man's athletic prowess at the Arroyo Tennis and Country Club, now was a memory. Abandoned by the other members for luxurious new locker rooms outfitted with massage tables, saunas and Jacuzzis, the Hall was left to molder silently, a mildewed dungeon riddled with crawling insects and peeling paint that draped overhead in serrated strips. Thick concrete floors and walls insulated the interior from outside noise and invasions of radical temperature; it was always cool and very quiet save the echo of dripping water from corroding pipes that drifted through, pacing the decay.

Tory was the Hall's sole tenant. His locker stood in a bank of rusted cubicles set against the west wall, where photos of Club champions long dead or grown old yellowed in their frames. His own picture, a self-tribute awarded after he'd won the previous summer's Fourth of July Tournament, hung nearby. The traditions of honoring Club champions had ceased three years before, after construction of the new sports facility was complete and the other men moved their gear into the new locker room. Tory always liked the Hall, with its history and character, and he was just starting to come into his own as a player when construction began on the new building. His reputation was established by then and as he turned fourteen, the age recognized by the Club as mature and worthy of incorporation in the roster as a Junior Member, they told him he would not be joining the others in the new facility but rather occupying a locker in the old Hall. He accepted his exile happily, though it was obvious the Club intended to demean him with the gesture. The secretary had conferred with the Sports Director then returned from her whispered meeting, handed him his locker number and remarked with a smirk that should the lock be frozen with rust, he could return and she's assign him one that worked. Tory had no intention of returning and settled into his own space quite content to be away from the other members.

Now he sat once more before his cubicle, relaxed and enjoying his odd euphoria. The ants were still hard at work and he traced their origins to one of the two potted palms that stood guard on either side of his eminent locker. It was a beautiful thing, this locker. Tory had wire-brushed the rust from its steel, oiled the hinges and dial and painted it a brilliant purple-yellow in tiger stripes. The naked bulbs above he'd covered with colorful Chinese lanterns that cast orange and blue light in surreal nimbus. Spiders crept in through small frosted windows to spin webs and Tory left them alone to thrive on the other invading insects. Their gossamer webbing clung to door jams and portals, contributing a haunting mystery to the decorating scheme, and as he cleaned out his locker Tory worried if someone wouldn't come in to clean up the Hall while he was gone, and kill all the spiders.

He packed his Adidas bag to bursting. He checked the strings of an old

Wilson racquet and noticed a crack in the frame; it was a practice racquet and so battle scarred one could hardly read the manufacturer's logo, but it had served Tory's brother Mike throughout his last Club seasons and after Tory retrieved it from Mike's trash can, his own. The cracked head sealed the fate of the old Wilson and it would not escape the finality of the garbage pail again.

A couple of short rolls of head tape joined the racquet. A pair of socks with fading elastic was similarly sentenced followed by three cans of dead balls, a copy of Sports Illustrated featuring Roger Federer, a scratched CD of Wagner that played "The Ride of the Valkries" until it wouldn't, the April MAXIM and an empty Gatorade bottle. He found a roach under a LaCoste shirt and smoked it, then dragged the palm trees into the showers, setting each under a slow drip. The entire picture wall called to him and Tory remembered, digging back into his packed bag for a Sharpie. He scribbled "R.I.P" under the photo of the recently deceased 1963 swimming champ, slung his bag over his shoulder and left the hall. He did not know when he would be back.

****

In the dim recesses of the bar the beleaguered Chair Umpire of the Memorial Day Tennis Tournament Men's Finals ordered another draft and idly flipped open the cover of a stray matchbook to read the advertisement printed there. The bar was nearly deserted save two women golfers chatting over a sandwich at a corner table and the Umpire himself, who was on his third beer and his fifth anxiety attack. " Why didn't I control that crowd, Jesus, they were getting those kids all riled up…shit." He took another long swallow and shook his head. "I should have shut them up. I should have done something…"

"MAKE BIG MONEY IN TAXIDERMY!" the ad screamed. Then the print became too small and the umpire tossed the matchbook away, too depressed to consider the rewards of stuffing dead animals. "Man, I should have underplayed the whole fight to those bastards. I should have passed it off as just another couple of players blowing off steam. I shouldn't have let them interrogate me like that." He stared into his beer. "They wanted blood.

They were just like that crowd. They just wanted some blood."

It was late in the afternoon. Through the bar's plate glass window the Umpire could see a group of young children bouncing precariously on the high dive over the pool. They were laughing delightedly, oblivious to his misery, enjoying the prolonged daylight offered by the nearing summer solstice. The Umpire remembered a cocktail party he'd been invited to, over at his ex-wife's. He motioned to the bartender who drew away from a golf match playing on the small TV and rang up the Umpire's tab. The Umpire paid and left a few dollars for a tip and the bartender said "thankyousir," then glanced quickly away to the bar door to wave at a passing boy loaded down with a stack of tennis racquets and white Adidas bag.

"You know that kid very well?" the Umpire asked.

"Yeah." The bartender brushed an imaginary crumb from the bar. "He's a good kid."

"He's a heck of a tennis player."

The bartender nodded and looked down the bar at the small television. After a moment he said, somewhat defensively, "Lewis can whip everyone here. He got a free ride to play at USC next year, but I don't think he'll take it."

"Why not?"

The bartender shrugged. "Who knows?"

The Umpire nodded, thanked him again, and left the Club. When he got home he showered and put on a new white blazer and went over to his ex-wife's. He told the story of the match to a pretty young woman, and she felt sorry for him and when he left the party she left with him.

<u>4</u>

<u>A Tale of Bad Companions</u>

At nine-thirty a.m. on the Sunday of Memorial Day Weekend Tory Lewis surrendered to the persistence of his doorbell and rose from a groggy sleep. He stumbled from his bed, pulled on a pair of swimming trunks and staggered down the hall and the twenty-four stairs to the first floor, where he crossed the sunroom on a shortcut to the front hall and yanked open the front door.

Now Sunday is normally a placid day, unhurried and uneventful, a day when a person can enjoy twenty-four hours of unmolested leisure to recuperate from whatever violations the week has dealt. And Tory should have recognized the ill bodings of the caller's urgent ring and ignored it, but being barely conscious his faculties were dull and reasoning unsharp, for upon opening the door he knew he had made a mistake.

A young man leaned numbly against the doorjamb, his face swollen and purple. Dark glasses hid two undeniably black eyes, their injury betrayed by the purple rings cresting over the plastic rims, and there was a pronounced cut creeping across his chin. Several stitches jagged the length of the wound, significantly adding to the hideousness of his countenance. "Holy Jesus," Tory muttered, and tried to shut the door but the visitor was quicker and pushed powerfully to prevent its closure; a brief struggle ensued as Tory dug in and pushed back. "You must have the wrong house!" he shouted. "I didn't order any chopped liver!"

The mangled man gave a mighty shove, knocking Tory aside. He stepped over his fallen host and grunted, then started for the kitchen on stiff legs. Tory picked himself and rubbed the sleep from his eyes, following his torpid guest into the kitchen. "Who are you and why are you here? Why am I confronted with the very face of death at…" he peered at the oven clock

"…nine-thirty in the morning?!"

The young man ignored him and popped a Budweiser he'd taken from the refrigerator. He nodded expectantly; Tory shook his head. "No thanks, I don't drink with losers."

There was a delay while the man drained half the can. Then he leaned against the island and gasped "…but I won!"

"Oh no you didn't. You got K.O'ed in the fifth, or maybe the ref stopped the fight, the cut or something, but you didn't win."

The man said nothing but straightened painfully and pulled off his t-shirt. "See that there?" he demanded, pointing over his shoulder to a long, serrated red lash crossing the length of his back. "Motorcycle chain!"

"Get the rest of those Buds and I'll find the ice chest. I think I need to sit by the pool to hear this one." Tory started away but Pietro grabbed his arm. "Have you got Vicodan or something…? I'm in a lot of pain."

Tory scratched his head and considered. "I do, but I don't want you getting sloppy here…is your pain acute or dull?"

"Acute!"

"Hmm. I'll have to go look and see what the good doctor has in his medicine cabinet." He disappeared in the far reaches of the house. Pietro moaned and turned away from the kitchen island with some difficulty. He moaned again when he opened the fridge door and again when he pulled two six-packs from the shelf. He was scooping ice cubes into a plastic bowl, moaning between scoops, when Tory returned carrying the ice chest and a handful of amber pill bottles.

"Here," Pietro ordered, "have some consideration." He thrust the scoop into Tory's hand and snatched the prescription bottles from him. "Alright, fun stickers!"

"Just wait. I haven't prescribed anything yet…are you going to operate any heavy machinery today?"

"Nah, just the television remote. What's 'Doriden'?"

Tory looked away from the ice bin and squinted at the label. "I'm not sure but I gave some to Courtney Kempner's brother and he ended up in jail."

Pietro laughed and tossed the bottle on the counter. "No thanks, I remember that. I also remember the time you gave me those 'ludes and told me they were vitamin C…"

"They made you forget your cold, didn't they?"

"Yeah and I forgot all my Chemistry too and flunked the final. Luckily they let me graduate…" He waved a handful of blue pills in front of Tory's face. "What're these?"

"Take those."

"How many?"

"As many as you like, but I recommend three." Pietro took four, washing them down with the last of his beer and fishing a new can from the filled ice chest. Tory closed the lid and hustled the chest out the back door, Pietro following in step.

They settled into matching chaises beside the Lewis's expansive pool. Though it was early the sun was beginning another relentless day of heat and a thin brown belt of smog floated on the horizon. The Ventura freeway hummed below.

"Okay, so tell me when they started allowing chain whippings in the ring."

Pietro reached into the ice chest to scoop a pile of cubes into his shirt, which he fashioned into an ice bag and applied to his face. "I haven't fought in six months. They suspended me, remember?"

"Oh yeah, you put lead in your gloves or something."

"Didn't help. All it did was make my arms tired." There was a pause while Pietro reflected. Tory waited. Finally…

"Come on, tell me the story!"

"Oh yeah. See I was at Gus's last night, shooting pool and having a good time, not causing any trouble, when my old crony Jim Coulter comes in…"

"Is that the guy who robbed the liquor store?"

"No, just shutup and let me finish. Anyway, Jim's hammered and starts making all kinds of noise, singing and yelling, so they throw him out and someone tells me to drive him home, 'cause I'm his friend."

"Right," agreed Tory.

"So we go out and Jim's got this old tow truck, I don't know where he got it, and he climbs in, insisting on going up to the Orbit or some crazy place, only we don't go to the Orbit we go to the Bull and Jim gets in a fight after one beer so they toss us out and we decide to go tow the mayor's car or some other crazy shit, and en route we pass by the Thirty-Fiver.

"It was a scene. Some motorcycle club had come into town for a Memorial Day ride and taken over the place so Jim sez 'hey, let's go inside and get some crank,' so like a dumbass I go along and while I'm inside asking all these goddamn smelly bastards if they've got any speed I suddenly notice Jim's not around anymore..."

"Holy Jesus!"

"Damn right! And just as it's dawning on me that I'm solo there's this HUGE crashing noise like six diesel trains coming through the bar! Everyone races outside to see this tow truck, fool Jim at the wheel, roaring down Colorado Boulevard with four choppers chained to the hitch smashing and sparking and getting all torn to shit...!"

Here Pietro had to hold his sides to keep from laughing. He choked and winced and gasped and sat up painfully, laughing as he wrung the water from his shirt, soaked from the fast melting ice.

"So anyway...(more laughter)...all these assholes start running after Jim, right down the middle of Old Town, and people are screaming and every restaurant slams and locks their doors, and a bunch of these idiots jump on the bikes Jim didn't steal or knock down and roar after him.

"Well it took about two seconds for the cops to jump in...they were hovering around the Thirty Fiver and from where I stood it looked like they were enjoying Jim's little show. But I guess they had to do something, so two cruisers took off after the parade, busted Jim for his own good, and gave the bikers a bunch of shit." Pietro dug into the ice again and replenished his cold pack.

"And…?"

"What?"

"What happened to you?!"

Pietro grinned. "Well, I was watching this whole scene, laughing my ass off, and it suddenly occurs to me that these fuckers are quite angry with ol' Jim and being that I'm his friend and all, will probably have something to say to me about Jim's antisocial behavior. As I'm running away…"

"They caught you and kicked your ass! Ah, that's hilarious!" Tory doubled over laughing. Pietro shot him a dirty look.

"Yeah, well let's see it happen to you. Anyway…" he muttered, draining his can, "…that's the end of it."

"Wait a minute," Tory protested, "how'd you win?"

"I got away of course. What are you, stupid? Have you ever been whipped by a motorcycle chain? Those fuckers were going to kill me."

Tory kept laughing, and when he could laugh no more he gasped "that's the best story I've ever heard," and high-fived his friend.

It was not long before the pills caused Pietro to fall asleep and Tory lay in the sun ruminating on Pietro's tale. He snickered to himself at the vision of Jim Coulter, drunk and wild-eyed, behind the wheel of a tow truck with a phalanx of angry bikers chasing him. He glanced at Pietro; the boxer was trouble but he had not been around for a long time and Tory's life had moved along on an even keel. Now he was thrilled at Pietro's sudden re-emergence. Saturday signaled the end of Club tennis for him, the end of his affiliation and the end of playing by another's rules. He thought about the euphoria he'd felt in the locker room the day before and realized it was freedom; the comatose figure in the chaise was the herald of adventures to come. Summer looked promising.

Tory got out of his chair and wandered over to the edge of the yard. The drone of rushing cars from the freeway below smothered the gentle whisper of a light breeze and he shook his head at his fellow Pasadenans frantic in their efforts to escape the San Gabriel Valley. Only a small minority had opted to stay home and brave the heat and smog, and he was one of them by virtue of his two commitments: the Arroyo Tournament and his cousin Cecelia's debutante party.

The first had backfired; the Arroyo members did not share his loyalties and had suspended him. Tory played tennis for many reasons, and he enjoyed being the premier player at the prestigious club. But there was CIF still to come so he did not dwell on his lost championship, and though the scene had shifted it was not a terrible change. He still had his skills and recognition in the tennis community and there would be many invitations to play in tournaments elsewhere.

The second was a more complex commitment. In a surprising gesture of family loyalty, Cecelia Lewis had asked him to be her escort to the Pasadena Guild of Huntington Hospital Cotillion. And in an equally astonishing gesture of constancy, he had accepted.

Cecelia didn't really like Tory. They had grown up close friends but teenaged Tory was very different from pre-adolescent Tory. He was arrogant, he was reactive, he was dumb. He was family and irritating. But whatever antipathy she felt for Tory Cecelia really hated Pietro, partly because of his unbridled behavior, partly because he had a penchant for violence and had once beaten the daylights out of a boyfriend. In addition his appearance was startling; his hair was jet black except for a shock of blond in front that was totally natural, a characteristic that earned him the moniker "Skunk" in the ring. Whenever Pietro was around there was action, his mere presence provoked people. More often than not he was cut and stitched, bruised, or drunk. His reputation for sexual conquest both repulsed and intrigued girls, and Pietro worked it. Women liked him and often went home with him, then found themselves dumped like yesterday's coffee grounds. Then they cursed him and cried to their friends, and those girls listening so sympathetically would make a note to one day experience firsthand the legend.

Tory thought about Cecelia's party and decided he should not go alone. It was weird enough being her escort to the ball; he might not have accepted had her father not been in jail. Crisis should unite families, he knew, and once he got over the initial shock he agreed to participate, partly at the urgings of his grandfather, partly because he would get to go to a lot of parties and meet a lot of girls. But tonight Cecelia was the hostess and she might expect him to stay sober and civil, and to combat this he needed a wingman…he leaned over and nudged his friend. "Hey, want to go to a party tonight?" Pietro moaned and opened one eye. "Hmmph," he replied. "Right, Tory agreed, digging into the cooler for another beer and hurling the empty across the pool, where it bounced off the doghouse of Klaus, the Lewis's German shepherd. Klaus, dozing inside to escape the heat, bounded out.

"Woof woof woof woof! Woof Woof Woof! Woof Woof Woof Woof! the dog bellowed. "Klaus," Tory roared, "Achtung! Mach schnell!"

"Woof woof woof!" Klaus barked in answer, straining at the end of his chain. Pietro sat up and rubbed his head. "Christ that dog makes a racket."

"Go tell him to shut up, then. Tell him you've had a rough night and that he's really rude for waking you. He'll understand."

"I'm not sure what's worse, the dog's bark or his master's voice." Tory ignored him and went over to unchain Klaus from the dog house. The dog panted patiently in the heat while Tory liberated him, then galloped across the pool deck to the lawn where he rolled happily in the grass, sneezed, scratched, and suddenly leapt to attention with his ears perked up. "Look at Klaus—the phone's going to ring."

Inside the house the phone did indeed ring. Tory grinned and headed off to answer it. "Klaus knows!" Pietro called out. "Devil Dog knows all!" Tory laughed and trotted into the house and into the kitchen, grabbing the phone on its eighth ring.

"Hello! Tory? Tory, are you there?" Tory waited a moment then chirped "Who's calling please?".

"You ass, it's Cece."

"Cecelia! What a nice surprise."

"Is your cell phone on? I've left you a couple of messages. Anyway listen, are you coming tonight?" Tory told her yes and then dropped the phone, grabbing for it mid-flight, knocking over a three day old cup of coffee. "Damnit!" he yelled; when he recovered the handset Cecelia said "Jesus, what's going on over there anyway?"

"Nothing, I just dropped the phone."

"Well you certainly make a big production about it. Look Tory, my friend needs a ride tonight, can you pick her up on your way?"

"Maybe, is she hot?"

"Of course darling, she's coming to a beautiful person's party where only beautiful people are invited. She lives in San Marino, her name's Margo, Margo Vitesse. Maybe you know her, she goes to Poly."

Tory searched his memory for a face to match the name and came up empty. Cecelia moved on. "Anyway, she lives at –write this down— 1492 Orlando Road, that's north side, big English Tudor, giant lawn. See you at seven!"

"Ciao." Tory hung up and considered cleaning up the spilled coffee, then glanced around and considered cleaning up the whole house. It had fallen into disarray since his parents left. The kitchen was presentable but just outside the entrance a cluster of kegs lay stinking, carnage from a party weeks before. There were beer cans and fast food wrappers in every room; dust blanketed the bookshelves. He searched the cork board for the business card of a cleaning service, found it under a Westridge newsletter addressed to his sister (who hadn't lived at home for years) and made a note to have them come out during the week.

After wiping up the coffee he moved the kegs out to the back porch. When he returned to the pool he found Pietro engaged in getting Klaus drunk; he knocked the beer away and kicked his friend. "Don't do that, it gives him terrible headaches."

Pietro released the dog's jaw. "It gives me terrible headaches too but I still drink it." Tory patted Klaus and pushed him away from his chaise then settled back into it. The Times was lying between the chairs and he guessed Pietro had retrieved it from the front drive while he was talking to Cecelia; he pulled the sports page from the stack while Pietro settled into the comics.

"Oh Mary Worth, I want you…" Pietro groaned.

"Grannygrabber. You just like her 'cause she's Italian."

Pietro laughed. "Anything in the Sports page about dumbasses who beat up their opponents on the tennis court?"

"Nope. Let's check the city section to see if there's a story on idiot boxers who get thumped by bikers."

"Seriously, what was that all about?"

Tory shrugged. "This guy I was playing provoked me so I pounded on him."

"Uh huh. Well, that was dumb. It compromises your sport."

"Wow, and coming from such a model of virtue as yourself."

"Civility is not a requirement for fighters but you should respect the conduct of your game. From what I heard in the bars the whole Country Club went insane but you lost your focus when you should have just finished the match."

Tory half rose out of his chair, bristling; Pietro assumed he was reaching for a beer and politely offered him one, a fortuitous counteraction. Tory resumed his seat and sulked. "Easy for you to say."

"True enough. And I won't say anymore about it." And he didn't, his eyes closed and he relaxed into the chaise. Tory saw he was on the edge of sleep again. After awhile he felt drowsy himself and closed his eyes as well. He heard Klaus barking and the phone ringing inside but ignored it and soon drifted off.

In her hotel room at the Carlyle Bonnie Lewis shut her mobile and stuck it back in her purse. After a moment she lit a Virginia Slim and paced the floor, then picked up the hotel phone and called the front desk to let them know she was checking out; lastly she asked for a car to JFK and a porter for her bags.

<u>5</u>

<u>Ergo, Margo</u>

"Margo!"

"Oh no, it's my mother!"

"Ssshhh…maybe she'll go away. Don't giggle!"

"Mmmph. I can't help it!"

(Kissing)

"Margo!!"

"Oh no, there she is again!"

"She is loud."

"She is very loud!"

(Laughter from both)

"I must leave. She'll find us together…"

"No, don't…"

The handsome Italian boy slipped away and vanished; his gentle whisper replaced by her mother's thunderous call. "Margo! Margo wake up! The phone's for you!"

Stuffing the pillow into her ears would not have helped. Her mother's voice penetrated the thickest walls, drowned out chainsaws and leaf blowers, muffled cannonades. "Margo, Cece Lewis is on the phone!"

Surrendering, Margo dispelled the dream and woke to roll over and grasp clumsily for the phone. "Hello…?"

"Margo? Hi, it's Cece. Did I wake you up?"

"S' alright." She yawned. "What time is it?"

"It's nearly the afternoon! Did you stay up all night? Listen, if you still need a ride to the party I talked to my cousin a little while ago and he'll come and get you."

Margo blinked and tugged at a crop of bangs dangling in front of her left eye. "Hmmph. What?"

"My party. Do you still need a ride?"

There was a pause. Finally Margo drew into reality and realized that her present conversation had nothing at all to do with kissing boys on the Riviera. "Uh, oh hi Cece. Do I still need a ride? Uh…yeah, my car's still in the shop."

"Okay great. Tory'll pick you up at seven thirty. Bye!"

Click!

Still in the opiate of sleep Margo flopped back on her pillow and nodded off again, but her pleasure was interrupted by the rude "beepbeepbeep" emanating from the phone. She groped for the noise, found the disconnect button and gave up.

She lay on her back and remembered her amorous dream and the handsome boy, his olive skin, his blond hair, his alluring whisper, the way he kissed her neck…

"…pant pant pant pant pant pant pant pant…"

Someone was gasping outside her window.

"…pant pant pant pant pant pant pant pant…"

The respirations faded away. Margo sat up in bed and craned her neck to look through her window, down to her front yard. A young man was trotting exhaustedly around the perimeter of her lawn, his red hair matching his red face. His heavy breathing swelled and receded as he passed by under her bedroom window. "He looks like a tomato," Margo thought.

Hugh March was returning from running however many miles he ran every morning and was cooling down before coming back into Margo's house. He was a nut about running though his addiction was justified: he was one of the best high school milers in Southern California. He and Margo had been dating for nearly a year, but Hugh had been running for four. Margo knew what came first on Hugh's list.

She watched him warm down a minute longer before climbing out of bed and heading for the bathroom. "Yuck, I look like shit!" The puffy faced girl in the mirror did not disagree. Margo ran a hand through her tangled mane and pushed a sheave of black tresses in a mass atop her head. She let the pile loose and pulled on a strand, measuring its length. Thank God her mother was letting her cut it before the ball!

She turned on the shower, let the jets steam up the room, then eased into the spray. She let out an "aaaahhh" of pleasure and switched on the waterproof radio she'd gotten at Christmas. The garbled chatter of the morning DJ mixed in with the noisy churn of water and she dialed in another station and then stuck her head directly beneath the nozzle. In the midst of shampooing the hot water disappeared and a blast of cold made her yelp and leap away, it lasted only a few seconds and Margo guessed Hugh had come inside and turned on the shower downstairs in the guest quarters where he had spent the night. A new pop tune came on the radio and Margo rinsed away the lather and danced in the spray. Feeling happy, she finished her bath and toweled herself dry.

As she dressed in front of the mirror Hugh's hoarse laugh sounded from downstairs. She felt her nipples grow pert; Hugh's laugh always excited her...she touched them, feeling aroused and sexy.

It was the most exciting thing about Hugh, his laugh...when Margo had met him at a beach party the summer before it was his laugh that led her to lure him into one of the cabanas to make out wildly. He was not as sexy as his laugh but he was cute and full of energy and she loved him. She flopped back onto her bed and started to entertain herself but shook off the heated pulse and jumped up quickly when Hugh's siren laugh urged her downstairs into the kitchen.

"Hi Hughie!"

Hugh March looked up from his plate and strangled on a mouthful of pancakes. He managed a clumsy pat on her hand as she plopped down between him and her father, who had his head in the middle of the Times. Margo tousled Hugh's wet hair and grabbed for his juice; when she had drunk a gulp she seized his fork and plunged it into his breakfast.

Antoinette Vitesse snatched the fork away. "Come on Margo, let the boy eat his own breakfast and I'll fix you some of your own."

Margo frowned, she didn't want pancakes. She wanted Hugh's pancakes. "No thank you Mother, forget it. I was just sampling."

"What?"

"I'm not hungry. Forget it."

The air turned thick. Mrs. Vitesse rotated a quarter turn at the stove, her knuckles whitening around the spatula. "Then leave his damn breakfast alone!"

After a stunning moment of silence Hugh cleared his throat and pushed his chair away. Antoinette Vitesse loomed in the corner, standing by the stove grasping a kitchen tool looking like she might topple over at any moment. "Thanks for breakfast Mrs. Vitesse, it sure was good. I'll see you later Mr. Vitesse. See you tonight, Margo." He waved and was gone.

"See Dad? See?!" Margo pushed her own chair away and followed Hugh. She caught up with him just outside the front door as the voices of her parent's rose into heated argument back in the kitchen. Hugh did not look back at her but made a beeline for his scooter parked at the edge of the walk. "Hugh! Hugh! Wait up. What time are you coming over to Cecelia's tonight, Hughie?"

Hugh groped for the gas switch and grabbed the scooter's handlebars. "Uh, I don't know Margo, whenever they close the store I guess…" He climbed on. "We might stay open later 'cause we're having a big sale, but ya know, I gotta train…"

"But you just ran this morning!"

"Yeah well, I have to bike too…maybe I'll meet you at Cece's at eight or nine…that'll give me some time to ride and uh, you know, get showered and all."

Margo sighed and Hugh started his scooter. "I got a ride," she said brightly. "I'll be there before eight," but Hugh only nodded at her and drove across the walk, out into the street and away.

Margo watched him go and frowned at his disappearing form. "Goddamn it," she sighed. "Goddamn it."

<u>6</u>

<u>Rose Queens</u>

Tory snipped a short piece of tape from the roll and carefully tacked a loose strip of gauze over the final exposed bit of flesh showing on Pietro's mummified head. When the bandage was secured he stepped back to admire his work.

"Life!" he screamed, throwing his arms heavenward. "I have created life!"

His creation laughed a muffled menacing laugh from behind the dressings, plunged stiff arms straight out and teetered forward on rigid legs. "Drink...need...!" the creature moaned, pushing Tory back against the toilet and grabbing a beer bottle from the bathroom counter. "Jesus Tory, I can hardly see." Tory picked up the medical scissors and after a few vicious eye-gouging feints carefully snipped a rim of gauze away from each eye. Pietro was satisfied after that and rubbed his hair briskly to stand up in a vertical clump, then added fixer.

"Come on Skunk, let's get the rest of our act together." They left the bathroom to search through his father's closet flush with green O.R. scrubs, white medical coats, and miscellaneous accessories. Tory found a knee length white coat for himself and gave Pietro a set of the green pajamas, along with a white butcher's apron he'd retrieved from the kitchen. Before they left they discussed Tory's street clothing, and Tory changed from his T-shirt and shorts into a pair of Dr. Lewis's red-checked polyester golf pants and purple Dacron shirt, a truly hideous combination that looked wonderful when topped with the medical coat. On the way downstairs Pietro caught sight of himself in a hallway mirror and burst out laughing.

"Come on Tory, we can't go to a party like this! Are you nuts?! Look at me, I look insane!"

"You are insane. Look Pietro, if we show up dressed normally everyone's going to stress, your face looks like a smashed grape. But in costume we'll be welcomed."

"Man, I don't think I should go to this party."

"Yes, you definitely should."

"Why? No one there likes me."

"Now you're getting it."

On the way out the door Pietro paused long enough in the kitchen to smear ketchup on his apron, then rejoined Tory outside and climbed into the jeep. Tory grinned and started the engine. "I can't wait 'till Cece sees you!"

It was just getting dark and a chill was in the Arroyo. Pietro loudly sang some Rolling Stones song he barely knew, alerting any persons who might be wandering in the street to their approach. But the streets were empty save a squirrel Tory tried to run down.

They missed the squirrel but hit a human, a bicyclist who shot through the intersection at the bottom of San Rafael. Tory didn't hit the brakes until he was thirty yards out of the intersection, his brain suddenly paralyzed by the rushing adrenaline. "Green light, green light, I had a green light..." The jeep skidded to the curb.

"Holy shit!"

Tory stared blankly at Pietro. "Should I bail? Did I have a green light?" Pietro's face, hidden by the gauze, drained to grey and his mouth hung slack. "Uuuuhhh" he muttered, glancing backwards at the stricken cyclist lying in the middle of the street. "Holy shit!"

Tory felt his aorta rising up in his throat as he ran back to the accident. The intersection was quiet; there had been no other traffic at the time of the collision and none had happened by since. His brain raced with plans of escape...a quick hop on the 134, down the 210, down Linda Vista, across Orange Grove Boulevard, a quick U-turn up San Rafael...anywhere, just punch it and roar away, leaving the corpse and its wrecked bike for someone who did not have so much to live for…

As he crossed the line, breathless, the corpse sat up, tossed the bike off its bloody legs, and gave a healthy curse. "Thank you God," Tory prayed. "Are you alright?! Jesus guy are you okay…?" The cyclist looked up at him confusedly. Tory saw that he was a young man about his own age and not dead. "Hey—are you alright buddy?"

"He needs to go to the hospital."

Tory turned and found Pietro at his side. "We've got to take him to a hospital," Pietro repeated. Tory looked back at him stupidly.

"What's your name?" Pietro asked the boy.

"Hugh March."

"Look at his pupils. He's in shock." Pietro reached down and touched the cyclist's ear, interrupting a trickle of blood. "He has a concussion, maybe a fractured skull. Hey—c'mon buddy, come with us. We're gonna take you to a hospital."

"Are you doctors?"

Tory looked at Pietro and they laughed, laughed happily with relief and the lunacy of the situation. Indeed, the sight of the mummified Pietro and Tory's weird golf garb accented by the white coat must have confused the boy even more than the crash. "No man, but we're gonna take you to some, just hang in there." Pietro stayed with Hugh March while Tory ran for the jeep. They belted Hugh carefully in the front seat and tossed the damaged bike in the back. Pietro seized Tory's arm. "Hey—"

Tory stared at him wildly.

"Tory chill out. Look at his bike."

"What?!"

"Look at his bike. Look at the rim here…" Pietro jammed his fist into the tangle of broken spokes and bent rear wheel. "You didn't hit him, you hit his bike…"

It was not clear whether Tory comprehended. Pietro grabbed his friend's jaw and pulled his face close to his own. Satisfied he was not in shock also, he released Tory and wrapped an arm around his shoulder. "You just dumped him Tory, don't worry about it. Can you drive?" Tory nodded. "Okay then," Pietro said. He climbed into the back of the jeep. In less than three minutes they were at the emergency entrance of Huntington Memorial.

"Oh my God!" gasped a nurse. "What happened?!"

"Not me damnit, him!" Pietro shouted, pushing the concerned nurse off his arm and gesturing at Hugh March. "Him, him!" Finally the nurse got the idea and helped Hugh to a chair.

"Okay, sit quietly here," she instructed. Hugh March began to drool and two other nurses and an intern converged around him. Tory and Pietro stepped back.

"It looks like he's gonna be alright."

"Yeah."

"So let's go."

Tory shot him a disturbed glance. "What?!"

"Goddamn Tory, the cops are gonna be called."

"I had a green light."

"What?!"

"I had a green light. I remember now. The light was green."

Pietro turned at the whisper of the double doors opening and saw the inevitable policemen enter. "Okay, that's the story. Got it."

****

Ginny Lewis sloshed vodka onto the sleeve of her dress while answering the door. "Shit," she muttered as the cold liquor sopped her wrist. She did not immediately address the new arrivals but instead unbuttoned her cuff to roll up the sleeve to suck the juice from it, patronizing her guests with an apologetic smile and dumping the remainder.

Vodka splashed all over Pietro's shoes. He turned wordlessly to Tory who retrieved her fallen cup. "Looks like you could use a refill, Auntie."

"Oh my God, hello Tory. I'm sorry, I was startled by King Tut here. Hello…" She shook Pietro's hand. "Well, you're finally here, come on in." She led them into the front hallway, dodging a young couple who whisked by. "I don't know what's going on here anymore," she told Tory. "And after my fourth drink I'm not sure I care." Whatever she said next was lost beneath the screeching treble of an electric guitar from somewhere out back; Tory cupped an ear and shook his head as the guitar was joined by drums and a bass. He and Pietro followed Ginny to a room in a quiet corner of the house where a small bar resided. "I'm going to fix myself another drink, but there's plenty of wine and a couple of kegs, I think, out back with that awful band."

"Where's the bete de fete?"

Ginny waved drunkenly. "She's disgracing herself with alcohol and boys. And speaking of disgraces, Mr. Lewis…" Ginny slurred, handing Pietro a bottle of Tonic Water to open, "I heard you were a shining star on the court yesterday."

"Oh you heard that, did you. Well, which version did you hear?"

Ginny splashed elements of her drink together and took a slug. "Something about a near riot incited, various vulgarities hurled about, you know, the usual caustic behavior from you."

"That's not the official version. Look, we're gonna go get a drink, since you're not offering us one."

"That's right," she sneered. "Private stash." She followed them out of the room, talking to their backs. "Tory, when you find Cece would you remind her that she's supposed to behave herself at her own party."

"I dunno Auntie, that'd be bucking convention."

"Look kid, I'm paying for all this, that's all that's expected of me. Just go and deliver the message."

"What happens to these Pasadena chicks when they hit forty?" Pietro asked when they were safely out of Ginny's earshot. "Do they all freak out, or is it just the ones you know?" Tory grinned and waved on a couple of girls who were side-saddle on the banister at the top of the landing preparing to slide down. "Get out of the way!" one of them yelled.

"Freaks," chided Pietro. "Let's bail."

"Let's go find my cousin." They passed through a mosh of teenagers dancing on the patio and made a quick stop at the keg, Pietro muscling in between three heshers and growling when they protested. He filled two cups then held out the tubed spigot, daring them to take it. Tory pulled him towards the kitchen on the advice of a pretty blond.

Cecelia Lewis was indeed stationed there, back against the sink, giddily conversing with two other girls. Tory recognized one of them and grabbed Pietro. "Look—see that brunette? That's the one with the body paints."

"Where?"

"There—in the sequined t."

Pietro squinted through he crowd and Tory pulled him closer and sighted him down his outstretched arm. "The one talking to my cousin."

"She's smokin' hot."

"Likes the toys too."

"Oh yeah," Pietro enthused.

"…and so Alison looks at him and says, 'Please Mr. DeSilva, you're too gross…you'll have to insert your own suppository!' Ha ha ha ha ha ha!" Cecelia fell apart laughing, as did her audience. She laughed and seized the lapel of a passing boy and shrieked in his face, then teetered backwards and leaned against the kitchen counter for support. Tory tried to sneak up but Cecelia saw him. "Oh my God, Tory and …ha ha ha…Rocky Bertolucci! Ha ha ha!"

"Ha ha ha," Pietro laughed, somewhat unjoyously. He eyed the brunette. The other girl, a pretty blond, smiled at him and said "You're Pietro Bertolucci, the fighter?"

"Yeah, that's right."

"My brother knows you. He says you're a punk."

"Oh yeah? Tell your brother I'll kick his fuckin' ass."

"Ha ha ha. Oh shutup Rocky." Cecelia threw an arm around Tory's shoulder. "Hey cousin, glad you finally decided to show."

"Yeah sure." Tory smiled and reddened and Cecelia laughed drunkenly. "You just missed Margo. Remember Margo? The girl from San Marino who needed a ride?"

"Sure," Tory nodded. "I remember Margo. I remembered her about half an hour ago, when her mother told us she wasn't home."

"Oh bullshit."

"No, this is fact," Pietro interjected. "We were on her porch and rang the doorbell, rang and rang, and about five minutes later the old bag opens a window upstairs and screeches 'Stop ringing that goddamn doorbell. What do you want?!'" The two girls surrounding Cecelia exchanged smirking looks and Cecelia giggled.

"…When we told her we were there to pick up Margo she freaked. She yelled at us in this rattling voice for us to go away. Jesus, I thought she was going to jump down on top of us." Tory nodded in agreement; the two girls smirked again. Pietro's spine rose but Cecelia was on guard.

"Oh relax Rocky, they're not laughing at you, they're laughing at Margo. She has this really strange family and her boyfriend got in an accident tonight and gave Margo's number as his next of kin, so Mrs. Vitesse called over here hysterical and told poor Margo her boyfriend was dead…"

"Geeze," muttered Pietro.

Cecelia gestured at the two girls. "The beautiful blond is Angela O'Donaghue, and the gorgeous brunette is Kelly O'Leary. They're debs with me. Angela and Kelly, the mummy with the mean streak is Pietro Bertolucci." She turned to Tory. "This is my cousin Tory," and she planted a smack on his cheek. "Tory, you might remember Kelly from the one rehearsal you made."

Tory smiled. "Hi."

Kelly smiled back. Cecelia took Tory's beer and drained it, then tossed the empty cup over her shoulder into the sink. "Would you get me another, Rocky?" she asked sweetly. Pietro nodded and looked to the other two; Kelly told him she'd like one and he headed off for the keg.

"How nice of you to bring your most charming associate to my party," Cecelia smiled, kissing Tory again. Tory pushed her away and grinned.

"He's a total riot, really."

"He's kind of cute," Angela smiled. "Why's he all bandaged up?"

"He had some work done."

"I suppose Pietro is kind of cute," Cecelia conceded, "though it's not often one says so."

There was a commotion outside. Cecelia pushed Tory towards it. "Go, save my party from your total riot." Tory hurried away through the crowded kitchen. Kelly O'Leary's eyes followed him.

"You like him."

"He's a total babe."

"Tory's okay," Cecelia shrugged. "He'd be a great guy if he didn't have such a rotten personality."

"Why's he your escort if you don't like him?"

Cecelia shrugged. "He's family, it's easier. At least he won't molest me."

"Does Tory have a girlfriend?"

Angela nodded and Cecelia said "Courtney Kempner." Kelly waited. "Courtney was away on AFS," Cecelia explained. "She got back Saturday. She and Tory have been going out about two years. I talked to her today to see if she was coming over but she said she was too wiped out and kind of into staying home with her family."

"She goes to Blair," Angela added. "She's not like us."

Kelly O'Leary shifted. "What's that mean?"

"Well she's not a deb, that's for sure," Cecelia said, digging through her pockets for a pack of menthols. "Wait, that's mean. Courtney's still seventeen, but even if she wanted to come out they'd never let her. Your mother wouldn't invite her...I doubt yours would either," she said to Angela.

"She's a trollop," sneered Angela, taking the pack from Cecelia.

"Oh she is not. Courtney's Playmate pretty, big boobs, sexy strut. Most girls are jealous of her, like Angela here."

"So not."

"Come on, let's engage." Cecelia directed the girls out of the kitchen and went off to dance with a boy she'd met at a rock concert a few weeks before. The two girls followed. They had crossed the threshold of the billiard room when Angela heard an urgent voice calling to her. "Over here!" the voice directed. Ginny Lewis waved them through a nearby door.

"Hi ladies, are you having a good time? Oh good, I'm glad. Angela, would you please tell Cecelia that I'm going over to the O'Malley's? This place," she waved, "is out of hand."

"Alright Mrs. Lewis. "

"Thank you. If anyone is too drunk please call the police on them. That's just punishment."

"Sure thing.

Ginny Lewis disappeared and the two girls rejoined the partying masses celebrating Cecelia Lewis's coming out.

<u>7</u>

<u>A Reasonable Search</u>

Tory woke up Monday morning with a dry mouth and pounding headache. He sat up in bed and stared thickly into the light that burned through the terrace windows. The room was stuffy, as bedrooms sometimes are in the early summer's heat. He climbed out of bed and walked over to the French doors, yanked them open, and stood naked on the terrace.

The air was heavy with heat and pollen. Orange blossoms perfumed the front yard and a light breeze, redolent of juniper, blew through the Arroyo Seco.

He rubbed his eyes, tugged at his penis, and scratched. He laughed lightly, feeling the stupor of alcohol still coating his brain, and picked up a stray tennis ball from the tile, tossed it high in the air and served it with a bare hand dead into a wicker trashcan forty feet across the room.

It was Monday but there was no school because of the Memorial Day holiday and given his condition he wouldn't have gone anyway. He and Kelly had drunk some wine back at her house and he was hung over from it. He had not gotten home until four in the morning; Kelly had kept him there fucking for hours in all positions and when he told her he could not go on, his dick wilted like a soggy sausage, she brought out the body paints and they lazily decorated each other. At last they climbed into the shower together and afterward Kelly sent him home; her parents wouldn't approve. He understood. Kelly O'Leary had an amazing body, her breasts were small and beautiful and she possessed the finest shell-pink ears. Her skin smelled like lavender. If Courtney Kempner was Playmate pretty Kelly was model gorgeous. Tory wondered if they knew each other.

A pair of tennis shorts were draped cross the valet. Tory pulled them on, found a clean LaCoste shirt and slid that on too. He brushed his teeth, washed his face, swallowed some Tylenol and headed downstairs to the kitchen.

The Lewis house, as described before, was large and old. It was cool in the summer and cold in the winter, when most of the excess rooms were shut off to save heat and thick oriental rugs laid across the floors. Now most of these were in summer storage and the windows left open to circulate air. It was comfortable, a house well suited to the mild climate.

He padded along the hallway feeling dizzy from his hangover. It was not until he passed the mossy pond at the top of the landing that he smelled cigarette smoke. He paused mid-step and gripped the iron banister; someone else was in the house.

He listened. Water gurgled pleasantly in the deserted pond. There were no other sounds, and except for the smoke he would have sworn he was alone in the house. Leaning against the banister at a precarious list, Tory dropped step by step down the staircase and crept silently into the kitchen where he found his mother reading the newspaper while she let a Virginia Slim burn itself to death in an ashtray.

"Mom!"

"Tory! Come here sweet!" She jumped up from the table and grasped her youngest in a tight embrace, and Tory loved it and was glad she had come home. Bonnie hugged him and rocked, murmuring how glad she was to see him, and finally she loosened her grasp and looked at him. "Christ Tory, you're even taller than when I left!"

Tory laughed. "I'm the same size Mom, you just forget when you're away."

"Well you look great. How are you? I tried to call yesterday but there was no one at home. I guess you don't use the machine either."

He shrugged and Bonnie dropped back into her chair and plucked the cigarette from the ashtray to drag the last breath out of it. Tory found a cup and poured coffee from the pot; he was happy to have his mother home, and pleased she'd made coffee.

Bonnie Lewis was in her early fifties and well preserved. She possessed a beauty unpromised in youthful photos and manifested the grace and attractiveness that came with her maturing womanly figure. She was dressed in a white gauze Mexican frock embroidered with orange and red flowers at the breast. It spoke of leisurely breakfasts and unhurried matters, and Tory knew she'd come home to stay.

He took a chair across from her and grinned sheepishly. "Sorry the place is such a mess. I was planning to call a cleaning service this week…"

She cut him off with a wave. "Don't worry about it. I expected much worse; the only thing I'm unhappy about is your collection of smelly kegs on the sun porch. Are those recent?"

"A few weeks."

"All right, mushing along, what happened to the koi?"

"Jesus Mom, they died months ago. I told you about them the last time you were here."

"Oh that's right, one of your friends peed in the pond…" Tory started to protest but caught the gleam in her eye and laughed. Bonnie grinned and pushed a stray bang from her forehead. "How's Klaus?"

"Fine."

"…and Tidbit?"

"Got killed by coyotes."

"Shoot!" She shook her head. Tidbit was the latest in a line of doomed beasts, barely seven months old before Tory found his carcass strewn all over the front lawn. His sister Janelle, upon seeing the animal during a visit, christened him "Tidbit" after wagering that the skinny grey kitten would not survive 'till Spring. Bonnie unsheathed another cigarette and lit it. "How's your game?"

"SC seems to think it's pretty good. They've been trying to get me to sign a letter of intent."

"Why don't you do it?"

Tory shrugged. "Hell I don't know. I'm just not ready to commit to anything right now. I've still got to graduate and all."

"Well take your time son. Youth will be served, especially youth that plays tennis well. USC will still be there later in the summer."

"Right," Tory agreed. He focused on a crust of toast and rolled it beneath his finger until it crumbled. "The Club suspended me though."

"Oh? Why's that?"

"Fighting on the courts."

Bonnie cast a disapproving look but could not keep her stern composure when she saw her son's embarrassment. "You goof," she said softly.

Tory looked away from her smile. He glanced at the sports headlines and scratched his chin. "Have you played recently?"

"No, darn it. Last month I got together with your father in Connecticut and we played a couple of times."

Tory was surprised. "I thought Dad was in Germany. What was he doing in Connecticut?"

Bonnie exhaled and leaned forward, both hands resting on the table. "I asked him to meet me there…

"…We're getting a divorce."

Outside Klaus barked at three small birds come to bathe in the birdbath. Tory imagined bees humming in the bottlebrush lining the hillside, pollinating the orange trees that cornered the drive. He looked at his mother; her face was composed but regret languished in her eyes. "What's up?" he whispered.

Bonnie shook her head. She sucked greedily at her cigarette and stubbed it out and Tory knew she was distraught; she only chain-smoked when troubled. Her look begged for him to be satisfied with the revelation and understand; he did not indulge her. "Maybe you should start over…"

"Maybe I should…" Tears welled up and escaped down her cheeks. She wiped at them after a moment and breathed deeply. Tory got up and retrieved the coffeepot, filled her cup and his, and replaced the pot on the burnerplate. He sat down across from her again. Bonnie nodded. "Thanks."

Tory took the ball. "Obviously you and Dad discussed this before you got together in Connecticut…"

"Yes," Bonnie sighed. "Many times." She cleared her throat. "Ours is a worn-out marriage…no matter how much you love someone or something, everything is finite. When your Dad and I separated that time three years ago and he went off to travel he discovered a new life, exciting and full of personal and professional interest. He discovered he liked medical research and travel and when he came back here he was bored. And he made me bored…

"When was the last time you saw him…Christmas? And the time before, was that two years ago in June? He stayed a month, right? Well, what kind of marriage is that?" She leaned back in her chair. "What kind of marriage is that for me?"

Tory squeezed his mother's hand. "Yeah I know Mom, you're not dead yet."

"Damn right," Bonnie said, ready tears breaking out again. "So that's why I left and started to travel." She blew her nose on a napkin and wiped her eyes with her sleeve. "See son, people change, and if you can't change with them, you'd better let them go. Your father didn't like being cooped up here, he became restless and disinterested in our family. You've gotten the wrong end of it too, he was here for your brothers and sister but not for you."

"I dunno, Dad and I talk occasionally. Look Mom, why don't you travel with him? You seem to have that in common, why the hell don't you just go around the globe together instead of getting a divorce?"

"Don't get agitated Tory, I'm doing my best to explain but getting you to understand is very difficult. You want a reason that's more concrete."

"It would help."

"Well I haven't got one, son. Just the one I told you. We've changed. We've grown apart." Bonnie studied her son's dark features; he possessed the genes of some old relation, of which side she could not be sure. Her other children were fair-haired; Tory was dark and much taller than they or her husband and she could not remember her own father as a tall man. But Tory was calm and self-assured, and he would survive this. "It's just over," she said simply.

Tory got up from the table. "Alright."

"See you later."

"Bye." He left the kitchen feeling worse than he had when he woke up. His head throbbed and he felt tired and angry. He walked slowly across the sunny hall and felt the warmth of the day through the glass, which ran floor to ceiling on this part of the house and bathed the long stretch of mosaic floor tile in brilliant light. His parent's had a flimsy reason for calling it quits. If his father gambled away the house or his mother was a closet heroin addict, well then maybe he could understand. But "change" and "boredom" didn't seem appropriate symptoms for a failing marriage, and Tory was dissatisfied with his mother's explanation. He felt stupid and confused.

The door of the dining room was open and it struck him as strange for he hardly had reason to use the room and had almost forgotten it existed. He went in and stopped a few feet inside. Dust covered the walnut table and it was hot and stuffy, one could open the French doors at the west end and air the place out and Tory decided to, struggling with the frozen bolts that locked the doors to the floor. When they opened they did so under protest, groaning and creaking. When the last pair of doors was freed he stood in the flutter of the dusty curtains as they caught the breeze.

He looked around the dining room. It was one of the largest rooms in the house and the site of festive occasions when the family would celebrate Christmas or the occasional graduation. It had also served as the family boardroom, when major decisions were announced or argued, as happened when his family convened to discuss his expulsion from Poly, his sister scolding "I told you so!" and his brothers telling her to shut up, his father's outrage and threats to sue the school, and Pliny's acceptance of the whole matter.

Pliny. Now there was someone Tory could talk to. Possibly the old man would know what his mother was talking about and agree with him that his folks were being foolish. And even if he didn't agree he might be able to illuminate their reasons…

Atop the ornate brass and crystal étagère stood a recent family photo taken last year at Christmas. His father's salt and pepper hair pushed thickly back, his mother's black hair graying at the roots…for Christ's sake, they were old! They might not be dying but they certainly weren't spring chickens! He shook his head and dusted the silver framed photo with his shirttail. Janelle looked pretty in a dress, better than when she wore her stockbroker suits. Tim and Mike were establishment in Ralph Lauren shirts and silk ties, but they both drank like fish and told dirty jokes, so the ties were props. And then him, wearing the holstered .357 they'd given him for Christmas. He put the picture back on the shelf and hovered near a collection of curios near the serving table.

Most were from far off places: a pair of silver owls his father had brought back from Amsterdam, his mother's African tribal dolls, knick-knacks from an Egyptian bazaar. There were many handcrafted sculptures from the Lewis children's art classes, none of them useful or beautiful but honored nonetheless by Bonnie, who was sentimental about such things.

Tory picked up a clay soldier Tim had crafted in the fifth grade and blew the dust off. It was a crude, ugly figure copied from a Revolutionary War painting and Tory decided it was fortunate that Tim had not pursued art beyond this because he had no talent whatsoever and deserved to be a lawyer. As he replaced the statue he heard his mother's peculiar gate pass by and fade into the recesses of the house. Though barefoot she walked as if in high heels, with a graceful balance. His grandmother had walked just that way up to the day she died, at eighty-three.

One of the French doors slammed against the wall and a strong breeze blew into the room. A fluttering curtain whispered its welcome, interrupting Tory's meditation; he replaced the soldier in the dust and left.

It was nearly ten o'clock when he arrived back at his room. His headache was in full force and Tory could not remember where he'd put the Tylenol, all he found was a pill bottle with aspirin and old vitamins getting smelly together. He manicured a big bud Pietro had left and rolled a joint, settled into a faded director's chair on the terrace and smoked. Today was not as hot as Sunday and there was a breeze. He heard the Annandale PA garble a tee time and decided to go to the beach later.

Tory was fourth generation Californian; the clan had lived in Pasadena since 1910 and had been called Lucciera then. Someone anglicized the name to Lewis early on, but this was reasonable as the Lucciera's were from Northern Italy and fair. Benito Lucciera sired fourteen children who he supported through a meager trade as a carpenter. His youngest son, a wild boy called Pliny, grew up to be very successful and a founding member of the Arroyo Tennis and Country Club.

As a youth Pliny and some other teenagers had taken sportsmen and women dove and quail hunting in the lower Arroyo basin for pocket money. Some sharp entrepreneurs capitalized on the boys' trade and organized fox hunting excursions under the guise of a club, thus gentrifying the concept and lining their pockets with membership dues. Most of the time the shooting parties brought back only skinny coyotes or squirrels, but the coterie of members in their riding couture felt more couth accompanied by baying hounds than scruffy teenaged boys. Pliny and his group were virtually cut out of the market, until a rash of brutal horse slayings plagued the club stables. Faced with a rapidly dwindling number of steeds and a terrified membership, the club's management hired the boys to teach members swimming and tennis, a timely ploy that satisfied the gentry, the boys, and the residents of the Arroyo, who were tired of losing their dogs to hunting parties that mistook them for foxes. The remaining horses survived.

Eventually the club evolved into a tennis and social clique, and with the acquisition of property, a country club with select membership. Despite their mongrel origins Pliny and his friends stayed on staff as recreation instructors, security guards, and waiters. College scholarships were arranged for some of the boys from mandatory tithes offered by the membership at the request of Pliny. Upon his graduation from USC, Pliny borrowed from the Club Treasury and bought a home on Oak Knoll. He married a beautiful Pasadena girl of good family and breeding and together they raised four sons and two daughters.

Pliny sent his children to the finest prep schools in the state and encouraged them to be good citizens. Two of his sons died in Vietnam and his daughters married badly. Pliny's youngest son, Tory's father, went into medicine and set up a good practice in town. His older brother operated a financial consulting firm in Los Angeles and did very well for himself and his clients, until his recent conviction in a bank fraud scheme that also took down several city councilmen and a real estate developer.

Pliny had suffered terribly when his sons were killed in the war. His daughters' failed marriages to a gay Hollywood actor and reprobate race car driver, respectively, shamed him and his involvement in their lives lessened as the years wore on. Tory had met his aunts only a couple of times and could fully understand his grandfather's estrangement; the women were hard drinking, worn-out dames whose bitterness made them very unpleasant to be around. When the final insulting blow was dealt with the bank fraud indictment, Pliny disowned his eldest surviving son and reduced ties with that part of the family. Cecelia, the apple of her grandfather's eye, was the exception and Pliny planned to sponsor her at her debut in place of her father who was unavailable for the next eight years.

Now Tory decided the old man would have to be told of his suspension from the Club and his parent's impending divorce. With his feet propped up on the iron railing he tilted the flimsy chair backwards and leaned against the villa wall, feeling the cool texture of stone against his skin. It would not stay cool on this side of the house long, the sun was creeping towards the high point of the sky and would shine hot on the west side of the house by one o'clock.

He felt stoned and uneasy. Thoughts of his parent's divorce raised many questions. For one, what would become of the house? They couldn't sell it. They wouldn't...or would they? With no practical income he and his mother lived off stock dividends and trusts, and he never questioned their ability to pay property taxes or utility bills. There was never any lack of money; they still had memberships in half a dozen clubs and his parents lived like kings when they traveled...still, Tory had observed the divorces of a few friends' parents. He knew things rarely stayed the same, and property was always the first to go.

Owing to the persuasions of Pliny, Dr. Lewis had purchased the villa in

1968 for a hundred and fifty thousand dollars. It had recently been appraised at five and a half million, though that was an over inflated figure given the monstrous amount of refurbishment and repair the house desperately needed. The tennis court was cracked in the center and slipping down the hillside, the pool needed a new filter and retiling, the grounds were overgrown and neglected. The house itself, while still grand, suffered smog erosion and needed patching and painting. The wiring, plumbing and heating systems were arcane and inadequate and water damage stained the ceilings; the roof cried for retiling.

These things had never bothered Tory, and his parents lived in town for so few months out of the year they viewed the villa's condition with insouciance. Tory casually adapted to the peculiarities of the old house, knowing which outlets could be trusted and how much topspin to put on the ball to keep it in play on the inclined court (needless to say the home court advantage was significant when he played friends there). It was arguably too large for a seventeen-year old boy to live in by himself, but Tory felt comfortable and enjoyed the privacy of the San Rafael Hills. It was home and he liked it.

After awhile it became very hot and Tory remembered his beach plans. Courtney Kempner was back from Brazil, maybe she'd be recovered from her jet lag and like to go…

"Courtney?"

"No, Helen."

"Hello Mrs. Kempner. This is Lewis."

"Hello Mr. Lewis. Courtney's back but she went the Jonathan Club with Cece. Want me to have her call you?"

"That'd be great. Goodbye."

Several of his friends were working and one could go but had to be back by three o'clock. "Solo," he directed himself, rummaging through the garage for his boogie board and fins. The Budweisers had been guzzled yesterday; Tory filled his cooler with ice, threw a sandwich on top and headed for the Cal Oaks Liquor store to restock.

The proximity of the liquor store to the hospital made him think of Hugh March, and he decided to stop in and see how the cyclist was doing. He bought an extra six pack ("It's for my Mom") and walked the few blocks over to Huntington Hospital, leaving the jeep in the Cal Oaks lot.

The hospital wards reminded Tory of emergency room visits from childhood. There was a sense of pain and the slow process of healing. After checking with the registrar he dodged a trio of wheelchairs and caught an elevator up to the sixth floor with a man whose wife was dying of cancer (he told Tory twice). "This was a bad idea," he grumbled to himself, but continued on his mission. A wrong turn, a right turn and he arrived at the room.

A girl was standing at the bedside blocking Tory's view. She turned when she heard him come in and Tory felt anxious when he saw Hugh lying dully on the bed with his head bandaged.

The boy grinned weakly. "Hey…" he glanced at the girl. "This is the guy who ran me down, Margo."

"Hello," Tory smiled.

Margo looked sour. She took Hugh's hand. "Hugh's not getting discharged until tomorrow." She glared at Tory. "He has a fractured skull."

"Wow, really? That happened to me once. You'll get over it," and he gave Hugh an encouraging wink. "Well look, are you feeling better?"

Hugh tipped his hand in a gesture of steady convalescence. Tory nodded and dropped the sack of beer onto the bed. "Here's a little something to help you on your way. I'm glad you're improving." He picked up a discarded unit dose off the bed tray. "Hmm, Percocet. These are kind of fun, right?"

But Hugh looked blank and Margo stayed silent. Tory shook his hand, then Margo's. "It looks like you're going to be just fine. Nice to meet you," he smiled to Margo. She smiled unconvincingly back and Tory waved and was gone. "Holy Jesus," he muttered, running down the hall, "that was the chick I was supposed to pick up!" He glanced back over his shoulder and escaped in an elevator.

Margo picked up the sack. "Beer. That's great." She dropped it in the trash.

"It wasn't really his fault, Margo."

"I know Hugh, that's what you told me. Only now you won't be able to run in the State Meet, and they've cut off all your beautiful hair." She took his hand. "I've seen that guy before, I wonder where? This has been such a terrible weekend. Did you know my mom told me you were dead?" Hugh rolled his eyes.

A nurse came into the room and said hello, then announced that Hugh was being discharged that afternoon, which brightened everyone's disposition. "Are you volunteering today?" she asked Margo, but Margo shook her head and pointed at Hugh. "My boyfriend." The nurse smiled and told Hugh he was lucky, Margo was the Queen of the Candy Stripers, always smiling and encouraging the patients. When she left Margo went to the windows and opened them. "I hate this place," she grumbled.

<u>8</u>

<u>The Elder</u>

Resting under the shade of three large cottonwood trees, Pliny Lewis considered the charcoal sketch of two cats fighting by a fishpond submitted for critique by a neighbor, a middle-aged woman with auburn hair who sat next to him in a cheap lawn chair, one of several that were set up in confusion along Pliny's back porch.

"This cat is much larger than his opponent, and should be on top by virtue of his strength and weight. You have the skinnier one dominating…"

"But they're rolling," the woman reminded. "That says maybe," Pliny told her. "Your sketch has frozen a second of feline battle, and the aesthete will assume the victor is the cat depicted here," he pointed to the animal, "…and scoff.

"You see," he saged, "art is mostly self-indulgent work, and 'art appreciation' is a thinly disguised attempt by man to overcome his petty hostility towards his fellow beings. Now people who see your work will criticize it for many reasons; your perception of depth and values, your choice of subjects, whatever detail you've emphasized or blurred. So you'd do well to stay within the lines of conformity when depicting givens, like stronger versus weaker, to avoid vehement attacks from critics."

"I see," said the neighbor, who didn't really.

"What else have you got?" Pliny muttered, flipping through the woman's sketch pad uninvited. He stopped at a cubist drawing and frowned. "Picasso-inspired," the woman offered. Pliny tore the sketch from the pad and shredded it.

The woman looked hurt and she reached over and retrieved her pad from the old man. Pliny laughed. "Look my dear, I'm doing you a favor. Don't paint like Dali, sketch like Picasso, update Rembrandt. They already did the work. An artist is an individual and uses his obsession with form and imagery to bully other artists; Picasso was the master of the brush-back pitch and the art world cowered before him. You---" he pointed," are an amateur artist living in a placid town with no reasonable quarrel with society and you've no business drawing naked men in cubist. For God's sake, if you want to draw a naked man draw the butcher naked, or the pimply teenaged boy next door, but not like Picasso, who was a terrible artist anyway."

But Pliny's well-intentioned gesture upset the lady and she said goodbye sourly, then left through the back gate. Pliny waved goodbye to her back and closed his eyes. He had just fallen into a light doze when the lawn chair beside him creaked. Opening one eye he expected to find the woman come back repentant, but found his grandson instead. "Tory, how nice of you to come by."

"Hey Pliny." Tory patted his grandfather's hand. "How're you doing?"

"I'm very well. You just missed Mrs. Jurzinksky…" he adjusted the thick bifocals that rested across his nose. "She came by to show me a new sketch. Not bad, but she hasn't the passion to be a good artist."

Tory nodded thoughtfully and shifted his weight in the chair. " I saw a show at the Autry recently by a group of New Mexico artists. My favorite picture was of a runaway horse pulling a wagon load full of screaming fat ladies through a frontier town."

"Who's the artist?"

"His name's Eric Meyerhofer."

Pliny nodded. "I've heard of him. He's quite mad. Well I'm glad you've taken more of an interest in art. Not that it will do you any good at all, and in a cultural revolution you'll likely be killed for it, but I'm glad all the same."

Tory became preoccupied with a crust of sand he found in his ear. Pliny looked up at the cloudless sky and listened to a mockingbird off in the furthest cottonwood. He did not feel so old. "What a beautiful day today was. You look like you went to the beach. Was it nice?"

"It was great, but I didn't stay long. Traffic and all."

"Well do you feel up to a quiver?"

"Sure!"

"Good. I've had this urge to try out a few of the new hunting arrows I've made. There's a noisy dog about two blocks down that starts in at two am every night and he may be soon silenced. I shot two doves yesterday, right over there." He pointed proudly to a corner of the yard.

While Pliny went indoors to fetch his bow and quiver Tory examined the clawfoot bathtub stationed in Pliny's yard. Inexplicably the tub was full of rocks; the level of the quarry increased each time Tory occasioned to look. Recently a layer of soft moss had formed over the rocks, but apparently Pliny had found a new collection he liked and there were scattered stones atop the mossy felt.

"Here we are," said Pliny, emerging from the house. Tory left the mysterious tub and they passed through Pliny's back gate and after a short walk arrived at the fence separating the Busch Gardens neighborhood from the Arroyo Seco; Tory gestured for his grandfather to go first, taking the quiver and bow from him. Pliny groaned as he stooped and went through the hole, then Tory handed the weapons through and crawled through himself. "Someday I'll be too old to crawl through that hole," Pliny said.

"Then what will you do?"

"Well I won't die in front of the tube, be sure."

A soft gold light hung over the gulch, the sun casting its long rays against the eastside brush and rocks. The sweet smell of marijuana wafted down as they passed beneath the birdbath and Tory looked up against the hillside to see if it was anyone he knew, but the partiers were three unfamiliar heshers who dangled their legs over and looked down.

When they arrived at the archery range they discussed positions and decided to shoot middle distances. The range was deserted save for a good 'ol boy in camo firing from a hundred yards at a target just beyond the Roving Archer's shack. The lot held the light trucks of teenaged partiers and a couple of old cars belonging to fishermen come to test their casts in the pond. The Arroyo Seco belonged to those who lived with it, did not disturb it, letting it grow wild. Somehow it remained tranquil and undeveloped for those people.

Tory and his grandfather took turns with the bow, warming up with a few arrows apiece. Tory's shots flew up and over the haybale into a brush thicket; Pliny's flew straight into the bullseye. "Is that about the size of a terrier?"

"I'd say that dog's in some trouble." Tory took the bow. "Say Pliny, did you know they suspended me at the Club?"

"Don't take such a deep breath. No, I hadn't heard."

Tory sent an arrow into the target's outer circle and lowered the bow to rest on his shoe top. "Yeah, well, they did."

"What was their reasoning?"

"Fighting on the courts."

"Who suspended you?
"The Chairman. Ed Gaffney."

"He's chairman now? Christ. Ed Gaffney is a two-bit nobody."

"Yeah well, he's someone at the Club, right?"

A small smile slowly broke on Pliny's face. He said nothing else.

They shot all the arrows and retrieved them as the long shadows spread over the basin and purple dusk settled in. "Let's turn it over to the night," said Pliny. He and Tory headed back down the trail. On the way Tory stayed in quiet thought and Pliny gazed off into the deep sky. A black horse and rider passed by on the opposite side, shadows in the failing light. Specters of coyotes trotted up the wash. Tory and Pliny stopped beneath the La Loma bridge to watch them.

"Look at them dogs," the old man whispered. "As cool as they can be. I once knew a black man in Mississippi with a pet wolf. They were a cool pair."

"Oh yeah? The wolf was tame?"

"No, it wasn't tame at all. It was a wild dog with wild eyes and everyone in the town was afraid of him. But the man was so cool and controlled, the dog just jibed with him. Coyotes are wily but wolves are sinister, and that dog was an evil spirit that sat there beside the man and watched the world going by, watched everyone with yellow eyes. The old black man paid no attention to the animal at all, but the wolf didn't mind. It went off to eat and came back to the man after. Everyday the wolf did this, the man never fed him."

"Uh huh. Just followed him around…"

"Right."

"What was the wolf's name?"

"His name was Satan." Pliny regarded Tory critically. "I thought you'd guess."

"I had a feeling. You seen that wolf lately, Pliny?"
"Often enough."

"Uh huh…I thought so."

"What's eating you, Tory?"

Tory shook his head. "I've had a strange weekend…the tournament was complete chaos, it was the first time I think I realized what a bunch of louts there are at the Arroyo, and that they really don't like me. It made me crazy with rage when the guy I was playing started dicking around, I'm usually not like that."

Pliny took off his glasses and wiped them on his shirt. He crossed his arms. "I think I know you as well as anyone, Tory. I know how you react under pressure, and I admire your verve. You must learn to exact your vengeance in subtler ways than fighting…but it's just as well you're out of there. You'll never improve your game playing that fat lot of weekend jocks at the Arroyo."

"I wasn't playing anyone from there. He was a ringer, he was pretty good."

"Did you win?"

"I was gonna."

Pliny nodded, smiling. "Well you need to go someplace where you will lose. The king only knows survival. You've told me you're not ready to go pro, so it's clear: you must go to college and play."

"Uh huh. Well I might."

"Just as I was glad Poly expelled you, I'm glad the Arroyo excised you, you will become smarter and more worldly by going to college; those institutions which nurtured you in the past have no place in your future."

Tory considered Pliny's rhetoric for a quiet moment, then: "There's something I don't understand, you sat on the board for thirty nine years and now you view the Club like it's hell on earth. Why?"

"Come on, let's walk. It's getting dark." On the way Pliny told his story.

"At one time the Arroyo served to further its members success. It was a good place for making contacts, meeting women, taking the kids to play and teaching sportsmanship, etiquette and decorum. All of which was lost on my daughters, but my boys, especially your father, grew up with social graces that allowed them to advance and I give partial credit to the Club for that. But the world changes, Tory. The city around the Club has become integrated, the tenor of the people has changed. There are still refuges for the elite, but the Arroyo is a haven for people resisting those changes. Christ son, look around you…Armenians, African Americans, Asians, Mexicans…and not one of them has membership at the Arroyo…not a damn one.

"In 1974 our society was on the edge of a quiet revolution. The influences of the young people of the sixties were still affecting the status quo; the government was reeling from corruption charges and people like me were looking very hard at our old values. I decided that mine were solid, but somewhat archaic and I decided that the Club, which I valued very highly for obvious reasons, was solid but archaic too. And a little radical change would be difficult but overall constructive and positive. So myself and a few others decided to do the obvious and integrate the roster.

"There was a black man, a middle-aged broker who applied for membership that year. He had a family, two daughters and a wife. Beautiful women. He was a likable guy, low key and very athletic. He played a fair game of tennis, you bet.

"James Jameson wanted him in. Sponsored him, helped him network a little with some of the more liberal board members, guys like Sam Row, Hiram Walker, Zeke Dunnahy—good guys, you know them. Anyway, this man, I won't tell you his name, he fit in pretty well and Sam invited him to the Club for drinks one night to introduce him to me; Sam thought he should start at the top. They gave me his dossier and felt me out for my reaction. I thought about it and decided it would be a good move.

"So that Sunday night after all the families had cleared out from dinner we all met for a drink. I liked the man, he spoke topically and intelligently, drank a stiff drink, showed a sense of humor. I answered a few well-disguised questions for him— he was feeling us out as much as we were feeling him out – and when we broke it up around midnight we made plans to meet his family… you know, the usual Club membership rigmarole.

"Anyway, some time passes and the board decides to admit three new members in June. James Jameson lobbies hard for this man. He didn't have to be too convincing; I mean the guy lived off Rosemont in a nice home, served on the Tournament of Roses, the whole Pasadena bit…I think people at the Club were finally starting to bypass the color issue at around that time, or making an effort at least…and it's not as if were afraid of being taken over, it's so damn difficult to get into that Club anyway. So the board gave the nod and the preliminaries started. The man had us over to his house to meet his wife and daughters and have a few drinks. It must have been pretty intimidating but they held their own."

Tory interrupted. "Just you men went over?"

Pliny nodded. "No wives. Just six guys in blazers and elitist attitudes. Well we had a great time. When we left we were so excited about admitting this family, I don't know, we just liked them as people. It sounds weird, but we all carry our prejudices around, especially us older guys, and here was someone who could beat down the door of prejudice for us, without us having to do any work.

"Belle was in Europe at the time, I think, so I didn't have to hurry home and I suggested to James that we grab a nightcap at Monahan's. And sometime during the course of our drink I sense something's up…I've known James for forty years, that's a long time. You get to know the idiosyncrasies of a man pretty well…and James was cagey, suspicious, and I began to wonder.

"So I checked things out. Checked land transfer titles, stock trades, anything that could hint of a financial interest for James, because James is a greedy bastard. Nothing stank. But it still bugged me the way he was pushing so hard, almost desperate for the man's admission. And then I discovered that James was having an affair with the man's wife, and was very much in love with her.

"No, stop. You're thinking 'so what?' Well it wasn't just any love affair, and it wasn't James's fault. Not entirely."

They reached the hole in the fence. Pliny bent down to duck through it but Tory grabbed his arm and stayed him. "Come on Pliny finish the story!"

"It has an ugly finale."

Tory nodded and Pliny went on. "You see, this guy's wife wanted to be in the Arroyo so badly she was willing to fuck her way in."

It was the first time Tory had ever heard his grandfather use the word "fuck" before. He stood quietly and Pliny sighed and re-shouldered his quiver.

"So I voted the guy down. When the time came for a black man to break the color barrier at the Arroyo, it was I who voted against him. Because no man should enter that Club a second-class citizen, and by virtue of his wife's ambition, desire for status, whatever, that man was unknowingly placed beneath James Jameson and reduced to cuckold, a stooge, someone who rode to glory on James Jameson's foreskin. And it made me sick but I did it for him and I did it for his daughters and I did it for his wife."

Tory shook his head. "James was a shit."

"He was. But he's not the first man to be made a fool by a woman, there's Marc Antony, Ulysses, King Edward to name but a few—and I wouldn't blame the wife too much either. She just wanted her husband to have that one last trophy, the last thing that said he'd made it in a white man's world, and she was going to use herself to help him get it."

"Did you ever tell the guy why he was voted down?"

"No, how could I? But I told that woman. I found out where she and James were going to meet for their next tryst and I made that appointment myself. Man, did she go crazy. She cried and wailed and…well, eventually killed herself. There. You know the story now."

"That's a bitter tale," Tory said after a moment.

"Yes, very bitter." Pliny handed him the bow and arrows and bent slowly to crawl though the fence. On the other side he looked tired. "Let's rest a minute," he said.

Tory dropped down and rested on his haunches. The old geezer had a code to live by. What was he doing, playing God? Nobody won. Was it for the best that the man was denied membership? Was it better for the Club? The man? Pliny left the woman broken and anguished, to live with her sin until she couldn't, while he protected James Jameson and the status quo. Only Pliny retained any dignity.

"So what was the backlash at the Club?"

Pliny registered mild annoyance. "There wasn't any."

Tory nodded. Of course not. He stood up. "You're a son of a bitch, Pliny."

The old man smiled. "It's a Lewis trait."

Back at Pliny's house Tory made a sandwich and took his snack and a beer out to the picnic table in the back of Pliny's lush, cool yard. He ate and drank and thought about things. After he was finished he went back inside the house and found Pliny cleaning paintbrushes in his studio. "Pliny, did you know my parent's are divorcing?"

Blue paint bled into a jar of mineral spirits. Pliny staggered, the color drained from his face and he cast his eyes down into the jar. "No."

"Yeah well, they are."

"What for?"

Tory shrugged. "I don't really know. Mom says she's bored."

"That's no surprise."

"Well…what should I do?"

Pliny regarded him sharply. "What do you mean?"

"I mean, what should I do? Let them divorce or try to keep them together…?"

"The first thing you should do," Pliny said slowly, "is get it out of your head that you are responsible for anything those two do. Got it?"

Tory was taken aback, but he nodded.

"Okay," Pliny said.

9

Tonton's

The chimes in the old Westmeuller clock rang with a dissonant clank, announcing the three o'clock hour. Coming through the door with shopping bags hanging from her wrists like so many bangles, Ginny Lewis wondered who had wound the clock and why. She set her purchases down on a table in the front hall and walked quickly into the living room to confront the timepiece. The Westmueller lived atop the fireplace mantel in earthquake-proofed obscurity (wired down for safety), it's hands frozen at seven minutes to midnight (one of her daughter's jokes). Once a week the maid scattered a veil of dust from its cherrywood case. Other than that the Westmueller saw no action; its purpose was strictly decorative and to serve as a constant reminder of the nuclear threat. Now it was ticking and chiming and Ginny Lewis was irked. "Cecelia! Cecelia!! Who wound the clock?!"

Cecelia either did not hear her or was ignoring her, but she was home for her car was in the driveway. "Cecelia!" Ginny Lewis called, "come down please!" She must have heard that time; Ginny was yelling at the top of her voice and she had a loud voice.

"What Mother? Stop shouting, what's the problem?"

"No problem honey, I just wanted to see you. Did you have a nice day? You know it's three o'clock…you have your photo session in half an hour."

Cecelia came downstairs. "I know. Where have you been?"

"Shopping dear, I had to buy some underwear for your father. Someone stole his. Hello." Cecelia had made it to the bottom of the landing by this time and Ginny kissed her. "You look nice. Are you wearing all that eye shadow for your picture?"

"Sure. What's the matter, you don't like it?"

Ginny gave her daughter's makeup a second appraisal and shrugged. "I don't know, it looks nice. Do you know who wound the clock?"

Cecelia glanced quickly into the living room and was suddenly aware of the ticking. "Gee I don't know…it must have been someone at the party."

"Well don't look so abashed honey, it's alright but I just wanted to know why. Where's your dress?"

"Upstairs."

"Alright, but don't leave without letting me see you."

Cecelia nodded and left to finish getting ready for her sitting. Ginny flipped through the phone messages in the kitchen, noting with interest the one from her sister-in-law and the telephoned quote from Jacob Maarse for Cecelia's bouquet. The message from her gynecologist was old news; she'd run into him at Magnin's as he was buying a gift for his wife. No, it was just a benign lump, very small, nothing to be concerned about. No, it wouldn't get any larger. The gardener had called to remind them to water the lawn twice a day because of the heat. Margaret O'Malley called to say she found a stray earring; was it hers? Her husband's lawyer called.

She returned her sister-in-law's call first, tapping her finger against the pencil sharpener in anticipation while the line rang and rang. Like herself, the other Lewis' hadn't the courtesy to use a machine so a caller was forced to suffer ten or twelve rings before giving up. Fortunately Bonnie picked up before that limit was reached. "Hello?"

"Bonnie? Hi sweetheart, it's Ginny."

"Ginny! Thanks for calling me back so quickly. How are you?"

"Fine, just fine. When did you get back? Tory didn't say anything to me about it…"

"Well it was a surprise to him too, I came in Sunday night, probably while you were in the middle of Cece's party. Had I known I would have come over and surprised the lot of you!" (laughter from both).

"Look Ginny," Bonnie breezed, "is Tory supposed to be photographed with Cece? He was uncertain and for the life of me I can't understand what he's saying today…he came home mumbling something and asked me to call you; is she getting her portrait done today?"

"Yes." Ginny shuffled her feet. "Um, I don't think Tory's in this one but let me ask Cecelia. Just a sec." She clasped the phone to herself and returned to her shouting post at the foot of the stairs. "Cece?! Is Tory taking the photo with you?"

"What?!"

She cleared her throat. "Is Tory supposed to be in the picture with you?"

"Hell no!"

Ginny stayed quiet for a moment. "Alright then…" she said to herself, then returned to the phone. "Bonnie?"

"I heard," Bonnie Lewis laughed. "Okay, just checking. By the way Ginny, was Tory acting strangely on Sunday?"

"Not really, no more so than usual. He was certainly dressed strangely, but he was pretty much himself…" her voice waned into uncertainty. "…Why?"

"Oh no particular reason. Look, I'm free for lunch tomorrow, want to meet at the Club?"

Ginny paused, unsure if she should bring up Tory's suspension. Did Bonnie even know? "Uh, Bonnie…"

"Oh don't worry, I know all about it. But now that you mention it, perhaps somewhere else is better…hmm, how 'bout Pinot at the Library?"

"That's not good for me. Too many attorneys."

"Oh right. Well, has anything good opened in town while I've been away?"

"Corporate restaurants."

"Well come on now, this is indecent. Ah, I've got it. The Raymond?"

"Fantastic." Ginny had been there the week before but they were running out of ideas.

"Shall I pick you up? Will you be ready in the early afternoon?"

Ginny giggled. "Well, for the moment I have a clock, so you can say a definite time. One-fifteen?"

"Great. I'll make the reservation. Tell Cece I said hi. Bye Ginny!"

"Bye!" She hung up and thought about her nephew. No, he'd seemed himself on Sunday night. She decided to ask her daughter and went upstairs and knocked at the door. "Cece? May I come in? Did you know Tory…"

Cecelia opened the door in answer. Ginny stepped back against the railing, overwhelmed by the beauty that flowered before her. The bouncy, slightly plain, somewhat ordinary daughter that had come downstairs earlier had metamorphosized into this lovely creature?

"Oh knock it off Mother." She picked up her purse from the dressing table. "What's this about Tory?"

"He's acting strange!" Ginny squeaked.

Cecelia stared at her mother. Was she taking pills again? "Are you alright? Stop staring, you're making me feel stupid."

"Oh darling, you look wonderful!!" She said it rapidly, her voice full of enthusiasm and buttery-smooth. "Jesus," Cecelia sighed. "I gotta run, bye." She blew a kiss and whisked downstairs, leaving her mother gazing after her.

Her car was parked under the porte cochere, out of the sun. A big black bug had dropped from the ivy onto the windshield and was endeavoring to rise to the summit of the car roof. Cecelia turned on the windshield wipers and smeared him across the glass.

The car had been a sweet-sixteen present, back in the days when her father spent his ill-gotten gains fast and furiously. It was originally black but Cecelia had grown tired of washing it and had it painted beige. So far she had no complaints. She slapped a disc into the CD player and gave the windshield one last squirt n'wipe before jerking the brake off and rolling backwards down the driveway. Near the bottom of the narrow drive she jammed the clutch and shifted; the starter coughed and the transmission went "whee!" and the Cabriolet jumped to life and rolled out into the street tail first.

The city had put as top sign in at about mid-El Molino but nobody paid it any mind, save for a slight deceleration. Its sole benefit was to allow Cecelia a quick second to check traffic; a light touch of the brake pedal and a 180 glance sufficed to assure her the street was clear (or not) before she zipped out. On this occasion there were no cars coming from either direction and after coasting into a turning radius she shifted into first and raced up the street.

It was another hot afternoon but Cecelia dared not put the top down. She had just measured the exact amount of mouse to fluff up her straight blond hair into something more exotic; what, she couldn't say, but at least it looked different. Her dress was off the rack but it was pretty and sophisticated. Less daring than some of the other girls' maybe, but she didn't have much to show off anyway, and it was comfortable. The gloves and pumps were de rigueur but not today; only the gloves accompanied her, safely folded in her purse. Her feet were clad in Reeboks.

At Tonton Portraiture she was stopped by a gaunt man in a ragged suit clutching a handful of Bible pamphlets. He had a filthy dog tied to a rope, the other end of which he'd wrapped around his left wrist. "Do you believe, Sister?," he asked with wild, frantic eyes.

"Believe what?"

"Why, in God…"

Cecelia looked him up and down. "Are you crazy?"

The man was uncertain. Cecelia waited a moment, then gave up and headed through the glass doors into the studio. A middle-aged blond woman was stationed at the reception desk. "Did he bother you?" she asked, obsequious. Cecelia hated her immediately.

"Who?"

The woman pointed out the window. "Him—that bum."

"No. Should he have?"

The woman pursed her lips. "I'll tell Mr. Tonton you're here." Cecelia sat down to wait. The reception area was a gallery of Tonton's work, glorious portraits of the loveliest of people. A haughty blond matron in a startlingly regal gown showed off a good deal of cleavage and dared anyone to touch her, and a retired couple celebrating their wealth beamed. At the other end of the hall stationed under her own spotlight a beautiful girl with rich brown hair made her debut. Cecelia got up and made her way towards the portrait to get a closer look.

"Hello Cece Lewis."

She turned quickly. A pleasant looking man about her father's age had come out from a side office as she'd passed and was extending his hand. She took it and the man smiled genially. "Paul Tonton. Shall we get started?" Cecelia nodded and gave a last backward glance at the photo of the debutante as she followed the man into his studio.

"I guess you got a little religion as you were coming in."

Cecelia shrugged. "Not really, I don't go much for religion."

The photographer chuckled and guided her to a stool in front of a stormy grey backdrop. "We'll do a couple of you seated first. Do you know who that man was…? The former chess great, Bobby Fischer. Handing out religious tracts. Too bad, isn't it?" He went behind his camera. "He's harmless enough, so my wife… you met my wife, she books all my appointments and receives clients…she just shoos him away after awhile. He was once a famous person."

"Did you ever photograph him?"

The pleasant man chuckled again. "Nooo, my goodness no. Who'd want to look at him?" He disappeared behind his camera.

Cecelia said nothing more. She adjusted her shoulders as the photographer directed and tilted her head in a practiced way that she knew would make an alluring photo. Paul Tonton loved it and took three pictures with her seated, unsmiling, then came over and guided her into a new position. "I take a lot of debutante portraits. Did you see the one at the end of the hall? Beautiful girl. She was the deb of the year last year."

"What was her name?"

"Um, Frances, I think. Frances Bonn. Okay, some teeth this time…"

When the session had completed Cecelia smoothed her dress and wondered how her hair was holding up. Paul Tonton collected his drives and touched her lightly on the shoulder. "These will be terrific. You're so pretty. Make an appointment with Mrs. Tonton to see the proofs. The ball's Saturday, right? You should be excited. Goodbye."

Cecelia wandered out, slightly bewildered. She felt as if she had just been awarded something simply for being alive and she was not used to the shallow folksiness Paul Tonton gushed. Probably most of his clients liked being gladhanded, but she had endured the session smiling like an idiot and being agreeable while posing and posturing in unfamiliar glamour. Oh well, it cost nothing to be friendly.

She waited patiently in front of the reception desk for the photographer's wife. The debutante's photo at the end of the hall caught her eye again. The girl was mysterious, alluring…Cecelia held no illusions about her own appearance, she only hoped her pictures would capture her healthy features and downplay her plain ones…she felt it unfair that Frances Bonn should take such a stunning portrait. Probably the girl's parents were good looking too, though genes only contribute some features. Frances Bonn's face held something only she could be responsible for.

Mrs. Tonton broke the spell. "Can you come in Thursday evening around seven?" Before Cecelia could respond she was handed an appointment card. "It will take about an hour to see all the proofs."

"Yes," Cecelia agreed, glancing back for one last look at the girl's portrait. She turned to leave, but something held her there; she was starved for substance, something real and human to take away from what had turned out to be such an artificial experience. "So that was Bobby Fischer?!"

A gleam appeared in Mrs. Tonton's eye and Cecelia knew she was going to get what she wanted. Mrs. Tonton shook her blond head. "Poor man. I always think of the Romans, who would position a slave at the victorious general's side during his triumphant entry into the City…while the people were going mad with praise the slave would be in the general's ear whispering 'all glory is fleeting…all glory is fleeting...'"

It was a windfall, a bouquet of deranged philosophy from the photographer's wife. Cecelia smiled. "Thank you." She went out into the street and looked up and down the avenue. Bobby Fischer was gone, shoo'ed away, probably. Indeed, all glory is fleeting. The Tonton's captured the moment and recorded it for posterity; once that moment had passed they looked to a new celebrity. Now she was it, more important than a Chess Champion. After Saturday she would fade off…and what of Frances Bonn? Would some new girl, newly crowned, hang from Frances's hooks? After her one-year reign would she too be replaced by another girl in virgin white? From Deb to Co-ed to Mother to Matron…the Junior League was full of them.

When she approached her car the top was down and someone was sitting inside.

"What the hell are you doing here Tory?"

Her cousin looked up from a letter he was reading. His eyes narrowed and Cecelia knew she had erred. Her mother had warned her that Tory was being weird; now he looked like he was going to unload on her.

"Shut up. Get in the car. I need to talk to you."

She did. "What's this all about?"

"Drive."

Midway down Lake Avenue Tory raised his hand slightly and Cecelia slowed down, though she was uncertain his gesture was directed at her, or if it even had a basis in reality. From the expression on his face he might have been trying to calm a storm or recede the tide…

"Mom said you were being weird. What's going on?"

Nothing from Tory.

"Great," she sighed. Cecelia had a feeling Tory wanted to go somewhere but he had issued no other directive other than "…drive," so she made a few knowledgeable turns around the hilly area north of San Marino and parked along a bridge overlooking Lacy Park. She tried not to make any sudden moves; she simply got out and sat along the ledge. Tory rummaged through her glovebox and found a spare pair of sunglasses. Then he grasped the roll bar and swung himself out of the car to join her on the ledge.

"Weed?" he offered.

"You're strange."

Tory lit a joint anyway and took a big hit. Again he held it out to Cecelia. This time she took it, deciding that the afternoon wasn't going to return to normalcy.

"Look Cece, what'd my Mom tell Ginny?"

"That you were acting bizarre. Truth, so?!"

"...and what did you tell Courtney at the Jonathan?"

"That you were an asshole. Look Tory, what the hell are you getting at? I don't like sitting this close to you. What's going on?"

Tory smiled behind the dark shades and rubbed his hands together as a fly would upon settling on a turd. "Cece, you should find someone else to be your escort."

"Oh shit." She slapped her knees. "Lovely Tory. A week to go and I should find someone else. Look, for your information I didn't ask you because I like you..." She turned away very angry and glared off at the smog in the west. Tory handed her the joint again and she took it and threw it down into the street. "Fuck fuck fuck" she muttered. Tory was a lot of bad things but at least he wasn't complicated. Until now.

"...And besides, who would I ask?! I don't like anyone right now and no guys are asking me out anyway."

"Come on. Lot's of guys like you. Flirt a little more and they'll ask you out. I know you like a lot of guys, I bet I could name about five of them, so ask one and if he's a total bore then it's only for an evening."

"An evening. Only a twenty-thousand dollar evening. Only my debut, for which I've volunteered about a thousand hours of community service, got my picture taken, gone to those damn rehearsals, and got a dress..." She began to cry. "The point of this whole thing is that you don't want to be seen with me, right?"

"Wrong!"

She looked at him hard.

"Wrong, Cece. The point I'm trying to make is that you'd make a lot better impression if you took someone outside the family. This big plan to showcase the Lewis kids is a little too weird for me."

Cecelia was dumbfounded. "What the hell are you talking about? It's a debutante ball…you can't handle that?! You loser!"

"Fuck you Cece, you and the rest of your tea-set friends can go, I'm sick of them and you. I just got wrung out to dry at the Arroyo, ran over your snotty San Marino friend's boyfriend, what a geek, got a surprise visit from my Mom who breezes in to tell me that she and the old man are splitting up, and a fucking letter arrives from Pliny's lawyers today saying he's changing his will to benefit me, providing I meet certain conditions like I don't know what..! Now you tell me with a straight face that I should escort you to this Cotillion…"

Cecelia sighed and hopped off the ledge, stooped down and picked up the discarded joint from the street. "Pliny wants you to take me to the Ball, Tory. He's almost ninety, for Christ's sake. Humor him, willya?! With my Dad in prison he's more than a little humiliated…" She took a few hard drags off the joint to see if it was still smoldering, then accepted a light from Tory. "Jesus," she croaked, holding in the smoke. When she exhaled she shook her head, hiked up her dress and climbed back on the ledge. "Now what's this about Bonnie and Frank splitting up…are we talking divorce?" Tory nodded.

"Well I can see you're freaking out. But Tory you can't skip out on me. Why should I bear the brunt of your troubles. None of this is my fault."

"Of course not. But if I go, see, all the attention's gonna be drawn to us, and then there's going to be more talk about how fucked up our families are."

"So what? They gossip about us anyway! Shit, you don't think I don't hear it every day?! 'How's your father, poor dear.' Poor dear nothing, he's guilty as hell and we all know it. Tory, everyone sucks. Don't be a bastard, come on. Pliny needs you to do this. I need you. You've gotta be my escort, it's too late to get anyone else, and besides, you promised…" Her voice trailed off. She saw Tory re-evaluating things and did not press her argument any further.

The sun burned red over the poisoned horizon, a warm spectrum of warm red, orange and purple hues. The two cousins stayed motionless on the ledge. A few joggers passed by, a few cars, and once two little girls on bikes pedaled up the street. But what mostly passed was time.

The marijuana made Cecelia more reflective than she liked to be, and the topic of today's stoned introspection was her relationship with Tory. She thought of what he'd said, of the gossip they would garner as a couple at the ball. Most girls took their boyfriends, or old family friends, but her decision to take Tory was influenced by Pliny. That she regarded her cousin as a somewhat immature, self-centered nutcase did not factor into it; he was blood, of eligible age, and male. That was enough for Pliny, who sat her down and issued his request. It was important, he said, to show his detractor's the future Lewises, two very fine, attractive and genteel teenagers who could weather their family's misfortunes stoically. She was uncertain at first, given Tory's proclivity for abandoning his dates at parties, but Pliny assured her that Tory would remain at her side for the evening unless given permission to roam. If Tory could survive the recent disruptions of his life and remain true to his promise to be her escort, then Pliny would enhance his will in Tory's favor. It was a good deal for him; why he was balking at the idea she couldn't begin to fathom.

"Who's my snotty San Marino friend?"

"What?"

"Who's my snotty San Marino friend?" she repeated.

Tory thought for a moment. "Her name's Margo, I think…"

"Margo? Margo Vitesse? You ran down her boyfriend?!" Cecelia turned excitedly to face him. "You ran down Hugh March?"

"Yeah," Tory grinned. "You mean she didn't tell you? That was me..."

Cecelia laughed, threw her head back and howled into the sky in wicked jubilance. "A-hahahaha! A-hahahaha! Oh this is great! This is rich!" Tory snickered and sat up, then looked down at his shoes and grinned sheepishly while Cecelia chortled and slapped her knees. "A-hahahaha! Tell me the story!"

So Tory told her the tale of his collision with Hugh March, of the encounter with the police at the hospital and the clash with Margo's mother under the window. They both broke down and laughed till tears ran down their cheeks when he got to the part detailing his visit to the hospital with the six-pack, of finding Margo sullen and bitchy and Hugh pie-bald. "Wonderful!" Cecelia cried upon hearing the story's end. "Tory, you are a character. A-hahahah! Oh my God, this is too much…!"

They shared another snickering spate of Margo-bashing and Cecelia grew red choking back another fit of hysterical laughter as she related the time Margo had tried to cut her own hair with the dog clippers. When they had exhausted themselves they sat back on the ledge to rest, giggling intermittently and daring not to look at each other.

"You know, Margo's going to be at the Ball on Saturday…wouldn't it be great if we got a picture of you dancing with her and had them run it in the Star News?!" Hahahahahaha!! They lost it again, regressing into hysteria. When she could muster control Cecelia blurted out her plan to contact the Society page editor and get the picture printed. Tory commented that Hugh would make a pretty picture as well, with his head all wrapped up in gauze, and Cecelia agreed and took her cousin's hand.

"Tory you've got to come with me. We'll have a blast, I mean it! Come on…"

Her cousin looked away. At last he looked back, grinning, and nodded his consent. Cecelia was all smiles and kissed him on his forehead.

"Hey Tory, when's the last time you danced a waltz?"

He thought about it. "The prom? No, maybe it was at that Morton wedding last year. I dunno. It's been awhile…"

"You're going to have to waltz at the Ball, you know."

"Oh yeah?"

"Yeah. Do you remember how?"

Tory shrugged. "I dunno. Maybe."

"Come on." Cecelia ordered. "Up." She snapped her fingers impatiently and held out her hand. Tory slid off the ledge and took it; he placed an awkward hand on her waist and after he was in position she put her left hand on his shoulder. "Step forward. Left now." Tory watched his feet as Cecelia called out instructions. They waltzed around the Cabriolet once, then out into the street.

At dusk they were still dancing, the deb in her white dress and Reeboks, her escort dapper in shorts and Schlitz t-shirt, laughing and dancing to the Acapella Waltz. It would have made quite a picture for the Star News.

10

White Gloves and Party Manners

"Get away from there!"

"What?"

"You keep your mitts off my clock, Tory Lewis!"

"Gee Auntie, I was only trying to help. You gals might be on time occasionally if you had a working clock."

Ginny slapped her nephew's hands away from the Westmueller, preventing a nearly-successful second effort. "We are fashionably late darling, so mind your own business. Look, get the hell out of my parlor said the spider to the fly. Go get a drink or something, talk to Pliny. I've got to finish getting dressed." Taking no risks, she pushed and poked him along, out of the living room and away from the winding key. Tory hopped a few steps up the staircase to escape her.

"I'm going up to see my date. Is that alright with you?"

"Snotnose." She stuck out her tongue and shrieked when he almost grabbed it.

"Knock knock."

"Some knock. Good thing I'm dressed."

"Shit, I've seen you naked before. Nothing special."

"Fuck you too." Cecelia closed the lid of her makeup case with decisive finality and stood up quickly from her dressing table to face him. "How do I look?"

She radiated. It was not so much the freshly pressed taffeta gown as the fresh young girl in it; her light brown skin, freckled at her bare shoulder, gleamed above the glistening white sleeve that crossed her upper arms. Her hair had been buoyed up with a generous amount of mousse, but it was fluffy and the highlights contrasted beautifully over darker roots. Each ear was set with a sparkling diamond and smaller sapphire, simple but elegant. Silver pumps, the standard deb shoe, encased her feet and white silk gloves pulled up over her elbows completed the outfit.

Tory squinted and tilted his head from side to side in critical appraisal. Cecelia looked away, exasperated, and folded her arms across her chest. "Come on Tory, don't be mean."

He bowed respectfully. "You look beautiful."

Cecelia rolled her eyes. "Did you bring me some drugs?" Tory tossed her a pill bottle, which she caught and emptied into her hand. "What're these?"

"Well I don't have these chick problems, so I just brought a whole bunch of stuff. The blue ones with the 'V' in the center are Valiums, pretty easy, right? The big white ones with the '4' are Tylenol 4's, and those should do you right up but they may be hard on the stomach and they do make one kind of groggy. The reds are reds, seconal, and I wouldn't recommend doing those for plain ol' menstrual cramps…they tend to get you pretty fucked up, but should the occasion arise you might want to barter them for some coke. There's also a couple of amphetamines, speed to you and me, in there too… heart shaped orange pills, 5 mgs. Dexadrine…I would recommend taking those, I think they're just what you need to keep on top of your game and mask the pain."

On his recommendation Cecelia popped one of the dexadrine spansules and washed it down with a gulp of water. She froze when she saw her cousin grinning hugely. "You son of a bitch, what did I just do?!"

"Nothing," Tory laughed. "Nothing, Cece. Just relax. Or rather, don't relax, now that you've just eaten that. Really, it's a mild dose, it's okay."

"I should have just said 'no.' Alright, where's my purse?" She found it in front of her. "Okay." She took a deep breath, sucking in air, exhaled and smoothed her skirt. "I'm ready."

Tory held out his arm and she took it. "You look very handsome, Tory," she smiled, and Tory acknowledged her with a grin. "We're going to have fun, Cece. You're going to be a big hit."

"Yeah, me and twenty-four other girls. Hey, what was Mom yelling about earlier?"

Tory shrugged and together they stepped down the staircase. "She got pretty riled up when I tried to wind that clock on the mantel." He searched her wrist for a watch and found none. "How come you guys are afraid of time?"

Cecelia nearly slipped and Tory grabbed her. "These shoes…," she complained. "Mom's been weird about clocks ever since Dad went to prison; she figures that time will go by quicker if we don't measure it. I never wear a watch. Pliny's given me about three Rolexes but I don't like them. Don't tell him," she added, whispering: "He keeps forgetting he's already bought me one."

"I hocked mine," Tory whispered back.

Cecelia gave a look of mock disapproval but she didn't really care. Pliny had a thing about giving cash gifts; instead he bought expensive jewelry. He probably already knew Tory had pawned his watch.

They descended the last step and went into the kitchen where they found their grandfather, distinguished in an old-style tux, popping the cork on a magnum of champagne. He poured three glasses and handed his granddaughter one. Tory helped himself and the three went outside.

It was a beautiful summer evening. The weather had cooled and there was a light breeze to blow the smog away and bring the sweet scent of snapdragons and crocuses over from the garden. Tory wandered over to look at a bed of roses beaming in red and yellow splendor. Pliny and Cecelia sat together in the porch swing.

They did not speak for a long time. There did not seem to be any reason to; the chaos of the pre-debut party, dress-shopping, photo sessions, rehearsals, all the organization and planning efforts had yielded to this one quiet moment in the afternoon sun with the young girl in the epiphany of her life and the old man measuring out his. Water rippled against the tile pool sides and the swing creaked in time. It was a moment of family.

Cecelia caught her grandfather smiling at her and blushed. He took her hand. "I'm very proud of you."

She looked down at her feet, feeling embarrassed. "I haven't done anything, Pliny. I'm just being presented, that's all."

"Well you're a fine girl. You have a lot of character and you've done well in school. That's all I expect of you." Pliny smiled and Cecelia smiled back. They clinked glasses and sipped their wine. Pliny looked off into the garden at Tory poking amongst the flowers and a sad look overcame him. "Our name has suffered some arrows recently," he said. "I'd like you and Tory to fix that...not by what you do, but by who you are."

Cecelia said nothing, puzzled by her grandfather's lugubrious tone. Granted, her mother was a dingbat and her father a convict...her aunts, whom she knew little of, had been disinherited long ago...Tory's father was a medical gypsy and his mother Queen of the Dilettantes; his brothers perennial frat house wild men and his sister a bitch...not a perfect family, but a family nonetheless and one she could live with. Maybe Pliny was tired of forgiving them...but didn't he know that she had yet to go to college and demolish her personal life? Fall down drunk at fraternity parties? Flunk classes? Get pregnant? She herself would have ample opportunity to ruin the family name, and she would likely achieve her own spot in the Lewis Hall of Shame! She decided to keep these thoughts to herself though, as Pliny had just produced a velvet jewelry box from his coat pocket.

"Here sweetheart. Sorry it's not gift-wrapped but your grandmother always took care of that and I make a mess every time I try."

Cecelia took it excitedly. The box opened like a newly hatched chrysalis revealing a string of graduated pearls brilliant against the black velvet. "Oh Pliny they're beautiful!"

"I think so too. Let me help you." He took the string from her wondering hands and Cecelia pulled her hair back to allow him to fasten the clasp around her neck. "You don't already have a set, do you?"

"No!" Cecelia cried, for she hadn't and was very happy to finally get some. She hugged him tightly and kissed him, murmuring her thanks. When she finally let him go she smoothed his lapel and got up, grinning. "I have to go see!," and she ran off into the house shouting for her mother. Pliny leaned back in the swing savoring her hug.

He opened his eyes when Tory came back onto the porch clutching a rose. "Is that for me?"

Tory grinned. "Sorry gramps, it isn't. It's a better flower than this old florist boutonniere, though…see?" He pulled out his lapel and bent down so Pliny could see, and the old man agreed. Tory went into the kitchen and returned with a knife and the bottle of champagne. He refilled his grandfather's glass and his own and set the bottle down beside him on the picnic table, then began to manicure the garden rose. When he had sliced off the thorns and clipped the step he grabbed the champagne and poured a splash on the bud.

"Whatever are you doing?" Pliny asked.

"Rinsing the petals."

"That's Dom Perignon you're pouring on the ground, Tory. Show some respect."

"Even better," Tory asserted. "I think the monk would approve. This is one gorgeous flower." He unpinned the old rose from his tux jacket and threw it away, then fastened the new one in its spot. "There," he said, proudly displaying. "Classier than some old store bought rose."

"Listen Tory, I'd like to ask a favor of you…I'd like you to avoid any confrontations tonight."

The kid looked at his grandfather. "Kind of 'out of the blue,' Pliny."

Pliny shrugged. "Maybe. But given your peccable nature you're going to raise hell at the opportunity and, well, please don't do it tonight. For Cece's sake."

"You mean, don't make fun of any old geezers tonight, don't beat up any geeks, and don't try to get any girls drunk and take advantage of them. Is that what you're trying to say?" Pliny laughed at his translation and Tory considered the request while gulping from his glass of champagne. "Okay Pliny, I'll hold up my end. Cece deserves it."

"Thank you. She does deserve it. She looks very beautiful tonight, doesn't she?"

"Yeah, she looks great. Did you see she's wearing Grandmother's earrings?"

"Yes, and I think I'll tell Ginny to give them to her. They look a damn sight better on a pretty girl than they do in some safety deposit box."

They were interrupted by the entrance of Virginia Lewis, herself looking fine in a backless lame gown with a diamond pave barrette pinning back her hair. "Well I'm ready!" she sang. "Shall we go?"

The two Lewis men complimented her several times and Ginny ate it up, reveling in their attentions. Together they walked around the side of the house and climbed into the Rolls Royce, the two younger Lewises in the back and Ginny up front with Pliny driving (Cecelia had already been waiting for them by the car). Halfway down the driveway Cecelia remembered her bouquet and Tory leapt out and ran back to fetch it, and when he returned the family drove off to the ball.

In the midst of dense freeway traffic Cecelia grimaced and doubled over; when Tory tried to assist she waved him off. "I'm okay," she whispered. "Just cramps."

"Didn't that speed help?"

"A little, but I get really mean ones. Should I take another hit?"

Tory shook his head. "You'll be bouncing off the walls. Just start drinking when we get there, maybe that will help." Cecelia nodded and continued to groan quietly.

When they arrived at the hotel Cecelia jumped out and quickly went in to use the ladies' room, brushing off queries by her mother, who started after her but was detoured by Tory. "Come on Auntie, let's go get a drink. Cece's alright, she just needs to chill out." He steered her into a group of proud deb mothers who quickly engaged her in admiring chatter, each taking turns receiving compliments from the others. Tory and Pliny stood by.

"What's wrong with Cece?"

"Women's complaints, Pliny. I gave her something to get her through the night and told her to have a few. She'll be okay."

But Tory was not aware that Cecelia's sufferings had compounded with a great flow that seeped beyond the tampon into her panties. She would have to make do with just a slip and hose and stepped out of her spoiled lingerie. "God," she sighed, throwing them into the trash. "What else?!" A fresh tampon, a vending machine pad for safety, a quick washup and she was ready. She checked her makeup, admired her new jewelry, then returned to the lobby.

"Hi."

Tory turned around. "Hi. You alright?"

"Yeah, fine. But a drink would be lovely." They excused themselves from the handful of parents around Pliny and headed off to join their peers at one of the ballroom bar stations. There they met Kelly O'Leary who was trying the patience of her date, a burly sophomore from UCLA. Tory moved alongside them and nonchalantly squeezed Kelly O'Leary's ass but she rebuffed him, grabbing his hand. "No no no," she smiled tersely. Tory shrugged and attributed it to her date's presence. When he got up to the bar he ordered a couple of gin and tonics for Cecelia and himself. Kelly O'Leary called over her shoulder to him. "Tory! We have a room! Come up with Cece!"

"Where is it?" he shouted across the mob.

Kelly conferred with her date. "Seven-twelve!" With a carefree wave she was gone.

"Ten dollars," said the bartender.

Cecelia had moved away from the crowd and was standing near the large doorway beside a potted palm, scrutinizing the nautical decorations dressing the ballroom. Most philanthropic galas attach a festive theme to the occasion; the Pasadena Guild of Huntington Hospital's June Cotillion celebrated the launching of the luxury liner Titanic.

This ballroom, however, bore no resemblance to the rusting hulk broken on the sand miles below the surface of the freezing Atlantic. Here the promise of lavish accommodation and catered whim thrived, surrounded by beautiful young girls embarking on their own maiden voyage into life. Ersatz portholes lined the walls, the stage was rigged with lines and moorings. A massive, craggy iceberg eight feet high menaced the hors d'oeuvres table and another smaller version floated in the punchbowl. The champagne, of course, was White Star.

It was a wonderfully decorative room but it could easily have been covered with posters of Lenin or camouflage. A group of Guild ladies dubbed "The Politburo" proposed a "Debs 'n Reds" party, with the ballroom done up like Moscow's Red Square complete with Kremlin spires, hammer and sickle flags, and murals celebrating the proletariat worker. They competed with the "Operation Freedom" squad, composed mostly of the San Marino wives of Halliburton and General Dynamics executives who waged their own war to muster toppled statues and mockups of armaments, but in the end both of these lost out the Titanic; the decoration committee opposed the limited beige and olive color scheme offered by Operation Freedom and there was too great a chance for unfavorable publicity from a Debs 'n Reds party. Besides, someone noted, the Communist Party wasn't all that much fun. The Titanic's detractors were consoled with assurances that they could design the Cotillion party favors, a concession the dissident's accepted readily; at each place setting was a little wooden lifeboat filled with chocolates.

Tory arrived at Cecelia's side and handed her one of the tumblers. "What's this?" Cecelia asked, pondering the tapered swizzle stick.

"It's an oar. Come on, let's have a look around."

They wandered amongst the other guests, stopping to say hello to acquaintances and to criticize the dress of enemies. Of the most ridicule was the attire of a fat man dressed in the full costume of a ship's captain, thematically appropriate but stupid nonetheless. Tory recognized him to be the oafish heckler from the Memorial Day tennis match. "That buffoon. I'm gonna sink his ship."

"Good," Cecelia said, knocking back her cocktail. "He was the President of the Tournament of Roses last year. Let me know if you want me to help."

"I will. Maybe I can dose him with a few ambien…"

Cecelia shook her head. "Too dangerous. Besides, that whole group is a bunch of drunks. Everyone would think he was just behaving normally. He'll disgrace himself on his own, just wait and see. If we alert the photographers, maybe we can get some photos of the old lecher trying to feel me up. I knew one of last year's Princesses and she said he was the filthiest old man she'd ever met…what?"

Her quizzical "what?" was in response to the look of astonishment on Tory's face. "Christ," he muttered, "I've never heard you talk like that before…"

Cecelia grinned, enjoying his unease. "It's cause I'm having my period. Can you imagine what you'd be like if your dick bled every month?"

Tory swallowed a mouthful of gin and tonic. "Let's change the subject. Sorry I brought it up. Oh, Kelly's having a party or something up in her room, do you want to head up there or hang around here for awhile?"

"What's going on there? Drugs, probably…"

"Seems like reason enough for me."

"Nah. You can go if you want. I don't feel like getting all coked up. You gave me that speed and that's enough, I feel pretty good now. But look, go on up. Kelly's with her jocko date, but I know she likes you."

Tory shrugged. "Not if you don't want to. I might want to check in on the Dodger game at the bar. Plus I should see how Pliny's doing."

"Alright, see you later." She excused him gladly, for at that moment Margo Vitesse had arrived in the ballroom and Cecelia wanted a private audience with her and to hear her full uninhibited version of Tory's hospital visit with her. Hugh quickly appeared, wearing a blue turban with a big jewel pinned to it. "Margo! Margo!" Cecelia called, and Margo saw her and came over with Hugh trailing.

"Margo, you look so pretty! What an awesome dress. Hi Hugh, how's your head?"

"He broke it," Margo sighed, perturbed.

"Did you see Steve Scott in the lobby, Hugh?"

"What?! Steve Scott's in the lobby?

"Yep, signing autographs and everything. Didn't you see him?"

"No!" He turned to Margo. "D'you mind if…" He needn't have even asked; Margo motioned him away as if she were shooing a pesky fly.

"I'm so embarrassed," she cringed.

"What happened? I thought you were going to bring that water-polo player?"

" I couldn't get rid of Hugh. He looked so pathetic, and he was so depressed about missing the State Meet. Besides, my mother wouldn't let me."

"Yeah, too bad. So tell me what happened…"

Margo scowled. "Don't you know?"

Cecelia was surprised, not by Margo's obvious resentment but by the fact that she had figured out the Tory-Cecelia relationship at all. She stammered and pretended to know only sketchy details, and eventually Margo's anguish delivered a torrid, embellished account of the accident that depicted the villain Tory as a hit and run drunk who left poor Hugh for dead in the middle of the street, returning only to steal Hugh's bicycle. Margo's account was so vivid that Cecelia felt a growing disdain for her cousin, and even muttered "what a jerk," during the telling, until she remembered the jerk was her date for the evening. "Well," she shrugged at the conclusion of Margo's tale, "at least you look great."

"Thanks," Margo said sadly. "I feel rotten. Hugh and I fought the entire way here. He looks so foolish! He knows it and I know it…I wish we had never come!"

Cecelia put her arm around Margo and felt guilty for having laughed at her with Tory. "Come on Margo, you look beautiful! Don't say stuff like that…come on, try to lighten up. Hugh looks okay…heck, with you looking so great and him, uh, well…so exotic, you'll be the center of attention!"

Margo started to cry. "I don't want to be the center of attention, goddamn it. I just want to get this stupid evening over with, okay?"

Cecelia steered her away from where they were standing, over to a wall where they could sit down in a couple of chairs. She took a Kleenex from her purse and gave it to Margo, who blew her nose. "God I've got such a headache."

"Shoot I don't have any aspirin with me, I just took my last Midol before coming in. I'm having my period, can you believe it? If I leak on this white dress it's the end of me."

"Too bad," Margo shuddered, curling up with her head between her knees. Cecelia glanced at her and stood up. "I'm starting to get a headache myself. Stay here, let me see if I can get us some Bufferin." She left and headed for a flock of misses gathered by the hors d' oeuvres table. Margo stayed curled up, staring down at her satin silver pumps so shiny clean against the mottled maroon carpet, like a glistening chunk of ice in a bloody sea. Nearby floated another isle, the plump silk clutch purse Cecelia carried and beside that the lacy nosegay she gestured carelessly with. Already Cecelia's flowers were wilting; Margo wondered what sort of condition they would be in at the end of the evening. Her nose started to drip again and she helped herself to another tissue from Cecelia's purse, uncovering the pill bottle stashed there.

She looked for Cecelia in the crowd, unable to spot her amongst the camouflage of white that buzzed around everywhere. Curious, she helped herself to the bottle and shook the pills out into her hand…maybe Cecelia had forgotten she even had aspirin…but what came out was not aspirin but a colorful collection in all shapes and sizes.

Margo felt a sudden urge to take them all. They were like precious jewels in her hand, their bright hues and inviting designs ignited her impulse to own them. She felt exactly like she had just walked into Nordstrom with her mother's credit card and pushed the little pills around in her hand for more specific scrutiny. Only the blue ones with the "V" in the middle were identifiable: Valium, the wonder drug. Her mother took them for migraines and stress…Margo had never tried them, but then, there was no time like the present. "Let's see, I take two aspirins, so I guess I should take two of these…" She washed them down with the remnants of Cecelia's cocktail and put the rest of the drugs back in the bottle. She felt dishonest and liked it, and slipped the bottle into her own purse.

She sat up, feeling better now that she had done something to help herself and giddy with the excitement of having been naughty. Her mother became a much nicer person, calm and sweet after having taken the tranquilizers, and Margo hoped they would have the same effect on her. Hugh came through the ballroom doors and stood helplessly off to the side; Margo waved and called to him and he came over.

"Hi.

Hugh sat down beside her. "Where's Cece?"

"She went off to find some aspirin. Did you have a nice time?"

"No. I don't know what she was talking about. There was no one in the lobby except all these people from this party and the desk clerk didn't even know who Steve Scott was…"

"Poor Hughie. Don't look so disappointed honey, maybe Cece thought he was someone else…"

"Yeah, maybe," Hugh grumbled. He looked at Margo suspiciously, for she had begun to rub his back lightly. "What are you doing?"

Margo felt mean again. "Okay, sorry, I didn't know touching you was off limits!" She looked angrily away. Where was Cece?

"Touching me isn't 'off limits' Margo. But make up your mind, are you gonna be nice to me tonight or act like your usual bitch self, huh?"

"Look I didn't even want to be here, but now that I am and you are let's make the best of it! In a few hours it'll all be over and then we never have to see each other again, okay?!"

It was Hugh's turn to look off into the distance. They sat there in their own wretchedness as waiters passed by dutifully bearing baskets of bread. Some couples had already seated themselves but they looked bored and unhappy and judging from the still-large crowd at the ballroom bar it would be some time before dinner began. Hugh shifted in his chair and addressed Margo from the corner of his eye. "I'm thirsty and I'm not going to sit here with my back against the wall all night. Do you want to come with me and get a drink?"

"No thanks, I'd better wait here for Cece to come back."

"Okay."

Hugh left and joined the crowd at the bar. Margo watched him edge into the fray. "I'm so stupid. Why did I say that to him?" She shook her head in remorse and hoped Hugh would forgive her. She still had her headache and neither the champagne nor the Valiums had made her feel any better; in fact she felt worse. "I need to take more." She looked for Cecelia and deciding the coast was clear, shook two more tablets out and furtively placed the bottle back in her own purse. The ordeal with Hugh had dried up her mouth considerably and the pills stayed stuck on the back of her tongue dissolving bitterly. She got up and bumped into a nearly handsome boy carrying a brace of drinks, but the boy anticipated the collision and stepped away. "Could I have one of those?" Margo croaked hoarsely. "Please?"

The boy was delighted. "Why sure, take this one."

Margo accepted the cocktail and quickly gulped half of it down. The bitter medicine residue was replaced by the pleasant juniper tinge of a good gin & tonic. "You're pretty thirsty," the boy observed. "Maybe you'd better have this one too." He extended the other drink but Margo blushed.

"I got a couple of aspirin stuck in my throat. Thanks a lot, that did the trick."

"Uh huh." The boy looked furtively around, then tilted his head suggestively toward the lobby. "Why don't you come with me and we'll talk about it." Without waiting for a reply he placed his hand on her back and guided her to the door. "I'm pretty good with throats."

When the shortstop's wild throw went sailing into the Pirate's dugout Tory turned away from the bar television in disgust and slugged the remainder of his half-finished scotch. He looked around the bar in vain search for someone to converse with and decided the inevitable had arrived; it was time to head back into the ballroom for dinner.

"Maybe it's not over," the bartender suggested with insulting piety.

"You already got me to pay twelve bucks for a watery scotch. I'll be lucky to leave with my cufflinks." With a last glance at the tv he surrendered a twenty. "I've got to learn to skip the home-team loyalty." The bartender laughed and collected the bet, wiping a wet rag over the spot where the money had fallen. Tory left the bar.

He joined a small bustle of people merging at the ballroom doors and glimpsed Margo Vitesse approaching from the opposite direction. This time Tory did not avoid her, in fact he wanted to get as close as possible. This Margo looked a very different girl from the peevish, buttoned-up shrew from the hospital…this Margo wore a spectacular dress that slipped far off her shoulders, revealing an eyeful of breasts. Brazenly confronting the congested doorway she caromed through with bullheaded determination, insouciant to the objections arising around her, and Tory recognized the glittering dilated pupils of someone just starting to feel the onset of a severe drunk.

In the wake of Margo's testudo came a young man, a casually projected twenty-one year old who disarmed the crowd of their resentment with nods and slightly unctuous hello's which he reserved for the especially pretty girls. As the parted crowd rejoined and Tory moved on he caught a glimpse of Margo crashing seat-first into a divan and her escort falling to his knees to the floor, and their sudden actions seemed more curious to him than anything he had ever witnessed. Then the dining room doors closed behind him, and Margo Vitesse was lost.

11

Picayune Things

"Tory, over here!" It was Cecelia, calling from one of the multitudinous tables. He scanned their line until he located the flailing ribbon from her waving bouquet and worked his way through the congested aisles, for many guests still stood in groups and continued to chat. Cecelia kicked the chair next to her out to one side. "Hi."

"Hi." Tory glanced at the little life preservers painted with each guest's name that served as placecards and flipped his over so the name would not show. "My name's not 'Victor'," he explained when Cecelia gave him a wary look. He sat down and slouched forward, his hands clasped confidently atop the table before him. Cecelia smiled briefly then looked away into the horizon.

"Do you like where we're sitting?"

Tory took his time answering, surveying the room to decide what constituted a good position. There had been much switching around of places and the Committee's spirited plan to seat old and young together was tossed as white dresses and black ties darted about in Cotillion anomie searching for the best tables. His eye fell on Pliny making time with a group of bejeweled widows and swept over to an area filled with cliquey boys from the Catholic schools. Not there. Moving on his gaze followed two very tan, very blond girls in black taffeta to a table nearly opposite his on the other side of the room. The blondes joined a thirty-something couple dripping with nouveau wealth and two other debs and their escorts. "How 'bout over there?"

Cecelia sighted down his pointed finger to the arrangement. "Pretty good. I like the guys…plenty of girls for you."

"What's good for the gander…"

"…Is good for the goose, yes I know. Alright, let's go." They threaded a serpentine path around the tables, stopping to chat with a very old man, a cohort of Pliny's from some ancient day. Their conversation was brief and friendly and might have gone something like this:

Cecelia: Hello Mr. Doubleday. Are you having a good time? I'm Cece Lewis, Pliny Lewis's granddaughter.

Doubleday: Hello Miss Lewis. You look beautiful. Is this your young fellow?

Cecelia: No, he's my cousin Tory. He's my escort this evening…no one else would have me. Ha ha.

Doubleday: Ha ha. I'm sure that's not true, a lovely young lady like you. Tory…

(Tory and Doubleday shake hands. Doubleday begins to cough mightily.)

Doubleday: Ack…cough…ack

Tory: Let's move on. He's going to die.

As they approached their table Cecelia noticed Tory checking out the two blond misses. "Ex-debs, from last year. They always wear black." Tory nodded and pulled out his cousin's chair. The two girls were conversing in private whispers and did not acknowledge the new arrivals but the wealthy thirty-something couple welcomed them as did Cecelia's fellow debutantes. Dinner was served.

The waiters brought out a cold avocado soup starred with almond slivers and sour cream. Beside the tiger lily centerpiece were bottles of champagne and the diners ate their soup slowly, sipping the wine between spoonfuls. All around the room rose the pleasant laughter and walla of animated conversation mixed with the clatter of cutlery against china. The two ex-debs broke up their intimate conversation and traded off telling a story of a star-studded polo match they had been to that morning. Over at his table Pliny entertained the widows with the story of a love affair he'd once had with a deaf woman. And Ginny Lewis, seated far away from her father-in-law and daughter (she had dismissed Pliny to sit wherever he liked and Cecelia wouldn't have dreamed of letting her mother near her) established herself as the belle of the ball with her bright laugh and flirtatious smile that captured the attentions of many of the men surrounding her, along with the ire of their wives. (It's safe to assume that Pliny and Ginny were too involved in their own ebullient parties to give two hoots about the younger Lewises.)

At the Cotillion to be quick with a placecard preserver was to be happy, and most of the guests seemed to be enjoying the company of their fellow tablemates. Those who stodgily stuck with their original assignment endured the infelicitous company of the unwanted or unaccompanied; fortunately the food was good and one could eat instead of talk. Following the cold soup was a light spinach salad and the main course. One could have veal, stuffed Cornish game hens or duck, and asparagus with hollandaise, or else peas. Tory and Cecelia both had the duck and it was good, with a light wine sauce and walnuts. None of the women ordered the veal, prompting a discussion on the pros and cons of red meat. Tory, discarding the mangled carcass of his duck onto a bread and butter plate, suggested the girls could go to a secret meat market he knew of in Koreatown where they could buy a pound of real human flesh, if they wanted a tasty meat that was tender, juicy, and low in calories. Appalled looks crossed the other diner's faces and Cecelia kicked him hard. Tory shrugged and said "just kidding."

And with this scenario established, let us retreat back to the moment the dining room doors closed on Miss Margo Vitesse.

<u>12</u>

The Duke's Tale

"Let me tell you a story," said the nearly-handsome boy. He and Margo were sitting together on a divan in the lobby behind one of the enormous elephant ferns stationed around the room. The boy, who called himself Duke, was leaning slightly forward with his knees apart examining a diamond the size of a large pea that he had found in the carpet moments before. It was a spectacular stone, a white multifaceted diamond in an old style cut. Its worth, the Duke estimated, was about fifty thousand dollars.

"You are so lucky!" Margo exclaimed.

It was then that the Duke told her his story.

"…Now I had an Uncle who once found a briefcase full of money at a bus bench on Figueroa, near Sixth Street," the Duke said. "He was a frequenter of the bars around there, a devout alcoholic who loathed work and enjoyed the company of distempered gamblers and street people. Anyway, on this occasion he awoke in a doorway from a blackout's night sleep and got up to wander down to the Rescue Mission, where he could join a few of his fellow Sixth Street citizens for breakfast and conversation, and maybe add his voice to the hymnal chorus led by the good Sisters of Mercy. *En passant*, he happened upon a briefcase sitting by itself at a bus stop.

"My Uncle stopped. Then he went on. Then he stopped. Then he went on. Finally, unable to ignore his obvious fate, he turned around and went back to the bus stop. The briefcase was still there, black and magnetic as Kubrick's monolith. Up and down the street he looked—no one. So very quickly he snatched up the case and ran off into an alley…

"…Now skid row alleys aren't the safest places, and being one of the more well-known lushes around the area, my Uncle couldn't exactly be seen lugging an attaché around. It would certainly around the suspicions of the local constabulary, they'd take the briefcase away from him and lock him up for theft or vagrancy…yet he had to open this briefcase! And he couldn't do it in the alley, it might have contained something important like Laker tickets or foodstamps or something…"

"Maybe it was full of money!" Margo shrieked.

Duke glowered at her. "I haven't got there yet."

Margo hung her head ashamedly.

"Now then, as I was saying, my Uncle needed something to put this briefcase in, something that would hide it until he could get to a safe place, something apropos like…like…" He looked to Margo encouragingly.

"Like a bag full of vomit!"

"Precisely," said the Duke. "And my Uncle knew exactly where to get one, for he had deposited a paper bag filled with said substance in a nearby dumpster the night before. So he retrieved his bag, slid the briefcase inside and ambled down to the Greyhound Bus Terminal to lock himself into a stall and open the case. Do you want some more?"

More in this case was more gin, which Duke poured generously from a silver flask taken from his inside jacket pocket. Margo nodded dizzily; it was her second helping. Duke filled her glass halfway, knocked the rim with the flask's silver mouth so that it sang, and recapped it with a crooked grin. Margo crossed her legs, tugged on her dress and concentrated on remaining upright, for she was definitely wasted by then and quite enjoying it. "So then what?" she chirped.

"Well what do you think? Here he was, some smelly old creep who bummed a drink far more often than he bought one and never held a job, and suddenly he's got a briefcase open on his lap and is staring at stacks of hundred dollar bills—fifty grand in all!

"Sounds pretty great, doesn't it?" (Vigorous agreement from Margo). "Ah, but there was one catch. Attached to this attaché, dangling from a strip of leather, was a nametag. With an address. And a telephone number."

"No!" protested the girl.

"I'm afraid so," said the Duke.

"He returned the briefcase?!!" Margo shrieked.

Duke crooked another grin and swung his knees back and forth. "Well, not yet. All that money made him afraid, and when he was afraid he drank. So he wrapped up the bag of money again and went off to get a drink. He was a nervous wreck when he left the bathroom…weaving around, bumping into people, muttering…by the time he hit the street he was in an advanced state of delirium tremens and his conscience was practically yelling at him. The poor man was so tormented he didn't realize it, but he was headed right back to the bus bench where he'd found the money, and damn if he didn't trip and fall flat on his face over another man who was crawling around on his hands and knees beside that very bench."

"Oh my God!" Margo closed her eyes tightly against the impeding revelation, fighting off a sudden attack of the spins. When she opened them again she found the Duke leaning forward, one eyebrow raised, examining her. She straightened up and blinked. Satisfied with her recovery the Duke went on.

"My Uncle picked himself up off the sidewalk. The man hadn't even noticed the old bum, so consumed was he with his search. He was on his knees wearing holes into his perfectly tailored suit, crawling amongst the dirt of the city looking this way and that, peering under the bench, delving into the gutter, looking up and down the street desperately…he just couldn't believe that there was nothing there. And my Uncle, who was standing there over him in his filthy Rescue Mission duds, my Uncle, who never had a cent in his life, who drank up the change people gave him and combed through garbage cans for food when he absolutely needed to eat, FELT SORRY FOR THIS MAN!!!

"Did you lose something? my Uncle asked.

"What?!' screamed the man. 'Did you lose something?' my Uncle repeated. The man didn't answer for a moment, so shocked was he at being addressed by this scruffy man who reeked terribly of vomit and mold, a down and outer with insurmountable problems who was likely better off dead…he waved him off. 'I lost my briefcase. I lost it right here on this bench…'

"Are you Harold Lyons?" my Uncle asked. The man jumped. He fixed his saucer eyes on the old bum and tried to speak, finally daring to gasp 'Yes!'

"It was the moment of truth for my Uncle. He looked at the man's face streaming with sweat and panic, and hesitated…he had fifty K tax free, no questions asked, right there in his hands, enough money to get off skid row and get going in the right direction for once in his life…and there on the other side was a guy who'd obviously been going that way for some time.

"Is your briefcase black, with gold locks and a nametag?'

"Yes! Yes!" cried Mr. Lyons. And there followed a terrible moment, a moment of such suspense and anticipation that to liken it to anything in history would weaken it, these two polar opposites with such dissimilar fates, suddenly crossed, neither daring to consummate the moment with further words that would bring defeat to one and victory to the other…and then he who had the most to lose spoke. 'Did you find it?' Harold Lyons gasped.

"Yes,' replied my Uncle. 'I have it right here.' And he reached into his sack and pulled out the briefcase full of money, whereupon Mr. Lyons dropped dead of a massive heart attack, right there on the sidewalk."

Margo stared, mouth agape, in stunned disbelief. "No!"

"Yes," the Duke said. "Yes indeed."

"What did your Uncle do?!"

"He went off and had a drink. Cheers!" He raised his silver flask and took a swallow. Margo did the same from her tumbler, desperately trying to focus her vision on the Duke and a girl in red who had just arrived on the scene. The girl lay her hand on the flask, arresting it. The Duke scowled, regained his manners and gestured an introduction. "Frances, magically delicious."

"I think you've had enough nastiness for cocktail hour, dear." She smiled pleasantly to Margo as she held out her hand for the Duke to take. He obliged her and stood up from the divan, bowing deeply to Margo.

Drunk as she was, Margo panicked at losing her storyteller to the sudden interloper. "Wait!" she blurted out, "What about the diamond?"

"Diamond?" inquired Frances, with a raised eyebrow.

"What about it?" shrugged the Duke. "Perhaps I should tell you the rest, that's only fair. You see, my Uncle took some of the money he'd found and got himself a bath and a shave and a suit of clothing, and he gave a little to a friend of his, fifty or a hundred bucks or so, and together they hopped a bus to Santa Anita, where my Uncle put every cent he had on the horses, and that very day, do you know what happened?"

Margo shook her head.

"That very day my Uncle picked six winning horses in a row."

Margo could not even respond, so stupefied was she at the enormous greatness of the Duke's tale. She fell back against the velvet cushion of the divan and slouched helplessly. Duke brought the diamond out from his coat pocket and held it up to the light. "You see," he said finally, "I can't return this rock, even if I found out who lost it. They might have a heart attack, or worse!"

"Goddamn!" Margo slurred.

"Exactly." The Duke grinned. "Now I have stumbled onto my own bag of money, not that I need it of course, my Uncle recently died of cirrhosis and left me a goodly portion of his estate...but one should never refuse a gift and as long as I don't care too much about money I will always have it. The lady who lost this diamond knows that, you know that, and probably everyone here knows that, being of the same ilk and breeding..." He waved his arm in sweeping gesture at the parade of people filing through the ballroom doors, headed for their tables and dinner. "She will discover a vacant setting on her tiara and suffer a mild spell, but it will be insured and a nice new stone will soon be set in its place. Meanwhile, I will have a new influx of cash."

"You have too much already," the girl named Frances objected.

"No, just enough." He turned back to Margo, slumped deeply on the divan, her eyes glazed over but still with a glint of comprehension. "Do you understand the moral of this story?"

Margo moved her head back and forth in approximation of a shake.

Duke pocketed the diamond. "Wealth perpetuates. The rich get richer." With a wink he was gone, headed off into the ever-flowing stream of Cotillion goers, the sudden girl in red coupled to his arm.

"Shit," Margo grumbled, trying and failing to stand. She was too drunk to eat and too drunk to converse. Luckily no one besides the girl Frances had come by to see her slumped in the divan with her dress rumpled and hairdo askew. A feeble remembrance of Hugh stirred weakly in her brain, but it was not enough to enable her to sober up and venture into the dining room…she was more wasted than she had ever been before and could not remember how she got that way, because everything preceding her encounter with the Duke seemed a vague dream. She closed her eyes and spun.

13

Margo Redux

"Margo!"

No answer.

"Margo!"

"Hmmph. What?"

"Margo!!!"

"What?!"

"Margo!!!!"

This time Margo opened her eyes. She looked around the ship at the waves of silently scurrying guests. "MARGO!!!!!" screamed the voice, ever more insistent. "WHAT?!!" Margo screamed back.

"It's time to go," the voice replied calmly.

Margo looked down and finally located the urgent caller, a large orange cat dressed in the uniform of a ship's captain, whose head just peaked above the divan seat. "Excuse me," she said, "but where are we going?"

"To the lifeboats," replied the captain. "The ship is sinking."

Margo looked up from the furry face to the ballroom doors where masses of people continued to rush out, making no sound. She looked for Hugh amongst the throng but did not see him. "I think I'll wait right here, thank you." With that she closed her eyes again.

A moment later she felt a soft brush across her cheek. The cat had jumped up to the arm of the divan and drawn its tail across her face. "I'm afraid I can't let you wait here," the cat said firmly. "The ship is sinking and

I'm responsible for you now."

Margo eyed the cat grumpily.

"Alright, though I do think it's weird to take orders from a cat, especially from one dressed up in a uniform."

"Don't be insolent," the cat hissed. Margo decided she had better do as instructed, for she was not quite sure of the situation and the cat was, after all, a captain. Once more she looked to the crowd of people leaving the ballroom but did not recognize a single face and their silence made her somewhat reluctant to call out. The cat leapt down and took a couple of quick hops stopping abruptly to look back at her. "I'm coming, I'm coming, keep your fur on." The cat, apparently satisfied, bounded off and vanished.

"Where's my purse? Ok, here…" She opened it quickly to check her makeup in her compact mirror. She brushed a little powder over her cheeks and was glad her eyes had not assumed their usual puffiness, for she knew she had been asleep for quite some time. Replacing the compact in her purse she drew her hands down the gazar skirt to smooth it and took a couple of steps towards the silent current, but noticing the bouquets in the hands of the other debutantes, realized she did not have hers and turned back to look at the divan. The flowers were not there.

"Oh! Oh!" Turning fretfully to the crowd she called out: "Has anyone seen my nosegay! Excuse me, has anyone seen my flowers? I had them right here and now they're gone!" Dropping her voice she cursed a little and wondered if the cat had taken them but dismissed the thought as silly for the cat had no way of carrying them and what would he do with a debutante's bouquet anyway? Use it to woo another cat? She smiled at the thought. "Pardon me," she called again to the crowd, " have any of you seen my bouquet?"

There was no immediate response, nor was one expected. After all, the ship was sinking and the guests seemed oblivious to her anyhow. Then, just as she was about to give up, from out of the crowd came the debutante mistress Agatha Grilover, who Margo at first did not recognize for she had changed from her evening gown into a man's tuxedo and was sporting a very thick, very black mustache that Margo thought looked quite ugly.

"Margo!" exclaimed the old lady. "What are you doing here alone? Where's your escort?"

"I don't know," Margo cried. "I was sitting here talking with a Duke, then a girl in red came and took him away. And then I fell asleep and a cat woke me up, and I don't know where Hugh is and he probably won't look for me anyway because I've been so mean to him and I've lost my flowers and I don't know what's going on and everything seems so strange!"

"Oh hush up!" snapped the old woman. "That's no way for a girl to talk on the night of her coming-out! You should be grateful to the cat, he very likely saved your life! The ship is sinking and you're sleeping away…! Shame!" Her mustache twitched and she licked a little fleck of spit that had slipped to the corner of her mouth. "Now get with it young lady and join the crowd!" With that, Agatha Grilover turned smartly on her heel and marched back into line.

"Yes'm" Margo curtsied, adding "you ugly old fag-hag." The insult and the curtsey were both wasted, however, for Agatha had long since disappeared. "Well," she sighed, "I suppose I should get going." With that she ventured forth across the lobby, brushing away the thick fronds of the potted ferns that seemed larger and more numerous than they had before and flapped like flags in a stiff breeze in her path. After a short time she joined the moving herd.

No one noticed her. She stayed in step with the rest of the patient collection of guests, speaking to no one nor being spoken to. The line continued its hushed journey down the hallway to the elevators where some of the ladies and gentlemen split off and entered the cars. Then a woman who looked very much like Cece Lewis's mother beckoned to her from a small alcove and Margo stepped out and made her way over.

"Hear the music?" the woman whispered, her tone lighthearted. "Listen!" Margo did, cocking an ear but all that was audible was a loud rushing of water, like old plumbing flushing very loudly.

"What, that?!"

"No! Shhh…" The woman put a finger to her lips and Margo listened again, this time picking up a faintly discernable minuet that played just above the noise of the water. "There!" Her slender arm extended across the corridor towards a closed stateroom door. "Go in there!" Margo looked past the blur of black and white passing by and wondered how to cross without being swept away again by the crowd. When she looked back to the woman there was no one there.

Margo felt disappointed. Quickly deciding to follow the woman's advice she pushed her way through the parade of guests to the opposite side of the hallway, but was confused by the sameness of the doors and was unsure which was the correct room. She listened again for the music…again, the same rush of water sounded. "Oh well," she shrugged, pushing down on the nearest handle, "nothing ventured, nothing gained." And with that she opened the cabin door and went inside.

Margo was not sure what she was going to find on the other side of the door, but what she did find was decidedly not a stateroom. It was not even part of the ship. A blank desert landscape stretched out, bisected by an empty span of concrete highway. Just to her right was a towering butterfly-shaped sign illuminated red with white neon piping, revolving lazily atop a very high pole. With every third turn the sign flashed "DUKE'S" in neat white neon script.

"Now a sign will usually lead you to something," she told herself. "And it says 'Duke's' so it probably has something to do with diamonds, or gin… so I'm certain I'll meet up again with the Duke." Hopeful that she would at last be able to recognize someone, even an accidental acquaintance like the Duke, she hurried and in no time arrived beneath the sign. What she found confused her even more, for her syllogism applied correctly to logical things in a logical world, and here on this barren stretch of highway reality had no business.

There was, plainly and simply, nothing there. The sign existed solely for itself, a neon monument in a rocky desert. Amidst the crackling hum generating from high atop its lofty setting came the faint minuet Margo had heard outside the stateroom door, and she recognized it and nearly leapt for joy—she had come through the right door after all!

"Hello! Hello!" she called to the sign. "Hello!" The sign made another lazy, crackling turn.

"Margo?!"

"Yes!" Margo answered excitedly. "Yes it's me! Who's up there?"

"Margo you've arrived just in time!" Cecelia Lewis's voice connected with Cecelia Lewis's face, and Margo saw her friend peering down from high atop the sign first in red, then in white, then in red again. She looked as if she were riding a carnival ride. "Margo, stay right there! I'm just about to sing my song!"

"Alright," Margo shrugged, a little miffed. "Gee, I didn't even know you could sing…" and she felt a little resentful that she had not known of this talent before. The light minuet grew louder, then segued into a tinkling piano that Margo thought somewhat hokey. She stepped several paces back to better her view. Cecelia was standing atop the sign, turning like a ballerina frozen on a music box. Finally she began, in a clear voice just one octave above the crackling hum:

"John Jacob Astor

shoulda spent it faster

cause he ended up in the drink!

Hail! Hail! Everybody bail!

The ship is sinking

And we're all thinking

Just one more dance before we go

Just one more dance before we go.

On her maiden voyage

She lost her buoyance

And kissed an iceberg in the sea.

Hail! Hail! Everybody bail!

It's freezing cold

And my mink's too old

I was gonna get a new one in N-Y-C

I was gonna get a new one in N-Y-C!

Oh my oh mi-a!

Where's the Car-pa-thia?!

Save a little boat for little ol' me…

Hail! Hail! Everybody bail!"

Cecelia's song ended with the dramatic banging of the lower keys. Margo clapped enthusiastically. The actual truth of the matter was that she didn't think much of the song, but Cecelia's enthusiasm and her Broadway flourish (one knee down, arms open to the world) instinctively led her to applaud. Cecelia acknowledged her praise with several bows; when Margo thought she had shown enough appreciation she stopped clapping and called up to her. "Cece! Come down and talk to me!"

"Sorry Margo, I've got to stay here! The ship is going down!"

Are you mad too? Margo thought. "Cece can I come up?" She had no idea of how she was going to get up there, but presumably Cecelia knew a way… "Cece!" she called again, "I want to come up there with you!"

"No!" Cecelia shouted down. "It's too late! You've got to get to the lifeboats! Go back!" And with that she vanished. The sign flickered and everything went dark.

****

"Margo."

"Yes?"

"Margo, it is I, the Captain. Why are you still here?"

"I don't know. Where are you?"

"Here," answered the Captain, and Margo felt a soft brush against her ankle. "Pick me up."

Margo reached down in the darkness and found the cat by her feet. She picked him up gingerly; she was unsure whether to pet him or not for the cat had admonished her in the lobby and she did not want to anger him again. However, the cat settled into her arms purring contentedly and Margo stroked his head gently which the cat seemed to enjoy. "Scratch me behind the ears," he suggested.

"I wish I could see you. It's so dark I can't see anything at all. Can you?"

"Of course," purred the Captain, for Margo had found a pleasurable spot under his chin. "Cat's can see in the blackest night, the darkest pitch, through intentions and souls…" He twisted and shifted in Margo's arms. "A little more there, please."

Margo indulged him. "Are you sure we have time for this? Didn't you say the ship was sinking?"

"Oh sure. But a Captain always goes down with his ship. We have nothing but time."

"What?!" She dropped him to the ground. "Wait a minute Sir, I'm not going down with you. I don't want to die!" Her voice rose excitedly. "I want to live! I still have to make my debut!"

"It's too late for that," mused the cat. "You should have thought of that before you acted so irresponsibly. Goodbye."

"Wait!" she cried, but the cat had seemingly run off.

"Margo!"

"Yes?"

"Margo!"

She was relieved, he had come back. "Yes Captain?"

"Captain?! Margo, it's your mother calling you. Now stop this silliness and come here right now!"

Enveloped in darkness, Margo began running blindly towards the boom of her mother's command. "Mother?!" she cried frantically. "Mother?!"

"Over here!" Margo floundered in the dark, panic rising in her chest. "Open your eyes, girl!"

"They're open Mother! I can't see anything, why can't I see?!!!" She began to cry pitifully.

"Oh you're so helpless. Here!" A strong grasp circled her wrist; despite the rough treatment Margo was relieved, someone had arrived to take her out of the darkness, someone cared…she stumbled along behind her mother's powerful tow. "Where are we going Mother?" she asked, choking back a sob. "To your debut," came the determined reply. "Oh," Margo said.

They ran for a little while longer and Margo heard that same loud rush of water that she had first heard in the corridor. Then suddenly they stopped running and Margo stumbled and fell and she lay on the ground unhurt but scared and anxious; she heard hushed voices unintelligible in conversation but distinguishable in tone, a woman's voice and a man's, though still she could not see in the unyielding black.

The roar of water sounded louder and closer; Margo felt afraid. Then strong hands were on her, lifting her, and Margo gasped as she splashed down in the icy sea…she struggled against the undertow and kicked hard, driven by panic and the shock of cold water all around her, fighting for the surface.

<u>14</u>

<u>Kelly O'Leary and The Short Shrift</u>

As the waiters began to clear the plates there was another massive game of musical chairs amongst the guests. Tory stood up and slipped on his jacket. "Want to go outside and get high, Cece?"

"No thanks. I think I'll stay right here. Maybe some of my friends will come over…come back in about half an hour to check in with me. I think the band's going to play awhile and then they'll do the presentations. I wonder where Margo is…?"

"I saw her before dinner began, oh look!" He pointed towards the stage, where twelve middle-aged swingers in tuxedoes were arranging themselves in Big-Band formation behind microphones and instruments. Cary Cohn's Swingmaster Jam was in the house.

"Good Lord," Cecelia breathed. "This is going to be nauseating. Please don't be gone too long, okay Tory?"

"Okay."

"And don't get too stoned."

"Got it. Ciao."

"See you." Cecelia waited a moment, deciding on her next move, and then crossed her legs and opened her purse to select a cigarette from an pack of Kools crumpled there. The amber pill bottle was conspicuously absent. Uh oh. She looked through the purse again, removing Kleenex, tampons, hairbrush, lipstick, compact, two five-dollar bills, and her lighter. "Shit!"

Did I even bring it with me? she thought. Yes, she remembered seeing it there on her first visit to the bathroom, obvious amongst the other items. Did I open my purse after that? Drinks…? No, Tory got those. Cigarettes? This was her first one… Kleenex? Yes.

Margo's tears, over by the wall. She hadn't remembered the bottle falling out but that was the only place it could have happened, and she had been so preoccupied with her distraught friend it was possible the pills had rolled out there…and also possible they were still there…as if on cue she was stricken by a painful cramp. "Oh," she moaned, hunching over, the unlit Kool dropping from her fingers to the tabletop.

"Hey-hey-hey! This first tune's for the kids so all you old folks stay seated, unless you're ready to ROCK!" Cary Cohn punctuated his leering fatuity by plucking his bow tie. Old ladies trembled, and the first groaning strains of "Rock n' Roll Music" reverberated through the ballroom. Cecelia shuddered and quickly gathered up her gloves and bouquet. "Excuse me," she smiled to her table. No one paid any attention as she stood up, grabbed her purse and quickly bumped her way through the obstacles of chairs and people to the place by the wall. There was no evidence of Tory's pills and the chairs had been removed. Cecelia was sorry she had brought the bottle and tried to remember if there was a prescription label on it—it could mean big trouble for Tory if someone traced it back to him, being that all of the pills inside were classified narcotics. There was nothing else to be done, however, and it was imperative she escape the band's crude attack on rock before she went insane…she hurriedly exited through the heavy oak doors.

Once closed they provided an excellent acoustical barrier to the Cotillion's musical miscreants, and teams of wild horses could not have dragged the score of debs and dates decumbrant on lobby couches back inside. Cecelia waved to a group of friends and scanned the area for Tory. She half expected to find him hooking up with some girl and was relieved when she did not, though the only other place he would be, outside getting stoned with a friend, was equally discomfiting.

Another searing cramp seized her and she staggered and tried catch her breath; she needed immediate refuge and the lobby was not it. There was a quiet ladies lounge on the second floor and she left the lobby in a stride just short of a run and headed up a flight of marble steps just as the ballroom dispatched a squad of Cotillion Guild members to coax their young refugees back inside. As Cecelia rounded the staircase's arc she saw Agatha Grilover pleading with a loveseat and was oddly grateful for the cramps that had driven her from the lobby.

At the top of the stairs she stopped midstep. A gasp had sounded from somewhere, from where she could not tell as the landing was deserted...but plainly, a gasp.

She heard it again, weaker this time, coming from behind a ficus off to her left. She stayed poised though the hazy yellow light from baroque wall fixtures cast an eerie illumination inciting fear and anxiety.

And then retreat was impossible, her muscles paralyzed and her bones fused. Her own body kept her there, a rigid prisoner, as a shadowy specter emerged from behind the plant. Like an angel cast from heaven the ghostly figure heaved another tormented gasp and swept forward in a roiling cloud of white.

It was a girl, a tormented apparition in a dress that billowed askew, arms extended in pleading gesture. The girl's head lolled to the side dangling brown curls. Clutched absently in her grip was a small purse, its jaws splayed open. The girl staggered forward a step, then rocked by some invisible wave she heaved to the side; she struggled for balance and recognition as her murky eyes met Cecelia's.

"Ack...Uhhhhhhh...Cece..." The purse dropped from her grip dislodging Tory's pill bottle which rolled away. Margo clawed blindly at the air; she shut her eyes tight, repositioned her head straight, and grimaced in a moment of desperate preparation. Then her knees weakened and bent inward, she shuddered in seizure and her eyes snapped open and rolled back in her head. Her body went limp and her mouth gaped out a whispered sigh as she tottered forward, a flash of white, to crash headlong at Cecelia's feet.

****

Finding no one agreeable to smoke pot with, Tory wandered the halls poking around various parties. He drank a glass of champagne at a wedding reception on the hotel veranda and checked out the hostess in the hotel dining room where a testimonial dinner for a retiring assemblyman was dying of boredom. Finding nothing stimulating and not wanting to get high alone he decided to return to the Cotillion and joined a dour bustle of people at the doors. A scratchy old voice from the back of the pack called: "After you've socialized a bit be ready to line up in the kitchen for your presentation, girls!"

"Shut up," came the quiet plea from a debutante at the head of the reluctantly moving bunch.

"Who's that?" Tory asked, tilting his head in gesture to the rear.

"Agatha," the girl sighed, and Tory aligned the scratchy old voice with the crone who ran the debutante rehearsals, who told him at his first and only session that his fingernails were dirty.

He located his table, now occupied by three women about his mother's age, a depressed boy wallowing his own self-pity, and a very old woman wearing a tiara who seemed oblivious to the goings-on around her. Tory approached them with his most charming smile. "Good evening, I wonder if any of you have seen Cece Lewis? She was sitting here a short time ago."

The three looked to one another. "Why I'm not sure who she is…do you know, Martha?"

Martha hadn't a clue. The boy looked up sourly. "I think she went to the bathroom."

Tory nodded his thanks and was about to go when one of the ladies spoke up. "Aren't you Tory Lewis?"

Tory hesitated between veracity and denial, but remembered his grandfather's wishes and nodded. "Yes. And your names?"

"I'm Mrs. VanHosen-Brown, this is Mrs. Cooper, and Mrs. Vitesse," said Mrs. Martha VanHosen-Brown, with a flourish to the other ladies. Tory bowed to them and shook hands with the morose boy. "Robbie Larsen," the boy muttered half-heartedly. A cherished foray into reality suddenly seized the very old woman and she ventured forth with gusto. "Tory!" she guffed. "Tory! Is that a sobriquet?!"

All heads turned, astonished at the dowager's coherence. Tory opened his coat and checked the label. "No ma'am, its an "After Six."" With that he made his departing bow; the dame slipped back into the comforts of Alzheimer's and the three matrons returned to their chatter. Robbie Larsen wished he was dead.

A passing waitress poured Tory a glass of champagne and he continued on through the ballroom looking for his cousin, but keeping an eye out for Kelly O'Leary. Maybe he could lure her someplace and seduce her before the presentations…but Kelly was dragging around her oafish date and it would be a task to separate them. He suddenly found himself in front of his aunt's table where she was conversing animatedly with a handsome gentleman. "Hi Auntie."

Ginny feigned annoyance. "Who are you?"

Tory grinned. "Have you seen a pretty girl, somewhat poofed hair, wearing the family rocks?"

"I think I did earlier darling, but she's been flitting around so I can't be sure. Do you know Mr. Walker here?"

Tory shook the man's hand and crouched beside his aunt's chair. "Cece is having some uncomfortable pains, Virginia. Someone told me she's gone off to the bathroom. Do you know anything about this?"

"Yes," Ginny whispered. "But it's not polite conversation. If I see her I'll tell her to stand by."

"Okay," Tory nodded. He toasted Ginny and Mr. Walker with his champagne and was off on his search when Hugh March crossed in front of his path. "Hi," Hugh heaved drunkenly.

Tory quickly glanced around for an escape route but Hugh was on him, breathing alcohol in his face. "Lishen," Hugh slurred, "lishen, I gotta find Margo…you know, my date? I gotta find her. You seen her?"

"um, 'fraid not. Say, have you seen mine?"

"Yeah, she went upstairs about five minutes ago…or maybe ten. Anyway, she went upstairs."

"You wouldn't happen to know exactly where upstairs, would you?"

"If I shaid stairs I shaid stairs," Hugh growled. He jabbed his thumb southward and Tory followed the sight line but saw no stairs, only the end of the ballroom. "Great," he said appreciatively, clapping Hugh on the shoulder and shoving him aside. "Oh, by the way, you're looking much better these days."

Hugh pointed to his turban. "Broke my crown."

"Uh huh. Well good luck finding your date."

On his way out of the ballroom Tory puzzled over the Hugh March Encounters, wondering why this strange young man had been injected into his life. Though clearly hammered he had correctly directed Tory to the marble staircase; as he started up them he heard his name: "Tory! Oh Tory!"

He turned. It was beautiful Kelly O'Leary. "Hi."

"Hi. Listen Tory, you have to get up to room seven-twelve."

"Good idea. Let's go."

"No no no," Kelly shook her head. "Cece needs your help, Margo Vitesse is sick or something."

"Oh Christ, are you kidding? Why's that my problem?"

"Hurry Tory!"

Tory grabbed her as he turned. "Do you want to meet me after the presentations? I've got some coke…" A lie, but he could get some.

Kelly shook her head and smiled patronizingly. "Tory I like you but you've got a girlfriend."

"What? No I don't. We're not going out anymore. Really."

"Sorry. Look, you'd better get up there. Cece's getting frantic." She headed back down the steps. Tory waited a moment, vacillating between chasing her down and charming her into another groveling session or answering his cousin's relayed distress call. But then Kelly's date appeared by her side and they went off together. That was that.

"Seven-twelve, huh?" He cleared the landing and punched up an elevator.

Ding. Seventh floor. Tory stepped out into the hall. Maybe Cecelia was playing a trick…she could get nutty sometimes…but Kelly's urgent message seemed on the level so it was actually possible that Cecelia really did need him.

He examined the cracking enamel paint over the numbers and chipped away at a sliver with his fingernail. The hotel would not repaint the doors until the paint noticeably peeled; by keeping their hallways dim the managed to hide such needed repairs and basted the hotel in an atmosphere of declining grandeur. Fine, old was in. His people felt comfortable with old. He knocked.

"Who's there?"

"Open up cousin."

Tory was not prepared for Cecelia's strained look. "What's wrong?"

Cecelia nodded to the bed. Margo Vitesse lay unconscious on it. "She got into the pills."

"Holy fuck."

<u>15</u>

<u>A Desperate Situation</u>

There was a pounding at the door. The Lewis' exchanged frowns. Cecelia swallowed hard and called cheerily "Who is it?"

"Hugh March."

She looked to Tory for direction, he shook his head "no" and Cecelia looked at the door, at Margo sprawled face-down on the bed, and back to Tory. She pushed her hair back and moved closer to the door.

"What is it Hugh?"

"Lemme in, I want to talk to Margo. She's drunk, isn't she? Lemme talk to her."

"She's in the bathroom Hugh. Go on downstairs. Margo will be down shortly."

"Margo's drunk. Lemme in goddammit." The handle began to rattle. Cecelia took a step closer towards the door and faltered; she glanced desperately at Tory. He waved his hand. No way.

"Margo's fine, Hugh. Go back downstairs."

Her assurances were for naught. Hugh began to pound angrily, mixing in curses with his relentless insistence. Tory sighed and pulled on his tuxedo jacket. If Hugh March did not succeed in beating down the door he would soon succeed in attracting hotel security. Tory pointed to the deadbolt on the door and Cecelia nodded. Then, in a reflex second he grasped the knob and flung the door open, swept through the hole and slammed the door behind. Cecelia bolted it fast and stood next to it breathing quietly.

Margo groaned. Cecelia went over to the bed and poked her. Receiving no response she rolled the girl over on her back and called her name. Nothing. Cecelia shut her eyes and prayed.

Even with her eyes closed the stark figure collapsed on the bed stood out horribly in her mind, a vision of shallow life inert and ghostly. Maybe she should call a doctor, or drive her to the hospital…tell Margo's parents, tell Agatha Grilover that Margo had become ill and would not be presented tonight…get on with it. "Damn you Margo, if you make me miss my debut tonight I will never forgive you!"

She did not hear the knock at the door, not until she choked back a shaking sob and opened her eyes. "Open up Cece, it's me, Tory." She brushed back a blurry tear and fumbled for the handle, then hesitated. Was she opening the door for Hugh too? What had been decided on the other side?

Tory guessed her anxiety. "I'm alone. Hugh's gone downstairs." It took a moment to free the sticky bolt and another for Tory to push the door open; he'd slammed it with such force it had stuck against the doorjamb. When it finally broke free Cecelia stepped aside to allow him in and Tory walked past without looking at her, following a line to a straight-backed cane chair in the corner of the room. He slid off his jacket and sat down tiredly.

Cecelia waited. Tory slumped slightly forward and clasped his hands across his knees. After a quiet moment he looked over at the bed, then to his cousin. "They're starting to assemble. You'd better go."

Cecelia stared him down. Tory squirmed, straightened, and finally addressed the vacuum: "Hugh March is going to be your escort."

"What?!" She had been betrayed. Refolding her arms across her chest she took a defiant step towards him and cocked her head, incredulous. "What?!! Hugh March?!!!" Resentment gave way to open hostility. "Hugh March, who caused all this? Who let his girlfriend drink and drug herself into a coma?!!"

"The finger's pointed at you and me too, Cece."

"Bullshit, this is totally his fault!"

"No, it's our fault! Margo took the pills from your purse and I gave them to you! Hugh's only guilty of being an asshole."

"I don't believe this!"

"Neither do I, damnit! Now look, Margo took at least forty milligrams of valium, and God knows how many drinks she had, but she's just not going to make it tonight and that's the plain truth. You, on the other hand, owe it to Pliny and your dad to be presented. Just forget about Margo and get down there."

"I'M NOT GOING!"

A terrible silence followed. Tory, rigid in his chair, Margo, passed out on the bed, and Cecelia, defiant in sweeping taffeta formed an incorrigible triangle, each stubbornly refusing to budge from their position. And while the two cousins stood in stalemate a fourth party introduced herself to the room, coming in through the open door Cecelia had neglected to close and lock, crossing quietly in a rustle of red silk to seat herself at the foot of the bed.

The girl crossed her legs and smoothed the skirt of her front-button dress. She rested her arms lightly over one another and looked from Cecelia to Tory patiently, as if she were waiting for them to resume their argument and could wait all night if that were to be. Cecelia became furious. "Excuse me, this is a private room."

It was a wilting declaration, icy cold. Tory did not add any additional comment; nothing he could say would equal the harsh admonishment his cousin had lashed out in a few curt words. He waited for the girl to get up and go.

But instead of leaving the girl smiled bemusedly and tossed her head at the unconscious debutante on the bed. "How did she die?"

"She's not dead!" Cecelia snapped. "It's none of your business so get the hell out!" She grew intensely aggravated…the girl made no move and Tory shifted to the edge of his seat and readied himself to spring across the room and separate the two. "WE'RE BUSY!" Cecelia yelled. "GET OUT!"

The girl looked first at one cousin, then the other. "What're you busy doing…?" She cocked an eyebrow and reclined leisurely, resting her weight on her elbows. "Hmmm?"

It was more than Cecelia could take and she lunged, missing completely as the girl rolled smoothly off the bed and stepped to the middle of the room. Cecelia's attack abated and then fell confusedly apart as she found herself blocked by the bed. "Tory do something!" she pleaded, bursting into tears.

Tory stood up. "Enough of this bullshit. Who are you?"

The girl did not answer him directly, but looked first to Cecelia with territorial warning in her flaring green eyes. Then she turned to Tory and in a sultry, confident voice announced "I'm Frances Bonn."

Her revelation startled Cecelia who took a small involuntary step back. Her hands dropped from her hips and hung loosely at her sides; Tory noticed his cousin's abrupt deference and relaxed. Whoever this Frances Bonn was, Cecelia respected her. He was unimpressed himself but grateful the hostilities had ended, for Cecelia's rage had brought a great deal of tension to an already desperate situation.

"Well look Frances Bonn, we've got a girl here who's drunk and isn't going to make it to the parade. The show's over, there's nothing else to see, so get lost."

Frances Bonn laughed. She stayed where she was, her lips pursed into a mocking smile. Tory felt a hot flush of embarrassment along his neck and looked at Cecelia to see her reaction, but she was quite docile. To hell with both of you, he thought. "Cece, if you're going, go. If you want to stay here with this tart, fine, I'll go down and tell 'em you're not going to make it either."

"Tory, let's call an ambulance."

He shook his head. "No way."

"Tory there's nothing we can do. Besides, Margo might die!"

"NO! Goddamn it Cece, if we let anyone onto Margo's condition or how she got this way it'll rain shit on both of us. You won't even make your debut either for all the cops questioning you, don't you see?!"

"She might die!"

"No she won't! She's just fucked up! Margo's body just shut down to prevent her from polluting it further, that's all. She's just fucked up!"

Finally overcome, Cecelia covered her face with her hands and sobbed into her elbow-length gloves despairingly. Surrendering to his own frustration Tory plopped down into the cane chair and hung his head.

He looked up after a few anguished moments, moments of defeat and fear scored to Cecelia's sobs, and saw Frances Bonn leaning over Margo examining her thoughtfully.

Frances placed her hand on the back of Margo's exposed ankle and feeling Tory's eyes upon her, looked over.

"She still warm?" he asked acidly.

"Yes…fortunately."

Frances straightened up and tugged on the dissilent portrait collar of her dress. Without further attentions to Tory she went over to the distraught girl in the middle of the room and touched her elbow; Cecelia responded and Frances Bonn pulled her kindly towards her and hugged her. Cecelia, to Tory's amazement, collapsed in the girl's arms and cried pitifully, and Frances said nothing but stroked her hair and held her. Cecelia quieted.

"Fix your makeup now," Frances said. Cecelia choked back a final sob and went obediently to the bathroom, shutting the door behind her. Frances looked expectantly to Tory. "Well?"

"Please get out of the way."

Frances bowed obligingly, taking a seat at a small wooden desk. "Would you like some help?" Tory ignored her and knelt on the bed beside Margo and began undressing her. When he succeeded in separating Margo from her dress he cast it to the foot of the bed and Frances leapt to its rescue, finding a hanger in the closet and slipping the gown over it. She hooked it over the door and returned to the bed. "Fill the tub with cold water," Tory ordered. When she turned away Tory considered Margo's bra and slip and then removed them too.

Cecelia, her face washed, her hair combed and coiffed to a reasonable facsimile of its set, stroked her lower lashes with a touch of mascara that almost bumped down her cheek when Frances came through the door. "Christ, you scared me!"

"It's okay," Frances soothed, bending over the tub to stop and drain and start the cold water.

"What're you doing?"

Frances straightened and smiled. "We're gonna get that chick to the ball."

Cecelia finished with the mascara and dropped the tube into her purse. She smiled weakly. "I'm sorry I yelled at you."

Frances waved her off. She nodded through the bathroom door. "Is he your boyfriend?"

"No, cousin."

Cecelia saw a flash of interest in Frances's eyes. "Aah," said Frances.

"He's my escort."

Another nod to the door. "Who's she?"

"Her name's Margo Vitesse. She's my friend."

"It seems more that you're her friend."

Cecelia acknowledged this, making no comment but smiling down the drain as she rinsed her hands in the sink and dried them on a towel. "Margo's really great most of the time, but she got upset tonight. Her mother's crazy and weird and her boyfriend's a dipshit."

"The mother's boyfriend?"

"No, Margo's…he's the dipshit." She giggled at the improbability of Mrs. Vitesse having a boyfriend. When she finished with the towel Frances Bonn handed her gloves. Cecelia smiled. "Thank you."

"You'd better hurry now."

With a nervous final review in the mirror Cecelia tugged the gloves on, stretching them up over her elbows. She and Frances exited the bathroom and found Tory sitting at the foot of the bed absently staring at the rose pinned to his lapel. Margo lay face up, looking sweetly asleep with the sheets pulled up to her chin, a pile of lingerie on the floor. They all looked at it. "They're usually awake when I take them off," Tory grinned.

Frances and Cecelia laughed, and the sudden levity relaxed them all and Cecelia patted Tory on the head. With curious stares following she scooped up Margo's panties and dashed into the bathroom. Tory shrugged when Frances looked at him quizzically.

A moment later Cecelia raced out and grabbed her wilting bouquet from the dressing table. "Okay, I'm ready."

"You look very beautiful," Tory said.

"Oh shut up. You won't drown her, right?"

"Not this time," Frances assured.

"Deb of the Year, huh?"

Frances made a small "mea culpa" gesture with her hands. Cecelia paused, then with nothing more to say darted out the door. Frances closed it behind her and leaned her back against it. "Having fun?"

"Like I said…"

"…I know, they're usually awake when you take their clothes off. All right Casanova, it's bathtime."

Tory rolled up his sleeves and scooped Margo up. He carried her into the bathroom, bumping her head on the sink as he negotiated the narrow doorway. Frances pressed herself against the wall, out of the way. "Ready?"

"Come on," Frances urged. Tory dropped Margo into the tub and Frances Bonn took over.

16

Debutantes

Cary Cohn had returned to his familiar Big Band Swing repertoire with no further disserves to rock and grateful parents and grandparents crowded the dance floor. The tables were spotty with sour boys whose dates had upgraded and pitied dowagers too old and senile to be tolerated. Cecelia hid behind the iceberg at the hors d'oeuvres table, out of view, until the whereabouts of her mother could be determined; she did not want Agatha Grilover spotting her and asking bothersome questions, like where she had been and if she'd seen Margo.

She looked around the room for her grandfather but the dim light of the chandeliers made one silverhaired old man indistinguishable from another. And she looked for Hugh March; at least he would be easy to pick out…she wasn't especially anxious to find him too soon before the presentations, but if she could locate him from a distance she could wait until the last minute, then swoop down on him quickly and get him on her arm before he knew what was happening.

There was Ginny! A flash of silver amidst the mix of dancers. If the tempo stayed fast another pass would bring her to the periphery of the floor and into Cecelia's range. Cecelia trained her eyes on her mother's bobbing barrette and when the accelerando sounded Cecelia dodged a rushing waiter and navigated the course of tables to the dance floor's edge. Her mother Lindy'd towards her and Cecelia hated her for having so much fun while she was saddled with the burden of Margo.

God in Heaven! Cary Cohn segued into a tango! Cecelia whispered a stream of blue invective at the bald bandleader and nearly abandoned the quest but considered the outburst that might result from an uninformed Ginny watching her daughter descend the steps escorted by a drunken fool with a cracked head… "Cece Lewis are you out of your mind?! Is this some kind of joke?!" That's right Mother, grab another handful of salt and rub it in…don't be shy now…she shivered at the thought.

She sensed the desperation of Robbie Larsen looming and immediately broke into a cold sweat. "Oh please don't let him ask me to dance, please don't let him come near…"

"Hi Cece, want to dance?"

She turned and smiled delightedly. "I'd love to Robbie but I can't right now, I've got to get ready. Say, where's Theresa?"

Robbie winced. "She ran off with some guy from Stanford. They're probably fucking in my car right now."

"Oh gee Robbie, I'm sorry, well maybe she went to the bathroom or something. Anyway…Mom! Hey Mother! Hey Ginny!"

"Oh hi Darling! Is that your new boyfriend?!" Ginny waved to Robbie and Cecelia felt sick and stepped on the floor to escape Robbie, who took the hint rather badly and sulked back to his table. Ginny was dancing with a dark man who wore glasses and a full head of wild black hair.

"Mom, wait! I have to talk to you!"

"Sweetheart, have you met Doctor Bendejo?" The swarthy Spaniard dipped Ginny and holding her there, kissed Cecelia's hand. Cecelia smiled charmingly and was grateful for her gloves.

"Mother," she whispered in Ginny's ear, " I need to talk to you – now!"

"Isn't he gorgeous?" Ginny whispered back. "Plastic surgeon!" She winked and poked Cecelia's left tit.

"Mother!"

"Tory was looking for you!" Ginny called over her shoulder as Doctor Bendejo tugged her to an upright position and tangoed her away. Cecelia watched them somberly. "Christ, she's already husband-shopping before the appeal." She felt disappointed and depressed.

The giant chandeliers in the great ballroom were dimmed and barely illuminated the lonely sentinels scattered amongst the tables. Occasionally one of these would flee, floating towards the exits like anguished souls turned away from God. Cecelia fled in the same way.

For every action there is an immediate and opposite reaction. For every divorcee enraptured by a smooth prospect dancing her to romance on the floor there is an ex-husband resting his foot on a bar railing. Uncomfortable in the presence of their once-family, they are coaxed into a tuxedo by the engraved invitation from their debutante daughter whose acquaintance has been lost throughout the years. Gravitating to the only setting they feel comfortable, these men talk little and say less while waiting for their moment at the foot of the steps when they take their daughter's hand for her final trip around the presentation arena. Until then, they warm themselves beside the glowing light of the bar tv, pools of hard drink before them. It is the bane of their existence.

And for every Ginny Lewis, effervescent, blushing with flirtatious smiles, there is an uninvited Bonnie Lewis who on this night sits in a comfortable chair reading some faded movie star's biography in her big, empty house, the house she has come to hate for all its quiet aging. Later, after she has smoked her tenth cigarette and grown tired of reading, she will fix her makeup and drive down to one of the good bars in town where they have jazz on Saturday nights. She has been to Cotillions before, her own thirty-two years ago and more recently her daughter's, but that too was some time ago.

And then there is the trouble in Paradise: girls accompanied by their boyfriends seek to break the bond, overcome by a sudden dissatisfaction with their safe, predictable guy in the midst of so many handsome, exciting newcomers…boys who cast interested looks their way, sufficient to unsettle a girl and make her suddenly bored with the compliant, ready-to-please boyfriend (who suffers her cold silence unhappily). Together they are disastrous, fighting in the car, lingering in romantic ennui at the dinner table or on a couch in the lobby, avoiding conversation until separated by one of the gregarious newcomers who lures the girl away and sends the boy to sit by himself at the table.

To these, the estranged and lonely, better luck next time.

****

Resigned to the ineluctable Hugh March, Cecelia searched the hotel before finding him weaving between the shelves in the Sweetshop. The British girl behind the counter was relieved when Cecelia came in to retrieve Hugh. "He looks out of it, what's wrong with him?" Cecelia ignored her and hustled Hugh out; he followed her like a guilty puppy, looking down at his feet the entire journey from shop to hotel kitchen, where the debutantes were lined up inside.

She stopped him just outside the kitchen entrance. "Let's have a look at you…"

"Cece I'm sorry I caused you all this trouble."

She shook her head forcefully. "Forget it Hugh, just perform. Okay…" She pushed down on his turban; Hugh winced and Cecelia said "sorry" then adjusted his bow tie and straightened his jacket shoulders. "You shouldn't drink anymore, Hugh," she stated firmly, a final addendum to his contrition. Then she turned him around to examine his back and when that was done, turned him forward again. "Okay, you know what to do. Smile." He did, unhappily. Cecelia smiled reflexively at his distress. "Come on Hugh, lighten up. I want to make a good impression. Just remember not to slouch and hold my hand firmly when I curtsey at the bottom of the stairs, these shoes are slippery. Got it?"

"Got it." Together they plunged through the door.

"Cece!" Squeals of delight. "Where have you been? Agatha's having kittens!" Cecelia tightened her grip on Hugh's arm to prevent him from staggering and brushed off the questions, saying "here and there" and "Agatha's always freaking out about something, it's her job." The excitement in the kitchen restored her energy and she smiled and giggled nervously with the other girls as Agatha Grilover bustled down the line, fixing immodest necklines and organizing her brood. Cecelia remembered Hugh and found him hiding shyly behind her. "Hugh, go on out with the other guys!" Hugh bumped himself out and Cecelia blew him a kiss when he glanced back for reassurance. The girls around Cecelia waited until he was out he door before they began their interrogations.

"Hugh's supposed to be with Margo but she's running late and Tory got caught up in something, so since I'm before her Hugh's with me."

"He looks so goofy..." opined Jennifer Marsden behind her. Cecelia frowned with no small annoyance and Jennifer shrunk back. "Where is Margo?" Alison Lark snarked. "Did she find Tory more interesting...?"

Cecelia flipped Alison Lark the bird and found Kelly O'Leary in her face. "Is Margo going to make it?"; when Cecelia shook her head 'no' Kelly grimaced. Just then the line of girls moved forward and Cecelia pushed her back to the O's, restoring order to the procession. Kelly's empathy was patronizing at best; she had been useless during the crisis, standing by inert looking horrified until Cecelia told her to retrieve Margo's flowers from the lobby and find Tory. Cecelia was the purest victim of Margo's inebriation and she had to suffer Hugh March as a result; she'd be damned if Margo was going to garner all the sympathy. "Stop it, stop it!" she ordered herself. Deforce resentment, move forward. Be poised, charming...you've done the best you could. It's time to shine.

"...Miss Nan Foley Kennedy..."

The K's. The line advanced a pace and Cecelia shivered, gripping her bouquet tightly, pressing it other stomach to dispel the frenzied butterflies. Each time a girl stepped through the kitchen door to advance to the penultimate spot behind one of two specially erected screens on the stage wings the debs in the kitchen grew more quiet, so that by now in the middle of the roll call there was only the sound of their hearts thumping furiously beneath their breasts. No one dared whisper, so transfixed were they by the applause rumbling through the walls every time the emcee announced a name. And the young lady waiting by the kitchen door for her cue locked her knees to prevent their buckling and promised herself she would not stagger as the girl before her had.

"...Miss Hope Louise Lapideaux..."

Alison Lark went unsteadily through the door; Cecelia was next. Her mind was wiped clean as she waited. Only sheer terror governed her and she could not conjure up a single thought of what she was to do next; her brain had shut down everything but the motor functions, which were vaguely operative from the adrenaline flowing.

"…Miss Jean Alison Lark…" The strawberry blond anorectic spindled out into the stage lights to meet her acolyte and curtseyed with princess grace to the thunderous approval of her audience. Cecelia went through the door like a dumb cow, lumbering behind the protective screen on the short path to the wings. She peeked past the curtain and watched Alison join her father at the bottom of the steps and slide her right arm through his crooked left. Directly across from her, Hugh waited behind the escort's screen and when Alison and Father Lark moved on Cecelia motioned him out. Hugh, Cecelia would later say, performed perfectly, walking straight out to center stage to wait for her. Cecelia knew that somewhere out there Pliny was waiting to take her hand for the final tour of the ballroom and requisite curtseys; she hoped he wouldn't balk.

"…Miss Cecelia Marie Lewis…"

Lights! Applause! All traces of fear vanished, she was an automaton who dutifully approached center stage. Hugh took her gloved hand in his and Cecelia curtseyed, rising slowly to savor her moment. Flashbulbs like lightning strobed amidst thunderous clapping. With all the sobriety he could muster Hugh March guided her deliberate descent down the stage steps, where Pliny stood by. Out in the crowd Ginny Lewis put her hand over her mouth and stifled a scream.

Alison Lark completed her trip around the ballroom arriving back at stage left as Cecelia performed her second blushing curtsey at the landing; Pliny replaced Hugh March at her side with precision timing, taking her right hand as Hugh abandoned her left. In this consummate moment celebrating the virgin rites of spring she was displayed for all to see and then sent around the room, for two more curtseys and public viewing. This was her apotheosis, and she relished it for its broad glorious display of her youth, beauty and purity. This was good breeding.

Pliny was the perfect man for this trip as he knew how to show off a woman, elegantly leading her at a measured pace to force the crowd to indulge her. For once Cecelia felt beautiful and the feeling was enthralling.

Ginny shoved her way through the crowd, heading Pliny off before Cecelia's final curtsey. Cecelia could not see her mother but sensed she was on her way; she had caught Ginny's look of outrage as she debuted with Hugh on the stage steps. "Faster Pliny," she urged, then resumed her glowing smile. Pliny acceded.

One could say that Cecelia and Pliny plain outran Ginny; Cecelia's last curtsey was more like a bob and Ginny would later complain that her daughter looked more like a servant girl rushing from her mistress's chambers than a debutante presenting herself to society, but that criticism mostly came from her annoyance at having been burned. Ginny's bitterest pill, Hugh March, had to be swallowed until after the Ball when she could vent her anger freely. For now Pliny and Cecelia had evaded her clutches. And while Pliny had no intention of letting Cecelia off the hook he did know when to play the game, however the rules changed on him. The goal of the evening was to get his granddaughter around the room in an elegant, dignified manner that would showcase her beauty and the Lewis name; whatever happened to Tory was of no consequence now, and Ginny's impulsive outbursts were to be avoided at all costs. They completed their tour and Cecelia practically spun from Pliny's side into the line of presented debutantes…the act had been performed, the lights gone down, the curtain closed. Cecelia Lewis had been presented.

It was an equally sublime parade that followed. Each fresh young lady provoked her own cheers and appreciative applause, each curtsey was confidently performed. Agatha Grilover had done her job well: the post Cotillion equinox would bring her accolades and thank-you notes, even the occasional gift. Then Agatha would languish in her paraclete status until a new crop of raw, boisterous girls were delivered to her doorstep and she undertook their finishing.

While Agatha dreamed her laurels a demure alumnus from her program slipped through the ballroom doors and stood at the back of the room behind the audience, unnoticed except by Cecelia, whose observant eye zoomed in on the red dress. Frances Bonn did not acknowledge her, her interest fixed on stage where Alexander Ulster's gloved hand coupled with her escort's for her first curtsey. Margo would be next; had Tory and the red queen Frances beat the devil? The odds were against it...Alexandra Ulster claimed polite applause for her willowy beauty as she changed escorts...Cecelia stared into the blackness at the rear of the ballroom.

Then Frances looked over and the two girls locked stares. The emcee announced Margo, hissing the surname consonants. San Marino cheered loudly with parish approval. Frances Bonn narrowed her gaze and told Cecelia no, Margo was doomed. Cecelia turned quickly away in anguish and watched her cousin Tory receive Margo's applause. The deb did not appear.

The clapping stayed constant. Tory remained steadfast at his post, ramrod straight, one hand tucked behind his back the other extended towards stage left fixing all eyes there. Cecelia stared him down but Tory, either blinded by the spotlight or the grievousness of the situation, failed to acknowledge her. She cast another panicked glance to the back of the room; the light was so dim Frances Bonn was but a shadow...but she too held her position. They had to have succeeded! Or was this some sick charade?! What happened to Margo? "Gee Mrs. Vitesse, she was supposed to have come out...I guess she got too scared." Or wasted.

Just as Cecelia was about to break from the line and rush up the steps to confess all, Margo debuted. Her dress was on straight. Her hair was fixed properly. She had her bouquet.

It was not graceful. It was not delicate. But it was a debut, an introduction to society of a young lady schooled in the established etiquettes that persist in these incestuous bastions of society, the resistant gentry for whom such rituals will endure so long as there is money in the family and an urbane eighteen-year old daughter to spend it on. Margo faltered a little as she advanced towards Tory; Cecelia hoped she would be invigorated by the applause as she herself had been. Like the twenty four times before, the debutante and her introductory escort joined hands and the girl turned to acknowledge her laudatory applause. Hidden beneath the flowing gazar of her fabulous dress, the unsteady machinations of Margo's curtsey began. Her left leg shook as she slid her right foot behind it. Tory gripped her tightly and the girl gently lowered herself. Out in the audience Antoinette Vitesse frowned and resolved to do something about Margo's posture…she smiled crooked, too.

From the dampness of Tory's hair Cecelia could tell he was sweating like a panicked horse. Did the rest of the Cotillion body see him tug Margo to her feet? A quick look at Pliny told her <u>he</u> had; the old man stood there arms akimbo, already confounded by the switching of partners, annoyed that his grandson had eschewed his date and allowed her to debut with some gangly raja…and here Tory was, yanking this floppy San Marino deb to a precarious standing position? Not exactly a shining moment for Lewis posterity…

"Come on Margo!" Tory hissed through his teeth. "Stand up straight! Smile!" She did. "Alright, down the steps now…" They were a short five paces away but to Tory they seemed a hellish horizon of threatening plunges. The awful consideration of Margo's father also loomed ahead. "Here's your daughter, Mr. Vitesse. Hold her steady now, she's kinda shitfaced." Tory moved them shakily to the precipice of the steps. It was fourth and goal…

But Tory did not know, as Pliny later acerbically remarked, that no good deed goes unpunished. Culminating in the most grotesque, heinous victimization of Margo that evening, the hand of fate reached in and gave her a good slap. Midway descending the first step Tory slipped on Margo's trailing skirt, the skirt she had forgotten to gather up for this very descent. He regained his balance but the damage was done, Margo tripped and lost hers. She went tumbling end over end, down the steps, Tory lunging vainly to her rescue and falling himself. Margo flipped completely over, corkscrewed as she grabbed for a handhold where none was to be found, and bumped the rest of the way down the steps on her stomach landing feet first with her dress pulled up to her waist, her panty-less butt mooning the crowd.

Antoinette Vitesse fainted respectfully.

17

Defeated

Wind. Wind like dry desert ghosts, wind that sucked the fronds from towering palms, scattering them across roadways. Wind that whipped the dust of the street through the air in clouds of torment, stinging eyes, dirtying hair, exciting the children to run madly about and scream from each torrid gust.

Tory staggered across the court like a drunken ox, halting and retreating, never following through but smacking the ball desperately, lunging after shots that torqued wildly across the court possessed by the wind. He was behind 5-4 in this third set of the Boys CIF Southern Section Prelims, exhausted and losing his confidence, angered at the vexing gusts blowing down on the court. His serves curved out and his backhand sailed long. Today he faced two opponents, the wind and a hotshot kid from North Hollywood High whose net play was exceptional; the boy was seemingly unaffected by the blow.

Tory lost the set to Kinnelly Brown, and with it the match. The last point Kinnelly sent was a crushing downward swat that bounced centercourt and caught an updraft of hot air channeled from the top of the stadium. Tory made a leaping stab but this bore no fruit, the ball had left his reach long before.

With the polite applause of the fans at his back Tory shook Kinnelly Brown's hand. "Good match," Brown said. "I was a little worried there when you took the second set."

"I let you win today, Kinnelly. You're gonna get killed in the Final."

"Yeah sure," Brown snickered. He shook the chair umpire's hand, then Tory did the same. As he headed for his gear Brown addressed him again. "I guess you won't be going to 'SC next year?"

Tory turned around. "I don't know. I haven't decided."

"They told me you haven't signed a letter of intent yet…don't wait too long Tory, they might rescind their offer. Especially after today."

"Look Kinnelly we went 7-5, 2-6, 6-4 here. Don't think you're anything special and don't give me any shit. I crushed you at Ojai and here last year. I'll beat you again the next time we meet."

"Too bad you didn't have all this game out on the court."

Tory dropped his racquet and started at Brown, but stopped and picked up a towel instead and wiped his face. "You're right. It was too bad." Saying nothing more he turned his back on Brown and went to the bench, nodding "good luck" on the way to his teammate Don Kim who was taking the court against a much stronger Palisades player.

He was exhausted and full of regret. Kinnelly Brown was his friend and his poor sportsmanship was inconsistent with their usual post-match exchange; Tory had held bragging rights before and Brown was just reciprocating. It was just the disappointment of going out so awkwardly… flailing around on the court, chasing unpredictable shots, clumsy returns, eight double faults…why did it have to end like this?

"Shit-shit-shit." He sighed and squinted up at the first row of seats where Courtney Kempner sat; she shrugged and gestured with her palms up as if to say "win some, lose some." He nodded and ditched his soaked shirt for a dry one. His shoes and socks were sopping as well, he took them off and stuffed them into a green and yellow bag with the scuffed legend "Blair Tennis" on one side and "Vikings" on the other.

"Ill wind, Tory."

Tory looked up at his coach's glum face, backlit by the afternoon sun. "Nah Coach, it wasn't the wind. It was me. Brown didn't have any trouble." He slipped on and tied a new pair of running shoes, ignoring his coach who ignored him back. Tory shouldered his bag and surveyed the stadium. Busy matches occupied courts all around and cheers celebrating a good point or dramatic victory drifted over. He listened to the applause from a match on

Court One and bit his lip. " I think I need to come to the net more."

"Eh? What was that?"

"I think I need to change my game—come to the net more…"

"Well you're a very mobile player, Tory. That's your strength, the way you hammer the ball from the baseline…your game is good, I don't think you need to change anything at all."

Tory shrugged, feeling impatient. "I got tired today, Coach. And I lost. I need to win again."

"You will Tory. Good luck." He held out his hand and Tory shook it, concluding their relationship.

****

Courtney Kempner managed a comforting smile. Tory crouched beside her but did not sit in a seat. "So, what are you going to do now?" he asked. Courtney patted his head sympathetically; Tory stayed her, then took her hand. "Are you gonna hang out?"

"What are you gonna do?"

"Go home and get stoned."

Courtney giggled. "I think I'm going to stay, I'm enjoying just sitting here in the sun. I'll walk with you to your car, though."

"Nah, it's okay. Thanks for coming to see me play."

"Oh come on Lewis, of course I was going to come. Look, go home and rest. I'll come over later tonight and we'll go to the movies or something."

"Okay. Bye." He stood up and walked stiffly out of the stadium, his muscles were tightening and lactic acid was creeping into his joints. A strong breeze lifted a hot dog wrapper up and swished it before him, he swatted it away on his climb up the stairwell and headed for the peristyle.

He paused out in the hub to check the draw—Kinnelly's name was already scripted in the advance bracket, with his match scheduled for the following evening. Tory's elimination became even more stinging; Brown's opponent was a tomato can.

"Tory!"

He turned, unsure where the call had come from. He heard his name repeated, mixed faintly into the voice of the wind and searched the complex for the voice. "Up here!" At the edge of the stadium rise a girl wearing sunglasses and a light colored scarf over her head was waving. He returned an indifferent wave and started for the parking lot. The girl called "Wait!" and vanished from her perch.

He sighed and dropped his racquet bag from his shoulder. He waited. And then after a moment of voice analysis he matched the girl with the name and started to run but Frances Bonn had already made it out of the stadium and was hurrying towards him. He looked for somewhere to hide but there was only open space and Frances was almost upon him. "Tory wait a second!" Then she was at his side and Tory surrendered.

"Hi, I saw your match."

"Uh huh."

"You played well."

"Thanks, but I didn't."

"I know. I was only being polite. You should try it sometime."

"Sorry Frances Bonn, politeness isn't my forte."

"It doesn't appear that tennis is either," and she made an L on her forehead with her thumb and index finger.

After a moment of standoff Tory grinned and pushed her. "You're a smarty one, aren't you." Frances smiled flirtatiously and Tory studied her features, noticing for the first time her full cheekbones and graceful neck that made her not just pretty but sensuous. "So really, what're you doing here?"

"I came to see you play."

The wind blustered around them, lifting Frances's scarf over her shoulder and laying it there. She let it rest a moment then casually brushed it off. Tory watched her, then reached over and brought the scarf back. She let it stay.

"Are you going home?"

"Yep. Nothing else for me here."

She pushed her sunglasses to the top of her head. "It was nice to see you again."

"Thanks, it was nice to see you too."

"Okay. Bye." She turned away and walked back towards the stadium gate. Tory watched her slim legs flashing beneath her white skirt that was tight against her hips in the wind. She was almost through the gate when he called "Hey Frances!"

She stopped, expectant. Tory waited until she made a full turn. "I'll see you around." Frances folded her arms. "Okay." Then she and Tory went their separate ways and Tory found his jeep in the parking lot and drove home.

<u>18</u>

<u>Pleasant Company</u>

Antoinette Vitesse came out of the study and caught the arm of a serving girl passing by with a tray. "What is this?"

The girl looked meek and struggled with a smile of ignorance. "No English," she said, pulling away. Antoinette tightened her grip and blocked the girl with her body. "Well you can't use this china with those hors d'ouvres, so take it back into the kitchen. Look—" To illustrate, she picked up an ornamented cracker and bumped the edge against the plate rim. Immediately the olive and cheese topping fell off. "You have to use a bigger plate, understand? 'Un grande platter,' so the guests have some room to select, see?" With a sweep of her hand and a firm push at the girl's back she sent her back into the kitchen. "Alright," the girl sighed. Antoinette smiled superiorly and looked around for another violation. Yesterday it was the carpet cleaners who tried to avoid moving the furniture, this morning the florist who mixed fresh flowers with wilted ones...

A drycleaning van pulled up and Antoinette met the boy at the open door. After scrutinizing for still-remaining spots and happily finding none she signed the invoice and took the tablecloths into the kitchen to give to the housekeeper, then took the rest upstairs. As she rounded the landing she passed by Margo's door and hesitated, unable to summon the courage to knock. She grew less bold every time she passed by the shut room.

Taking the clothes into her closet Antoinette hung them on a valet hook and began to strip them of their plastic coverings. With careful precision she placed each garment in an area hosting similar fabrics and when she got to Margo's debutante dress she left the drycleaner's bag on it and set it aside. Unless Margo wanted it in her closet the dress would go to storage. Maybe it would be sold. Either way it was a white elephant, much like the girl who had worn it.

While she was deliberating fabrics the truck from the furniture rental arrived and Antoinette hurried through the rest of the clothes, then rushed out to the backyard to supervise the arranging of tables and chairs. She followed the two deliverymen around, ordering them here and there and wiping everything with a damp dustrag. When the younger of the two men exasperatedly claimed they were only obligated to deliver the items, not decorate, Antoinette read him the riot act until he tired of her haranguing and said "okay okay lady whatever you want." There was no time in her schedule for uncooperative servicemen; the guests were due to arrive in three hours and there was still much to be done.

She was not a last-minute hostess, despite this rushed schedule. On the contrary, this party had been planned for six weeks and attention paid to the smallest detail: every piece of silver was polished, woodwork and cabinetry washed, a superb menu planned with the caterers right down to mounds of Beluga caviar in crystal bowls, and the engraving of invitations on fifty percent cotton rag paper. These also had been sent six weeks ago, the R.S.V.P's indicated three hundred guests. Privately, Antoinette had her doubts.

One hundred? Fifty? If twenty five came she would make a go of it and put on her best party dress. If less than twenty-five…well, toss on an old shawl, darken the house, and answer the door with a widow's visage. No one had called her to reassure her and she held no quixotic notions that all the invitees would honor their commitment. If it were she on the guest list she would stay respectfully away and later send a note for the etiquette breach. A sudden migraine, husband walked out, the dog was run over before her eyes…any excuse would suffice, it was just a formality.

Margo was a pariah, plain and simple. Her odious debut made her the object of scorn throughout the community and a party to celebrate such a girl was a party to be shunned. Antoinette considered canceling the affair, printing up three hundred notes expressing regret but nothing else. However it was too late to attempt such a socially difficult task and the selfish motive alone would further deride her family's reputation. Profaned as it was, this was not an acceptable option so Antoinette did the only thing she could do, and carried on deaf to the gossip. She proceeded with the party's preparations; the guests would arrive at six for cocktails and when it got dark at eight everyone would sit down to dinner. Decorum would prevail, there would be no defamatory remarks and Margo would be a coquettish celebrity, providing she could be coaxed from her room. Antoinette knew this was her paramount task.

When Margo crumbled on the stage steps her spirit followed. The only sound heard in the stunning silence was the sobbing of the damned; Antoinette lost her composure but her husband held his and quickly lifted Margo from the steps, but she wrenched herself from his arms and ran screaming through the hotel, hysterical and intent on killing herself. Fortunately she was prevented from accomplishing this by a quick-thinking bellboy who grabbed her as she made for the path of an oncoming Hummer. After two days in the hospital she had come home and locked herself in her room, not eating or venturing out for any reason. Nor was she responsive to visitors; Cecelia Lewis had come by a couple of days before but Margo would not speak a word to her, instead lying flat on her back staring blindly at the ceiling as if Cecelia did not exist. After an hour of this treatment Cecelia left in tears and Margo stayed vapid, registering no emotion, revealing no thought. The doctors said she was in shock and Antoinette accepted this condition for about half a week until her tolerance wore thin and she demanded her daughter snap out of it. Still there was no change, the days gummed together and a sepulchral gloom seeped beneath the shut door and spread through the house. In a silver bowl downstairs Margo's bouquet wilted and died; after much agonizing Antoinette threw the flowers out and decided to go ahead with the party and draw Margo out of her disabling funk. Either that, or ship her off to an insane asylum.

When the deliverymen left Antoinette decided to take a break and went to the kitchen to have a glass of water and a couple of aspirin. She leaned back into the human-sized swinging basket chair and closed her eyes, letting everything flow over her, relaxing into a malaise and drifting as the kitchen melted into a silvery white mirage. Like a Viewmaster advancing another slide the scene in her mind abruptly disappeared and she was bobbing alone on a raft, thick clouds hanging over her, listless on the silent sea. Here was the dream she dreamed when she needed tranquility, and if she was still too stimulated she added Mahler.

Antoinette luxuriated in the dream for a few minutes, enough to reset her energies. When she opened her eyes she fixed a stuporous watch on the caterers and kitchen help until she tired of it and reached for her cell phone, dialing her daughter's friend Cecelia.

"Hello?"

"Hello, Cece?"

"This is she…"

Antoinette kicked her foot out and pushed off the leg of a hutch to spin the basket away from the help. "Cece dear, this is Mrs. Vitesse. I'm trying to get an accurate count; are you coming tonight?" She listened to a long pause, finally broken by a regretful sigh.

"I don't think so, Mrs. Vitesse."

There was another long, involuntary pause, this time by Antoinette. "Alright, I understand," she said with no recrimination. "Well thank you for stopping by the other day. Perhaps you will visit again."

"Yes," Cecelia assured her. Mrs. Vitesse said "Thank you I'll be grateful if you do," and hung up.

So that was that, and the great question had been answered. None of Margo's friends were going to come, not even Cecelia Lewis. Antoinette grasped the sides of the basket and hefted herself out. She pulled the back of her blouse down and marched out of the kitchen and up the stairs to her daughter's room. She tried the handle of the door but it was locked. Undeterred, she knocked loudly and called "Margo! Margo!"

There was no reply.

"Margo! Listen dear, there are going to be people arriving shortly, and they'll want to see you. You are the reason they are coming, so get up from your bed and start getting ready."

Silence from behind the door.

Antoinette took a breath. "Margo, no matter what has happened in the past it is over with. You must dress and come down and greet your guests and be a proper hostess. No one likes a loser, Margo…"

On the other side of the door Margo shut her eyes tight and shifted to a fetal position on the bed. Her mother's voice continued on. "..If you continue to stay locked in your room you will find you have no friends at all and once you stop this silliness you will see the errors of your ways but it will be too late to ever hope of being in any club or getting a man to marry you!"

"I don't want to get married!" Margo screamed. "I want to die!"

"That's nonsense!" Antoinette retorted. "And what's the point of dying if you have no friends left to come to your funeral?! Margo, if you dress up nicely and come down to your party and are gracious and pleasant company all your embarrassing moments will be put aside and forgotten! I promise!"

Hail the versatile tongue! That messenger of taste, that sender of thought, the organ of love and hate which can both kiss passionately and lash like a barbed whip! And oh the tongue of Antoinette Vitesse, from whose tip such redemptive wisdom flowed and unblocked the ears of poor Margo. That which could not be accomplished by doctors or friends or the powerful team of love and understanding was successfully achieved by Antoinette's well-chosen words of social pre-eminence.

Curled up with her face stuffed in a pillow, Margo gave up trying to suffocate herself and gasped for breath, her chest heaving as she lifted her head and gulped for air. Antoinette's promise of redemption salvaged her corroded spirit, dragging it up from the depths of despair. If what her mother said was true, that a strong showing of congenial, effervescent celebration would erase the Cotillion catastrophe from Society's memory, then here was a reason to live. With the longing for death waning from her heart, Margo knelt tiredly amongst the rumpled sheets and surrendered her exile. Slowly she crawled from her bed and padded through the deep carpet to the door. Unlocking it, she met her mother's hopeful look with a tired nod. "Alright," she said softly. "Leave me alone. I'll be down in an hour." Then she closed the door.

In Antoinette's eyes blazed the light of pure jubilance; in her walk was the carriage of mighty accomplishment. She grasped the banister and descended the stairs with her head held high, feeling complete. As she rounded the landing she bumped into her husband coming out of the library and seized him, gripping his arms tightly. He was startled by her sudden action and the rapture on her face. "What the…?!"

"I am a good mother!" Antoinette exalted, shaking him and laughing joyously. "I am a good mother!"

Up in her room Margo leaned against the back of the door staring fixedly across the room at her reflection in the mirror. She stayed like that for several minutes looking at her tired nightgown and her ankles that showed beneath the hem. Finally she locked eyes with the girl in the mirror and they watched each other for a time, but neither would make the first move. At last the real Margo turned her face away from the mirror and with small deliberate steps walked into the bathroom to start the shower and prepare for her debut.

<u>19</u>

<u>Up Off His Ass</u>

On a hot July morning Tory Lewis fulfilled the demands of his schedule and served a hundred balls to a frantic Klaus, who could not keep up with the challenge of chasing and retrieving the rocketing orbs and howled and barked in German Shepherd angst. That done, Tory swept up the balls and dove into the pool to cool off and work on his tan; there was nothing else pressing for the rest of the day, here was his calendar: drinking beer, napping, watching TV, and calling Courtney Kempner up to screw the afternoon away.

Since graduation weeks ago this had been his routine. And while Tory knew life seldom offered such extended periods of irresponsibility he was bored, stagnant and soft. He craved action but was irresolute in seeking it, tossing invitations to tennis tournaments that arrived in the daily mail into the trash. His loss to Kinnelly Brown played over and over in his head during anxious moments of indecision prompted by recruiting calls; he had been admitted to three universities but committed to none, staving the coaches off with promises to notify them "the moment I reach a decision." The coaches thought him callow, but closer to the truth was the overwhelming uncertainty that he would ever win again…and in his present state he was honest enough to admit that he could not concentrate on his game, his universe was in slow chaos. Thus he sought solace in physical pleasures to blank out his mind, but on this particular morning with the sun rising once again to bake the day away and the pool raft drifting him into ennui the ether was beginning to wear off Tory's brain.

Seizing a thread of sudden vigor he rolled off the float and submerged, came up again and shoved the raft out of his path. For the next half hour he swam laps and when he tired he rested a moment in the shallow end, then swam over to the pool's edge to pick up the cell phone resting there. He dialed Courtney's number and got her voicemail, speaking rapidly he told her not to come up that afternoon, something had come up. Then he dialed Pietro.

After three rings the machine at Pietro's picked up and a woman shrieked "Why are you calling me?!! Stop calling me!!!", lines from a horror movie Pietro had recorded off the tube. Tory hesitated, thinking what rude message he could leave, when Pietro picked up and huffed "What?!" into the line.

"Hey!"

More huffing, he was breathing hard. "Hay is for horses. Who's calling?"

"It's Tory. Don't you have caller ID? What's up?"

"Hey dude, what's going on?"

"What are you doing? You sound all out of breath."

"I'm fucking. What do you want?"

"She must be a lousy fuck if you'll answer the phone."

"I'm not really fucking," Pietro admitted. "I'm jumping rope."

"Oh yeah? Did you get a card?"

"Yep," panted the voice. "I'm on an undercard at the Olympic in three weeks. Three weeks! There's no way I'll be ready."

"Who's the matchup?"

"I dunno." There was a pause while Pietro gulped a drink of something. "Dan Goosen's got the main bout, two welterweights I could kick the shit out of. Get this…I have to fight Super Lightweight."

"How're you gonna do that?"

"Hell, I don't know. I guess I've got to starve and work out like crazy. Dan hates me, I know he's getting back at me for all the shit I gave him. Anyway, it's a fight, right?"

"Well yeah, I guess…but they're not telling you who you're fighting?"

Pietro drank some more before answering. "I've got this new manager, a Mexican guy in Highland Park. He set it up with Ten Goose, he thinks they're bringing in someone from Argentina who's a terror, figures if I can beat the guy I'll be back in everyone's good graces and be a contender again, instead of a bum."

"Hmm, what you need is a big brother to look out for you…"

Pietro laughed. "Felipe, my new manager, is alright so far, he used to box himself out of some Frogtown club back in the sixties so he knows all the dirty shit and he's seen this Argentine fight before. He's got some footage of his last fight and I'm gonna pick it up this afternoon. Listen Tory, I've got to get back to jumping rope."

"Wait, uh oh, hang on a second…" Klaus had come up from the hillside carrying the remains of a dismembered animal as a gift and deposited it before Tory. "Klaus just killed a rabbit, no yech, it's a cat! Get outa here Klaus!" Tory pushed the dog's bloody muzzle away and picked up the corpse by the hindleg to heave it over the hillside into the brush. Klaus sulked off, feeling unappreciated. Pietro snickered on the other end of the line.

"You're dog's a killer, Tory. You shoulda known when you name an animal after a Nazi war criminal chances are they're gonna be a little vicious."

"It was my brother's idea. So look, want to come over and get high?"

"No!" Pietro answered irritably. "I've got a fight in three weeks! I can't party at all. Not at all."

"Okay, how about you bag the rope and let's go run…"

"Now that's an idea. I'm sick of it anyway. I'll meet you down at the Casting Pond in ten minutes."

"Okay, bye." As Tory hung up there was the ching of the gate latch and his mother came around the side of the house.

"Hi! I'm back from the Club!" She was in her tennis dress but without her racquet. "I just came home to change, I've got a lunch date." She waved and went inside. Tory wondered who the lunch date was and guessed from Bonnie's bouncy step it was probably with some new man. She was full of life these days, the decision to dissolve her marriage a tonic to her spirits. Since the filing of the divorce papers a few weeks ago she'd been out on one excursion or another every night and had even reconnected the answering machine. Before, Bonnie's periodic visits were short recuperative vacations during which she lounged around the house taking care of necessary business; his father was the same way, dropping in for a few weeks at a time to touch base and say hello. Neither parent had really lived at the house for years, they used it as a comfortable hotel and then left him alone. Now Tory was beginning to resent his mother's intrusion.

He hurried up to his room and changed into his shorts and running shoes, grabbed his keys and headed back downstairs. Bonnie whisked by in a bright summer dress and they nearly collided. "Oh hi honey, listen can you clean up your room today?"

"My room? What for?"

"I'm having some realtors in tomorrow. That's a good boy. Bye!" She gave him a quick peck on the cheek and was gone. Tory frowned.

He met Pietro at the Casting Pond and they stretched. Pietro told a few jokes and they started to run down the path that bisected the dry gulch. While they were running Tory told Pietro about his mother's homecoming.

"Sounds like she's gonna take the money and run, sport. Too bad."

Tory jumped a pile of horseshit and agreed. "I wish I knew where the old man was. I'd call him up and tell him what she's up to. I wonder if he even knows…?"

"Doubt it," Pietro said. "Your Mom seems like the kind of lady who dictates the action in that relationship." Tory said nothing in reply and they did not talk for the rest of the run.

They had gone about three and a half miles into South Pasadena when Pietro directed them up a steep street into Highland Park, where the graffiti became more prominent and the houses reflected the shabby lives of their occupants. At the top of the hill both stopped to rest, sucking in the hot air, then Pietro beckoned Tory into a slow jog down a narrow side street that wound through the Monterey Hills, finally arriving at a dirt path that led them into an enclave bordered by prickly pear cactus; in the center of the yard a small weathered barn endured in the sun and off to the side sat a rectangular wooden house shaded by oaks. "Hey Felipe! Hey, it's Pietro."

A moment later a small Mexican man came out of the house to greet them. Pietro introduced Tory and they shook hands; Felipe did not stand over five foot four but he was well muscled with piercing black eyes that probed the strengths and weaknesses of his visitor in quick assay. He said something in Spanish to Pietro who shook his head "no," then nodded and disappeared around the back of the house.

"What'd he say?"

"Nothin'. He's kind of a caustic fucker and doesn't like white people too much, if he says anything don't let it get to you. Come on, let me show you something." Walking straight to the barn Pietro paused to dial the combination on a cheap lock and unlatched the door. Sweeping it broadly aside he led the way into the cool, dark shed. A small boxing ring had been cordoned off with old ropes and a heavy bag hung from a roof beam near the door. Pietro crossed the room and unlatched another wide door, swinging it outwards into the afternoon sun and inviting a breeze that happened over the hills.

The extra light made visible a weight bench and barbells by the south wall and a speed bag hung in a corner. Pietro went over to an old doctor's scale and weighed himself. "One forty-four," he announced. "Five more to go." He stepped off, set his arms akimbo and looked at Tory. "This is the last one, man. I don't win this time and it's all over."

"This is the first time you've ever said that."

"Shit, I don't want to say it. This is my sport, I've been thumping heads since I was eleven." He shrugged. "Maybe I've gone as far as I can go."

Felipe's silhouette appeared in the doorway holding a struggling chicken; Pietro groaned. "Oh no man, I just ran here…not today." But today it was and soon Pietro was scrambling around the yard in pursuit of the frantic red rooster Felipe had let loose. Pietro darted this way and that, swatting harmlessly where the bantamcock had been only milliseconds before. Tory leaned against the barn's splintery wall laughing and shouting encouragement while Felipe urged his fighter on and grinned maliciously every time Pietro fell in the dirt. When it looked like the boxer was going to drop dead from exhaustion Felipe called on him to put his heart into it and Pietro wiped the sweat from his eyes and made a final charge, confusing the bird with a few deft moves and seizing its trim feathers to successfully end the exercise. His audience applauded and Pietro fell down in the dirt gasping for breath, the red rooster clutched tightly to his chest.

The Mexican freed the chicken from Pietro's embrace and took him back to his coop. Pietro stretched out on the ground, then hefted himself up and brushed himself off. "When I win this fight I'm gonna come back down here and eat that motherfucker with mashed potatoes and gravy, then pick my teeth with his bones."

"Stuff him and mount him instead. He'd look great over your Dad's fireplace."

"Not a bad idea," Pietro laughed. "Really, if you want to improve your footspeed this is the way, you're always moving left, right, backwards, all that. Felipe thinks I'm quicker already."

"I prefer to chase pussy, but if you're into cock that's cool."

"Shit the pussy you chase is so slow and dimwitted they're hardly any challenge at all. Man, I need a drink."

He went tiredly over to a patch of weeds by the house and dug up a hose, which he ran a minute to get rid of the hot water before drinking. When he was finished he offered it to Tory who had a drink also. Felipe came around with a DVD; Pietro took it and he and Tory said goodbye and left. They walked for a while then resumed a jog, taking a shorter path through Highland Park that led them up the wash and back into the Arroyo.

Both boys were dog-tired after their run and when they reached the Casting Pond they flopped down on the grass to rest. Pietro seemed the worse for wear and when Tory chided him for it the boxer reminded his critic that he had been working out continuously since three days before, whereas Tory had just dragged his slothful self away from his bed. "But anytime you want to run during the next few weeks let me know, I hate it and if I can get a partner it makes it better."

"That guy we ran over, Hugh March? He can run twelve miles a day and not be tired."

Pietro slapped at a fly come to drink of his sweat. "Yeah, but can he play five sets of tennis or get into the ring to fight another man? No way. There's all kinds of shape."

Tory stood up and wiped his face with his shirt. "I'm gonna go home and get some lunch. Come over later if you want to."

"No thanks, you'd have me smoking weed before the day's out. Tell you what though if you want to go to B.C.'s for a beer later I'd be up for that."

"I thought you couldn't party at all!"

"Well," Pietro grinned, "within reason…" He lifted himself up from the grass, about to say goodbye, when a horse and rider came galloping up the trail towards them. A smile crossed his face; Tory wondered who it might be that elicited such a benign response.

It was a girl, riding a large black horse. She wore a helmet and jodhpurs tucked into black riding boots and her t-shirt advertised tequila. With dramatic flair she reigned the horse to a walk and trotted him around the two young men. Pietro folded his arms across his chest. "Hey Frannie."

"Hey Skunk, how's tricks? Well well, Tory Lewis…"

Tory nodded a casual greeting though his heart thumped hard in his chest.

"What're you two mugs doing here?"

"Running," Pietro told her. "I got a card."

Frances Bonn's horse snorted and stepped back but she put an end to his recalcitrant behavior with a whack of her crop. "Oh really, that's good news. Are you going to cheat again?" Pietro scowled and Frances leaned down from her mount and tapped him lightly across the cheek with her stick. "I'm only teasing…my my, sensitive, aren't we?"

"Sensitive, aren't we?" Pietro said, slapping her horse hard across the rump, causing him to rear and sprint away with his mistress fighting to remain in the saddle. She regained control of the animal and brought him around again. Tory did not try to hide his amusement and Frances shot him an icy glare.

"That wasn't nice. So who are you fighting this time, is he any good?"

"I don't know, I'm going home to watch his last fight now," Pietro said, waving the DVD. "Think you'll stick around long enough to come see me?"

"Possibly. Let me know when it is, maybe Mr. Lewis here will take me." She straightened up and adjusted her seat in the saddle. "Well, be seeing you."

"So long Frannie. Be careful, remember what happened to Catherine the Great."

"Charming." She drew the reins to her and turned her horse. "Come over to see me this afternoon, Tory." Then she spurred her horse and disappeared through the brush. Tory waved at her back.

"So," Tory said en route to their cars, "how do you know Frances Bonn?"

"She and I go way back. How do you know her?"

"I met her at Cece's Cotillion. What's it to you?"

A knowing grin lurked at the corners of Pietro's mouth. "She's out of your league."

They stopped at Tory's jeep. "What makes you say that?"

"Experience. But suit yourself."

"No, I want to know. How come you say that? Was she your girlfriend or something?"

"Or something, yes, but not my girlfriend. Look Tory, if you want to get mixed up with her be my guest. But she's out of your league." With that Pietro thanked him for the run and strode over to his car, a black convertible Corvette with a white stripe painted down the hood. "You're a dick," Tory told him. Pietro waved and flipped him the bird.

20

An Afternoon Off

Frances Bonn lived in a large modern house surrounded by a twelve-foot high wall the same construction as the house, which is to say, formidable. It was a huge white block: corrugated concrete and steel set with rectangular panes of glass that ran forty vertical feet and the wall anchored in front hid from public view a most lush garden and pond. It was an impressive piece of real estate, though contrasting with the rest of the Craftsman bungalows and Mediterranean villas of the rest of the neighborhood.

Even Tory was intimidated when he pulled up in front of the Bonn's in his jeep; the wall crowded the sidewalk, urging on passerby. A nimble burglar could scale the wall, but what vengeance would he find on the other side? The house implored thieves to stay away lest they end up barbecued by high-voltage security wire or torn to ribbons by a kennel of vicious attack dogs. The common burglar might dream but never dare, the mortal karma so warning. But Tory had an invitation and as his intentions were somewhat good he felt justified in approaching the solid oak gate set into the wall at the west end; this was the single entrance. A driveway ramp dipped from there into the street.

The wood of the gate was old and scarred but solid as the giant trees it had come from. From end to end it was about twenty feet across and hinged on giant steel; two iron rings broached at handlevel. Beside them, fixed into the wall, was an intercom and buzzer. He rang it and a moment later a static voice crackled "yes?"

"It's Tory Lewis. Visiting Frances…"

The intercom went dead and a new frequency hummed. A latch released. The gate cracked open.

Tory pushed against its impressive weight and slipped through, shoving it closed from the other side. Then he turned and the house revealed itself.

It was even larger from inside the enclosure and bleached white. Five or six graceful willow trees rustled in the breeze at various positions in a courtyard landscaped with rolling mounds of dichondra. The pond was infused with lush green plants, dragonflies hovered over lotus atop the water. It was a serene yard, manicured and quiet, and Tory took all this in before walking the pebble path to the front door.

If there was a door. There was certainly an entrance, a vaulting portal thirty feet high opening over a polished black granite stoop. Two massive black slabs presiding over either side of the entrance functioned as doors when folded inward and a video camera ogled visitors from on high. Tory waved to it and a deep voice called "Come on in."

A man in swimming trunks appeared and beckoned. "We're out back." He drank from a tumbler and waited for his guest; Tory took his time walking through the vast entrance for there was a lot to see. Enormous sculpture lined the way and several large paintings hung from the walls. "Do people really live here?" he thought.

"Glad you stopped by," the man said. "I'm Jack Bonn." He was as tall as Tory and about thirty years older and fifty pounds heavier with thinning brown hair pasted back and he sported a belly that looked the product of too much good living rather than too little exercise. He gripped Tory's hand and smiled a familiar smile. "You came by to see Frannie; she went out on an errand but should be back before long. Come on out back."

Tory smiled, drawled "all right," and followed Jack Bonn out. They passed through a room the size of a small gymnasium, stark like the exterior but tastefully furnished with ultra-modern design and art, everywhere art. "You have some house," he told his host appreciatively. Jack Bonn thanked him over his shoulder. "You ever see any James Bond movies? We're in the next one." He said it with pride neither overbearing nor subdued, but rather familiar to a man who felt comfortable in his wealth. They passed from the large room through a set of glass doors onto the patio veranda, overlooking a sparkling Roman pool and thriving lawn. At the southwest corner was a tennis court rolled out with no fences or surrounding windscreens, a lined grey surface divided by a net.

"That's a Har-Tru, isn't it?"

"You bet. Do you play?"

"A little. Not much clay."

"That's because you're a Southern California kid. Nothing but hard courts around here. When Frannie comes back maybe we can get some doubles going." Tory was about to inquire who the fourth might be when the pool splashed and a beautiful woman broke the surface. "That's my wife, Jeunesse," Jack Bonn said, dropping fresh ice cubes into his glass from a nearby bucket. "Want a drink?"

"What?" Tory tore his gaze away from the beautiful woman who was pulling her beautiful body onto a shelf in the pool to rest. "A drink? Okay." Jack Bonn picked up a remote control from the picnic table and with the aid of a joystick directed a motorized liquor cabinet over from its place in the shade. "Frannie gave me this booze cart for my birthday, she said it would save me from staggering into anything valuable on the way in to get a drink..." The robot whirred its way over and parked at its master's feet. Tory took a Bud Tall from inside the refrigerator door and Jack cranked open a bottle of Tanqueray which he splashed in a glass along with a little tonic; he held up the tumbler to his wife who nodded vigorously from across the pool.

"I must say Mr. Bonn, your wife is about the best looking woman I've ever seen."

"Thanks Tory, thanks very much. Coming from a young buck like yourself, she'd be flattered." He prepared an identical gin and tonic which was ready by the time the woman climbed from the pool and came over, toweling herself dry along the way. She took the drink from her husband and smiled. "This is Tory Lewis, a friend of Frannie's."

"Hello." She was even more beautiful close up, late twenties with sun streaked hair and her silver bikini did nothing to hide her virtues. Tory felt his dick harden.

"Is it cocktail hour already? My watch must be broken." Frances came out to the patio. She was wearing a blue sundress and beamed when she saw Tory. "Hello Tory. My my, G&T's and it's not quite three o'clock." She gave her father a kiss.

"Highball?" asked Jack Bonn.

"Sure." Frances turned to Tory. "Hi."

"Hi. Nice place."

"Thanks. Want to see my room?"

Jack handed Frances a Meyers and O.J. and she inspected it curiously before shrugging and taking a sip. Tory moved over and took her hand; Frances said "well excuse us" and the two headed into the house.

"I went to see my mother after riding," she told him as they passed through the large room. "As you can probably guess J'taime is not her."

"I did guess. She's some piece to be married to."

"Did he tell you they were married? Usually he's not a liar. She's just the current samba, nice enough and as you witnessed, quite stunning." The topic seemed to bore her the way any oft repeated speech bores the speaker. "Here's my room."

She let him in and Tory went over to the desk and sat in a chair. Frances shut and locked the door, then turned on the stereo and leaned back against the door. "How did you find out where I lived?"

"I googled you." Frances didn't blink and Tory picked up a pen and tapped it against the desk blotter. "I looked in an old Westridge directory," he confessed.

"Oh," Frances nodded. The music played soft, the Rolling Stones "Gimme Shelter." Tory came over to her but she held out her hands and kept him at arm's length. "That's not what I want."

"I know."

"I just want to be friends."

"Okay."

He took the hem of her dress and pulled her over to the bed. Frances lay on it, her brown hair fanned out and Tory slipped off her sandals. He lay next to her and pulled off his shirt, then lifted the skirt of her dress over her hips. She was not wearing any underwear, her hair was smooth and dark brown over her pussy. Frances unbuttoned his shorts and pulled down his boxers; when he was naked she slithered out of her dress and pulled him onto her. Frances' skin was cool; the air circulated around her. She kissed him while he stroked her back, following the trail down her ass to her hot damp sex. She moaned when he touched her and kissed him harder, when he entered she gasped, breathing hard. He told her she was hot, wet, her flesh made him huge like a horse, wouldn't she like to kiss the horse, wouldn't she? He pulled out and she sucked him greedily then ran her tongue along his shaft until he nearly came, then rolled over for him to take her again. They fucked and fucked until they came in writhing, bucking orgasm.

They had sex the rest of the afternoon. When it got to be about five o'clock they went outside and had a swim; they were alone in the house, Jack and his alleged wife having gone to the beach for dinner. Tory thought the vision of Frances swimming naked in the pool mysteriously beautiful, she was so smooth and sleek, moving swiftly with arms outstretched as she cut though the water. Their swim lasted an hour; when they pulled themselves onto the edge it was nearly dusk and wonderfully cool beneath the trees. Frances then told him everything about him.

"Your real name is Victory America Lewis, after your father's disillusionment and subsequent abandonment of this country. Your mother is a woman of indifference and slight domesticity, she likes to be carefree and unattached to home and husband. You're seventeen, a Leo and tennis *wunderkind* but totally shallow when it comes to relationships. Your brothers and sister are the same, all of you just lost souls. You like me because you think I'm the same. I'm a Scorpio," Frances cautioned. "I do everything as I see fit and have no established moral guides. Tory, if you can hack it I want to spend time with you but I am not like you in any regard…I've powers unlike any girl you've ever known."

"What's your scene Frances?"

"Action."

Tory looked her up and down and she allowed it. "I like the feel of your body and you have a lot of money. Alright…"

Frances laughed.

21

Pietro Fights

The gutter in front of the Olympic was a ribbon of broken bottle shards guarding pockets of filth and the stench overwhelmed Frances as she opened the cab door. "Hurry," she commanded and Tory paid the cabbie quickly. Together they rushed to Will Call for the tickets Pietro had left for them; once inside they made a beeline for the bar.

Pietro "The Skunk" Bertolucci did not care that Tory and Frances had come to see him. After making weight that morning, at one hundred and thirty-seven pounds, he stopped caring about his diet and breakfasted on a large steak and three baked potatoes followed by a large bowl of linguini at noon. At three o'clock he ate three pears and a carrot. At four o'clock he made for the bathroom and had a long shit, took a cold shower and then a half-hour nap. When he woke up he stopped caring about food or rest and started to rev up.

At six-thirty p.m. Felipe picked him up in his van. Pietro nodded and climbed in, sitting not in the front seat but far back in the van against the rear doors. Felipe drove straight to the Olympic and pulled up in the lot directly behind; Pietro grabbed his gym bag, pulled the hood of his robe over his head and climbed out, entering the back entrance and following the labyrinth of tunnels to the dressing rooms in the catacombs.

A security guard stationed in the hallway opened the door for him and Pietro entered without acknowledging. He shut the door behind him and glared at the fight poster taped to the wall. There the flat, pitted faced of Aguilar de Los Hermanos dared him to fight, ugly face skewed up in hatred, mean black eyes promising violence. His own picture, positioned beside his opponent's, seemed languid. Pietro tore the poster down.

He boxed because he was good at it and did not hurt easily. A true welterweight at one hundred and forty-seven pounds, he was the proud owner of a 7-1-1 pro record, a nickname, one disqualification and subsequent suspension, and seventeen cumulative stitches (from ring fights). He had been kicked out of two excellent stables, Crown City first, then Ten-Goose. No one believed he would ever be anything more than a journeyman; he had neither the roots nor the savagery to be Class A. But Pietro worked at being a boxer, one who hits and dodges, jabs with his right and hooks with his left to close eyes and ring bells. He had the advantage of being a southpaw; nothing else distinguished him from the packs of pugs and wannabees. He had no KO's in his pro career but had never been knocked out himself, in amateur or pro bouts. Angela O'Donaghue's brother's remark that he was a punk was undeserved; Pietro had fought thirty six amateur bouts and won them all, honing his skills during three-rounders with headgear and oversized gloves, winning always on points.

Tonight it was all going to change. Los Hermanos did not box, he slugged. He did not dodge, he took what he had to and delivered worse. That was evident from the tape but more telling was the look he gave Pietro that morning at the weigh-in and it was this killer look that bore into Pietro's psyche and turned him scared. This was okay, it was early…scared would be followed by mean, and mean would climb between the ropes and be ready to fight.

"I'm gonna rock him," Pietro assured Felipe when the veteran arrived at the dressing room carrying his fight kit and Pietro's gear.

Felipe grinned. "You're fuckin' A hijo, remember what he is, a scum sucking fucker who's trying to hurt you. You can't spar with him, I see you sparring I'm gonna throw in the towel 'cause I didn't take you on to watch him beat your ass. You gotta go in there and pound him, never let him rest, pound his nose with your jab and then hook his ribs; if you can bang on his kidneys it's gonna be your fight."

"Truth. I'm gonna put him in dialysis."

The third card of the night was in its final round when Tory and Frances arrived at their seats in the second row ringside. A black junior-welterweight

had his opponent up on the ropes for a quick beating which the man, a
Korean boxer, was unable to defend; when the lights went out on the boxer
the referee pushed the black fighter away and counted out the fallen. The
Korean's corner came out to retrieve him while the victor celebrated with
arms thrust up. Tory took a swallow of beer and setting it under his seat
commented "I hope Pietro's is that easy."

Frances shot him an annoyed look. "Don't be simple."

The smart money said Los Hermanos. The Argentine slum rat had
everything to gain from this fight and his opponent nothing but the chance to
continue his negligible career. A millionaire's son versus a hungry violent kid
with a shot at the wealth and fame of American sport? Pietro would be beaten
like a dog…Palooka Joe, slow freight, another rung on Los Hermanos'
ladder. The Argentinean looked like a killer. He had what the great ones had,
a mania that predisposed him to murder and a total disregard for his own
life. This Pietro knew, knew it that morning when he weighed in, knew it all
day, knew it now. But he was no longer scared; scared had become mean.
Pietro was ready to climb between the ropes with all the angry force he could
mete out, crush the guy's kidneys and jab at the scar tissue Los Hermanos
called eyebrows, turn the black piercing eyes bloody red. So the line said Los
Hermanos? Pietro said different.

A boxing commission official watched Felipe taping Pietro's hands.
Pietro steamed all the while, feeling angrier and madder at everybody
and everything so that when Felipe tore the tape from the roll and tucked
down the end Pietro broke free and threw a flurry of shadow punches. "The
gloves," the official reminded.

"Wait a minute, I gotta take a leak."

He went into the bathroom, freeing his dick from the uncomfortable
confinement of the cup. He sighed and rolled his shoulders to keep them
loose while he peed, the next time he urinated it would be a public occasion
with several people watching, waiting to take his fluid to a lab. The pre-fight
piss was the last private moment he would have for a while and he let his
guard drop for a moment, summoning vague religious natures. "Please God.
Don't let him mess me up."

When he came out Felipe was waiting with the gloves. The official briefly inspected them for foreign objects and finding none, allowed the manager to fit them over his fighter's hands and tie them up. When Felipe finished the official signed the taped wrists and Pietro slid into his robe, pounded his fists together and said "let's do it."

"Okay, let me see if it's time." Felipe and the official left, closing the door behind them. Pietro stood still for a moment breathing in air. His chest filled and stretched his ribs; he watched them move in the mirror. He was ten pounds leaner than usual and liked it but did not know if the drop in weight would fatigue him in the later rounds or cause his skin to cut more easily on the gaunt edges of his face. Felipe had the cut kit ready: Vaseline, styptic pencil, adrenalin, needles…don't let him hit your face. Felipe came back and motioned him out and together they headed for the arena.

"Ernie Ramirez took it in four, the ref let 'em throw anything they wanted and Ernie dickshot him twice. Rakim says we gotta give him something if we win."

"Okay." Pietro moved ahead of him.

The journey through the catacombs to the ring thrilled him, thousands of people screaming shouting and luring Pietro to their arena to do his duty…it made him intense and excited. There was a yellow bulb glowing at the maw of the hysterical animal and he passed beneath it and was swallowed into the noise and smoke and sweat of the fight house, the fourth act on this hot Friday night. "HEY SKUNK YOU STINK!" someone shouted. Applause, boo'es, a cupful of beer that fell from the darkness and splashed harmlessly several paces ahead…and the appreciative applause of those lining the fight path, who admired any man coming to battle another man with just his fists.

Frances strained in her seat for a view of her friend and when he appeared she leapt to her feet and cheered. Tory joined her and they yelled into the din, praising their champion. Pietro had told Tory he never heard anything more than a guttural roar when he was about to fight so it never bothered him if the crowd was against him, but tonight they seemed to favor the Skunk. Still, there was scattered opposition that chided his family, his life, his boxing skills and whatever else could be defamed while he worked his way up to the ring. "CESTUS YOU FUCKING CHEATER! HEY REF, CHECK HIS GLOVES!" Frances turned and searched the crowd for the antagonist. "Asshole," she muttered.

It was the one heckle Pietro heard. "Jesus, they're calling me 'Cestus...'" As he reached the ring a big hand came out of the crowd and seized his wrist. "Whaddayasay Pete? Are ya loaded?" Pietro shook off the bookie's grip and ducked between the ropes; the man leaned back in his chair, confident. "I got you for a grand, Pete. Take it the distance and we're square." He said this to Pietro's back though it was later apparent that Pietro had heard him clearly –just before the opening bell Pietro would lean over the ropes and sneer "Only a grand?"

When Los Hermanos came into the ring he did it with professional élan. He was cool and in control of his entourage, a trio of men who quickly set up his corner and rubbed him down. He had a separate trainer, manager and cut man while Felipe was all that rolled into one. The advantage was Los Hermanos'; the more people to take care of you the better off you were – a universal axiom. Los Hermanos shucked his robe and accepted their treatments, giving Pietro the murderer's stare. Pietro returned it with venom. The bookie's claim on him had fueled him with more anger and adrenalin so that he was a bull who had already been through the piquadors. When the introductions, instructions, customary glove bump and last second spurrings had been completed the fighters stood, waited for the bell, then got to it.

The Argentine scored first, two sharp jabs that popped off his opponent's chin. The jabs went unanswered, both fighters eyed each other and Pietro dared him to try again. Aguilar did, a left jab to open Pietro for a right hook. The first punch scored, the second missed as the Skunk sidestepped and lashed a stunning blow on target, the kidney. Aguilar winced, Pietro hit him low again then came across his face with the hardest right he had ever thrown, a solid cross that crashed into the pitted face. Aguilar de Los Hermanos took the shot and staggered, moved sideways, then crouched with his hands held at his face and his eyes burning. Pietro knew things were going to change then, Aguilar wasn't going to box anymore after that showing up.

With twelve seconds left in the first round Aguilar and Pietro punched for each other's eyes but each landed only a small percentage of blows before the bell sounded. "Too bad," Pietro told him when they stopped. Aguilar grinned and offered more, stepping back into his pose and beckoning with a flourish of his hands. The crowd loved it, they roared with delight and Pietro smiled to himself and headed back to his corner. It was an even round, he was not afraid, the crashing right he delivered gave him credibility and Los Hermanos would have to watch himself.

"How's he hit?"

Pietro spat out his mouthpiece. "He's okay."

"Watch your arms, those chin pops were nothing. He's gonna try to kill your arms this time and take you out of your strength. Rattle his head with a right again, he's watching for your left."

Pietro took a swallow of water and Felipe shoved the mouthpiece in; when the old pug stepped aside Pietro saw that Aguilar had stood the whole minute and in fact didn't even have a stool in his corner. "Damn" he thought and felt his confidence blip. The bell rang.

The fighters met center ring but the momentum was lost and they circled each other predatorily, searching for an advantage. Pietro saw it first when Los Hermanos retreated a step and feinted; the Skunk moved in with a maelstrom of lefts and rights that pounded the Argentine back to the ropes, but the ruse was on…Los Hermanos broke free and clocked Pietro with an uppercut that staggered him back; reeling from the blow and surprised by the disregard Aguilar had for the punches he had taken, Pietro was suddenly on the defensive and winded from his offensive strike. Los Hermanos set in for the kill and slugged Pietro with the hardest punches he had taken in his boxing career. To him they felt like hammer blows, each sharp and penetrating to his bones. He countered with sloppy jabs that mostly missed, for Felipe's precognition of Los Hermanos' strategy was correct and Pietro's arms turned to lead as Los Hermanos pounded on them.

He took a couple of more blows before wrapping Aguilar in a clinch, forcing his head down to fatigue him. When the fighter broke free Pietro popped him with the heel of his gloves across the eyebrows, digging for a wound. A small scratch appeared and Pietro worked at it for the rest of the round.

"Head butt him!" Felipe hissed as he slathered Vaseline across Pietro's face. Don't let him get away!" Pietro listened to the rest of Felipe's staccato advisement without comment; his arms ached and his jaw felt torqued from the uppercut. He was not rattled but he knew he had lost the round and it was bad to get behind in a bout designed to eliminate him from boxing entirely. Unless he won by knockout the points would go to Los Hermanos; he knew this for weeks before but only now did it become clear that he might take a beating for nothing.

The third round was unmemorable as both fighters avoided each other. Felipe had restored Pietro's confidence so that he was not prey, but Aguilar was skilled at dodging him so Pietro could not score either. Three minutes passed by with only a few punches thrown, most of those defended by well-positioned gloves.

When the fourth round rang in Pietro felt better about his chances and decided to try combinations again. He lured Los Hermanos in and let him have a couple of shots, a strategy that did not exactly work. The blows came in hard and sharp and Aguilar closed up afterwards, Pietro had to drive him to the ropes again and pounded and pounded until the Argentine weakened, then hammered on his kidneys. Aguilar suffered under the blows, he stood against the ropes protecting his head and face, recoiling under the doubtlessly cramping kidney shots. When Pietro ran out of gas he backed away and Aguilar broke away running for his corner to recover and repair his offense. Pietro followed, jabbing all the way. When the bell sounded the Argentine quickly turned away and went to his corner wearing a dazed and fearful look.

Felipe berated his fighter for allowing Aguilar to escape. Los Hermanos was on the ropes, nearly defenseless and Pietro had allowed him to break away and last the round. Pietro did not want to win, he was too much of a pussy. Well, was he?! Is that what he wanted people to think? He'd better get someone else to manage his punk-ed out career if he wasn't going to finish the guy off. When the bell sounded he told Pietro to get out there and beat Los Hermanos to the canvas. Pietro pounded his gloves together and set out to accomplish just that.

Los Hermanos had other ideas, he let Pietro come at him and then attacked with stunning head shots. White flashes exploded in Pietro's brain, blinding him and bloodying his nose and mouth. A right hook knocked him back and he felt his legs go to jelly; Los Hermanos slugged him across the bridge of his nose and his face exploded in a mask of pain. Aguilar fired a thunderous uppercut…Pietro flopped backwards and fell.

He landed on a glove, fortuitously breaking his fall so that he was not counted "Knocked-down," and the second or two he stayed there allowed him to switch his focus from pain to surviving. Los Hermanos stalked him to deliver the killshots.

Pietro scrambled up, the ref grabbed him, and satisfied he was not loopy stepped back. Los Hermanos closed in but the weeks of running and skipping rope paid off and Pietro was able to evade the attack. The fight crowd was screaming at the top of their lungs so that when the bell rang it was a mere chime under the arena's roar. Pietro fought the gray vagueness before him and hesitantly headed for the least populated corner, his whole body shaking. Felipe directed him over with a wildly waving hand; clutched tightly in the grip of the other was a towel.

"Don't even think about it you fucker."

"Okay boy, okay." Felipe sponged the blood off Pietro's face and swiped the shock of blond, now thick with sweat and blood, off his forehead. "You did okay hijo, you lasted…"

"Fuck you man, it was his round but I can do it, I can win."

"Okay okay, just get your breath back. Work his body this round, work that cut over his left eye." Felipe continued to ladle out advice but it was the patronizing chatter of a coach who no longer believes in his athlete and finally Pietro told him to shut up.

In his corner Los Hermanos still stood, though he faced the crowd now. Pietro watched him while the seconds of his respite ticked away and suddenly he stood and kicked the stool away. The crowd roared its approval. Los Hermanos turned quickly and Pietro saw acknowledgement flash across his ugly, pitted face. Pietro stood defiant, Aguilar did the same and the sixth round began their battle anew.

Pietro ran from him for two minutes. He bobbed and ducked the shots, never allowing Los Hermanos to achieve his goal, though he was still woozy from the fifth's beating and could not see clearly. At one point the referee told him to quit running and fight, but it was a directive without backing. Pietro kept moving, trying to frustrate and tire Los Hermanos. Fans screamed, Felipe shouted, Aguilar de Los Hermanos chased him and threw blanks; Pietro stayed on his feet, gathering strength.

At last Los Hermanos caught up with him and Pietro stepped in and pounded him across the ribs with mixed combinations; Aguilar took the blows and jabbed at Pietro's broken nose, landing excruciatingly painful hits. They were potent shots, sure-winners guaranteed to send the victim reeling unsteadily away in classic "no mas" fashion. Had Pietro not forbidden his manager from throwing in the towel Felipe most certainly would have done it, saving his fighter from more savagery. Pietro, however, had never been a quitter and at this moment he endured the jabs to work his punches to Aguilar's ribs then groin where he dickshot him hard.

Aguilar crumpled, the wind went out of him and he buckled forward into a crashing uppercut that caught him flush on the chin, cracking teeth as his mouthpiece flew out. Pietro reared back and slugged Los Hermanos into insentience, stopped only by the referee who pushed him away screaming that the round had ended.

Two more rounds were scheduled. At this point neither Aguilar de Los Hermanos nor Pietro "Skunk" Bertolucci wanted one more second, so badly beaten they were. Their bodies were lumpy with swelling bruises and streams of blood ran down to the waistbands of their trunks. Fatigued and disoriented, each faced the seventh round with dread, though Los Hermanos was at more of a disadvantage having barely lasted the brutal sixth. While his cornermen were screaming about the below-the-belt punch Aguilar staggered into the ropes and clung there; for his part Pietro crossed to his stool and collapsed, hiding under an ice-packed towel that Felipe held to his swollen face. Their minute passed by quickly.

The intensity of the battle that was the seventh can be ascribed to each pugilist's honor; it had been too great a fight to be decided on points—when the call came Pietro and Aguilar met toe to toe at center ring and pummeled each other with abandon, crashing lefts and rights and hooks with almost no defense. Blood and sweat mixed and flew, and in their final throes each hammered the wounds of the other, until Pietro landed two successive left hooks on Aguilar's temple and the Argentinean terror blinked and dropped onto the canvas thirty seven seconds into the round. The fight was over.

****

Coins rained from the stands thrown by the appreciative crowd, true fans of the sport who had been entertained by a very good undercard. They cheered on their way to get beer and hotdogs, hoping that the next bouts would be equally entertaining and the restroom lines short. Tory and Frances joined the exodus but instead of queuing up for food they left the Auditorium and stood outside. One of the event staff hailed a cab at Frances's request; when it pulled up she turned to Tory. "Look, why don't you go on without me…"

"It was a tough fight Fran, but he won."

"I know." She wrapped her arms around him and began to cry. Tory hugged her, letting her tears run onto his shoulder. She cried softly, then kissed him on the cheek and stepped away. "Call me tomorrow. I'll be okay, really." Tory decided to go on without her, feeling a need to be by himself.

22

Tropism

Pietro screamed all night, screamed and yelled and cried from the pain of the beating he had taken. His arms swelled with fluid and the tendons torn from his ribs burned with the fire of pain. Pain was everywhere and it lived in him like a tortured, panicked animal fighting and kicking against his bones. His hurt did not consolidate, it rebelled and fought from every cell independently and each pulpy part throbbed and drove him to despair.

He screamed and sat up quickly in his bed, his anguish did not startle Frances but she noticed the time, three forty-five a.m., prompting her to give him another Percocet even though he had taken two an hour before. The pills would not cure him, only prevent the pain from becoming worse, though that hardly seemed possible. He was beat black and blue from his trunk up, and what wasn't purple was seeping blood.

Still standing in the ring the crowd assumed he was alright but in reality Los Hermanos had beat him nearly to death. He could not see beyond a spectral fog; referee, manager, ring announcer and opponent were shadows jostling him back and forth, parading him around to victorious applause, applause which he was barely conscious of given the thunderous pounding of his heart pumping blood out his open wounds. He did care about Aguilar de Los Hermanos who lay unconscious on the canvas through the ten count and finally was raised with the help of his entourage. He did not care about Felipe, who held his arm high for all to see nor did he even care about the fight promoters who swarmed into the ring to congratulate him and seek his commitment to future bouts. He cared about his blood, which was all over the ring and his body and had seeped down into his shoes so that each step was wet and squishy. His precious blood.

"Frannie! Frannie!"

She slid into bed next to him. "Yes Pietro, I'm here." Pietro quieted and let her dose him with another painkiller. She put the glass of water up to his swollen lips, he tilted his head and drank it all. When he had to pee she held a Gatorade bottle next to his penis while he tried to urinate without screaming.

Every moment was a crucible of pain and after he finished peeing he lay back down and moaned. Frances emptied the bottle into the toilet; when she returned he told her to take him to the hospital. Frances shook her head. "No, I will take care of you."

"Fran, I can't see…" Pietro started to cry. " I can't see anything!"

Frances took his hand and kissed it. She touched his forehead lightly while he sobbed about Los Hermanos. How strong he had been, how his punches were like hammer blows. "He was so tough, I really hurt him…oh man, I'm gonna die. Take me to the hospital Frannie, take me now."

Frances lay her hand on his chest, letting it rise and fall under his sobs. "No Skunk, you'll be fine. It was a good fight. You can take a little pain."

"I won this one Frannie. Remember when I lost? I wasn't half as beat up." He lay quiet for a moment. "Eight wins. One loss. One draw."

"Shhh. Be quiet now." After awhile he said "yes" and fell asleep. Frances went to the bathroom, wet a washcloth and returned to his side. Ever so gently she blotted the places where blood had crusted. She rinsed the cloth out and dropped it into the hamper, then washed her hands. Dark circles had settled under her eyes and her blouse was spotted crimson where Pietro's blood had flecked on her. There were more this time than ever before.

She had left Tory and returned to the Arena, making her way back to ringside to follow Pietro to his dressing room. She was unhindered; Pietro had left specific instructions with Felipe that Frances Bonn be allowed access. When the fight doctor had examined him and the boxing commission obtained its sample, Frances and Felipe helped Pietro into the shower and afterwards wrapped him in his robe and took him back to his house. Frances put him to bed; Felipe took her aside and quietly advised that the boy should be taken to the hospital, he had taken a hell of a beating…

Frances turned out the bathroom light and went back to her chair. She watched Pietro sleep for awhile, marveling at his bravery. He was always so ugly after a fight but she was never repulsed by him, only by the men he fought. To her they were roaches, disease carrying and filthy, and they were almost always poor and stupid. Pietro once told her that some of them failed the California Neurological Exam from sheer ignorance and were disqualified for fighting in the state because they could not identify which animals on a list could be found in a zoo. But the other roaches that knew about zebras and lions scrapped, slugged and headbutted in desperate yearning for something better than the wretched cracks they crawled from, and it was Pietro's job to drive them away.

After a short time she fell asleep and dreamed of being a little girl at the beach, sitting in the sand with her mother who was crying silent tears. The day was sunny and they were the only two there, and she played all day in the sand until the sky grew purple and pink with the setting sun. When it was nearly dark her mother took her by the hand and led her into the water, deeper and deeper, farther out into the turbulent crash of waves.

The dream startled her awake; she drank a glass of water and moved to the foot of Pietro's bed, where she lay until the sun broke over the mountains and light streamed into the room. Then she got up and made coffee in Pietro's small kitchen, read the paper, and waited. Pietro woke a short time later complaining and cursing; she gave him another Percocet and refilled his water, helped him pee again, and after he fell asleep she gathered up her things.

She shut the door quietly behind her. It was beautiful and clear, the sun was high in the east and it was very quiet.

****

"Where have you been?"

"Up all night with a sick friend."

Jesus, thought Tory, she thinks I'll buy that one. "Hey Fran, how about coming over for breakfast? Afterwards we'll go visit the Skunk."

"No thanks Tory, I'm really tired. But if you want to see him in the evening I'll go with you."

Frances hung up after a few more evasions and went out to the pool, squinting in the bright sun. Jeunesse was swimming and Jack Bonn had the newspaper and a Mimosa in front of him; when Frances came out onto the patio he looked her over. Noticing her bloody clothing he asked simply, "Been fighting?"

"Yes, and I won."

"That's my girl. Hey Frannie, can you come with me to the Equestrian Center tomorrow morning? I'm playing at nine."

Frances shrugged. "What's in it for me?"

"I'll spring for a dinner party."

"Sure, I'll do it." She looked at the beautiful woman swimming under water. "How long is she going to be around here?"

"Probably only long enough to introduce me to one of her friends…" Jack hit off his drink and dropped the newspaper onto his lap. "How much of Tory Lewis are we going to see?"

"Probably enough to make us want to kill him. " Frances grinned, sliding around her father onto an adjacent chair. She folded her arms across the glass tabletop and rested her head on them. Jack unclasped her barrette and lifted her hair from its bunch, spreading it freely across her head and shoulders. Frances closed her eyes and rested in the morning sun, feeling drained and happy.

She was dreamily aware of footsteps and opened an eye to find her father had turned his attentions to the beautiful woman, fresh from the pool and now standing beside him. Frowning, Frances got up to go but her father stayed her with a gentle hand on her shoulder; she resumed her restive pose. The beautiful woman moved to the side and along with Jack, caressed Frances' hair.

She bent down and kissed Frances softly, continuing to stroke her head and nuzzle her neck. Frances squirmed, she felt the woman's soft breasts brush against her ear. She smelled the scent of her hair and the heady breath of her desire. Quick hands turned over the buttons on Frances's blouse, letting it fall away from her shoulders. Frances opened her eyes; her father was nowhere in sight. She took the beautiful woman's hand and followed her to the edge of the pool, shedding her skirt along the way. They slipped into the water together.

In the late afternoon a gentle breeze blew into her room, bumping the curtains against the window and stirring Frances from her dreams. She rolled over and sighed, enjoying the luxury of being alone and in the comfort of her bed. After a time she got up, wrapped a silk robe around herself and went downstairs to the kitchen. Jack Bonn had left a note on the refrigerator—he and Jeunesse had gone out for the evening, he would wake her in the morning and together they would drive to Burbank for his polo match. Frances crumpled the paper into a wad and threw it away. She sliced an avocado and took it out to the patio where she ate it while gentle breezes blew leaves into the pool and the light turned golden.

"Call me…call me…" She fixed on Tory's face and whispered into the wind, concentrating her desires. Message sent, Frances opened her eyes and relaxed in the shade.

A little while later her phone rang. "Hi."

"Hi. I was just thinking about you."

"What're you doing?"

"Nothing. What're you doing?"

"Nothing."

"Well, come on over and we'll do it together."

"Okay."

Frances hung up and cheered.

****

Tory came over later that afternoon bringing with him a few joints and a handful of flowers. Frances met him at the gate, kissing his face and telling him how lovely it was to see him. Once inside she grabbed his waist and stuck up against him. "Let's get pleasure out of the way so we can get down to business." Tory dropped the flowers and his shorts onto the carpet and worked on getting Frances out of her robe. They wiggled over to a sofa and commenced fucking.

In the aftermath Tory caught her smirking. "What's so funny?" he demanded, growing more puzzled as Frances burst out laughing. When she had her fill she rolled over onto her elbow and said "This is my second time around today…J'taime did me earlier! She told me she wanted to do you too." Frances laughed at Tory's surprise and licked his ear. "How does that turn you on…?"

"Quite a lot," he replied on the way down between her legs.

Frances howled and writhed for the next half hour and finally gasped and passed out, exhausted from coming. Tory tried to provoke her further but she seized his hand. "Later," she murmured, then fell asleep. Tory drifted off soon after.

They awoke at about midnight and went for a swim, then sat at the edge of the pool and smoked one of Tory's jays. They felt good together, hugging by the water in the cool night air, young and fine. "Rate me," Frances cooed.

"Wild, with a smell of sweat and perfume. I love to kiss your tits, your pussy is like a hungry animal. When you climax you grip me like your whole body's wrapped itself around my cock. I like the exercise."

"Good one! Now me…you don't make love, you rut. I love you jamming it in me deep, I came so hard I thought I shook the discs loose in my spine. You have great lats and a tough, meaty butt. And Jesus, you sure do have a way with your tongue." They fell to fucking again, rolling onto the damp grass. After hollering like nightbirds they rested again and Frances lay her head on his chest. "Tell me your dreams."

"I'm down love-forty in the fifth set at Wimbledon, the Finals. It's certain death at five games to six. Then I serve two back-to-back aces and follow 'em with a net cord miracle, serve and volley my advantage and follow it with a lightning rally and I nail a backhand volley that hits chalk."

"Wow," Frances said admiringly. "Do you win the match?"

"I don't know. That's not my dream. I only want to have the poise and control to come back like that."

"You don't have it now?"

"No."

Frances was thoughtful. "You know, when I was Debutante of the Year I went to a lot of parties and enjoyed an elitist celebrity, and then the season ended and so did that life. The question I faced was my future and after mulling over the choices from a small list I decided to go to cooking school in France."

There was a significant lull in the conversation before Tory confessed "I don't get it."

"Well if you want something you just have to decide you're going to get it and then you can have it. If you want to be a tennis player famous for glorious defeats, or one who comes back from a deficit to win, then that's what you'll be. But wouldn't it be better to be a player who sets out to win?"

"I do play to win, I'm the Ojai champ. I don't need a sports psychology lesson from a debutante baker."

"Chef," corrected Frances. "And it's obvious your incorrigible nature prevents you from forming an operating philosophy because you lose your cool and get tossed out of country clubs and you blame the wind for unforced errors and you won't make a decision about college, because you're afraid of the future. Hence you drift like a leaf in the wind, spiraling downward. It's okay to have poise and control but without a burning passion for victory you will be a subaltern player, an opponent instead of a champion." She stood up and began to pace the deck. "It seems to me that you are too easy on yourself. If all you want is poise and control then you should hire a private coach and practice a lot. But if you want to win then you need to live like a champion, exalted in life as well as in sport and never compromise. You should demand all to serve you and belittle pretenders to your throne, both challengers and hapless amateurs. The best table—demand it! The best clothes—insist on them! Banish all who would prescribe their mediocre morals and values to you. Stamp out familial aggravation; if your family doesn't support you one hundred percent then they're against you.

"Root out the distractions that prevent you from achieving your ultimate goal—to be the number one tennis player in the world! Disdain advice from those who were never at the top and purge your mind of self-doubt. If you want to master the game then first master your life. Above all, know that you are superior to everyone else." Frances paused and smiled gently. "It's really easy, Tory."

Tory was chastened; his head rushed with arguments for his defense but his heart ached with acknowledgement of failure and Frances' censure, coupled with her prescription for glory, awed him. He knew that the confidence she spoke of required frequent success and said so. Frances agreed but reminded him that he had tasted success before, and was thus familiar with victory. "Besides, it is your name."

Her proselytizing left him weary and he wanted to remove himself from scrutiny. "So, now that you've told me how to live the rest of my life why don't you tell me how you're going to live yours?"

Frances shrugged carelessly.

"Don't give me that," Tory laughed. "Tell me how you're going to become the Five Star Chef / Bon Vivant nonpareil goddess of the world?"

"I dropped out of cooking school," Frances said simply. "It wasn't for me. And I already reached the apotheosis of bon-vivantdom, I was the premiere debutante of the whole country last year. That's all I ever wanted."

Tory was dumbfounded. "That's it?!"

Frances nodded.

"Well what about the rest of your life? What are you going to be?"

"I don't know…a toy for rich men?"

<u>23</u>

<u>Sonofabitch</u>

When the sun came up the next morning Frances traveled to the Burbank Equestrian Center to watch Jack play polo, and afterward take care of his spent horses. Except for a frightening collision that sent Jack Bonn headlong the polo match was uneventful; Jack was unhurt and immediately climbed back in the saddle and resumed play. Frances went back to her daydreaming and the chukkers continued; no one thought much about the fall except for a passing groom who considered Jack lucky, such falls often yielded broken necks.

The groom's comment made Frances curious. She thought of death's finality and it occurred to her that she had never experienced it up close and personal. Her mother was still alive, Pietro had not succumbed to a brain hemorrhage, and Margo Vitesse had survived her overdose (though Frances did not love Margo one bit the girl fascinated her). She had never grieved, never wished someone dead, never contemplated suicide. "If I could experience death, maybe I would understand it…" She wondered if she could arrange a tour of the coroner's morgue, and if Tory would want to visit it with her.

While Frances was contemplating the Reaper Tory slept and when he awoke it was eleven o'clock and Courtney Kempner was in his room, wandering around examining the trophies and photos clustered atop the flat surfaces. He blinked when he saw her, unsure, but Courtney anticipated his question and said simply "I followed the realtors in." Then she picked up a silver photo frame hosting her picture and threw it hard, hitting him in the knee.

"Jesus C.K. what's your problem?"

"What am I Lewis, some dumb hole? All of a sudden you stop calling me and then I hear all over town that you've been banging some society chick. Huh! I should have figured it, the way you've been prancing around with debutantes." She said it with scorn and folded her arms to await his denial, his dismissal of the whole affair, his plea for forgiveness and affirmation of his love.

Instead he shrugged. "So?"

"So are we done or aren't we?"

"We're done." He threw back the covers. "Want to get high?" And then he was up and digging through his drawers for clean clothes and his stash. Courtney turned away so she would not have to see him naked.

"I don't know Tory, is it me? Did I change? I don't remember you being this irresponsible and mean…or is that the way you've always been and I've been blinded by love…?"

Tory found shorts and a Nike t-shirt. "Come on C.K., you went away for six months and now all you want to do is go to concerts and the beach."

"Hey Lewis, that's all you ever wanted to do, that, screw me and hit tennis balls. And now you don't even want to screw me or go to the beach, you just hang around your house and cheat on me."

He rolled a joint on a silver trophy plate, took a hit and offered it to Courtney. "I don't even want to play tennis," he admitted.

She took the joint. "I guess we don't have much in common anymore then."

"Nope."

She sat down at the edge of his bed smoking dope and feeling sad, unaware that Bonnie Lewis had brought a group of realtors across the threshold.

"As you can see," she offered cheerfully, "this is quite a large bedroom with its own porch and bathroom, a very masculine arrangement that's perfect if you have pot-smoking sons who like to bring their girlfriends up for a joint or two."

"Hello Mrs. Lewis. Tory and I are just breaking up."

"Hello Courtney, I'm sorry to hear that, you seemed like a nice girl. Hello Tory."

"Hi Mom."

"Sorry for the intrusion, I just wanted these people to get a good look at your quarters." She smiled apologetically and pushed her group towards the bathroom two at a time, the realtors examining it with approving nods. "Okay, let's get a look at the downstairs now," Bonnie directed, and she waited by the doorjamb until all of her visitors had filed out. "They love it!" she whispered to Tory happily, then slipped out.

"Why's your Mom so hot to sell your house?"
"She's divorcing my Dad."

Courtney nodded and exhaled a cloud of smoke. "Make's sense." As much as anything else did. "Lewis, do you ever think of anyone but yourself?"

"Sure."

"Who?"

"You. Sometimes Pliny. Sometimes Frances, or my Mom, or my cousin. Once in awhile my brothers and sister, though not very often."

"That's not exactly what I meant. I mean, do you ever, like, consider humanity as a whole, people who have never met you, heard of you or acknowledged your existence? Anonymous individuals like a grocery clerk stocking vegetables in the middle of the night so she can make tuition money, or a gang member being sentenced to prison, or soldiers at war?"

"Never."

"You're being facetious."

"Not really. They don't care about me. If they met me they wouldn't care. You've heard that expression, 'no man is an island?' Well that's a load, we're all islands, we only acknowledge people in our immediate orbit. That's about it. I guess I learned that intuitively a long time ago, but it's been hammered into my head a lot lately."

"But what about people who try to do a greater good for the world, charity workers or diplomats, some altruistic someone who might want to help you reach your goals or save you from starvation or something?"

"I wouldn't trust them. Look, I once tried to help this girl who'd overdosed, and it backfired hugely. I couldn't believe it, I was so stunned that my good works preceded total disaster I kept trying to find the reason why... and then I considered my reasons for wanting to save her life and it basically came down to saving my own skin, because somehow she'd gotten into a bunch of pills I'd given Cece. She didn't die but she might as well have, for all her life's worth now. At least I escaped unscathed."

"So what you're saying is that you deluded yourself into believing you were helping this chick and all you did was help yourself, and that's a universal axiom?" Courtney was confused and not a little stoned.

"Let me put it another way. You know those groups you read about in the newspaper who work for a cause, like AIDS or the homeless or political prisoners, they're serving others in order to serve themselves. If a person is a model of virtue then they're denying themselves one thing or another while at the same time helping themselves to a generous portion of self-righteousness. Look, you go on a diet sometimes, right? So if you skip a meal because you're dieting you're depriving yourself of food, a basic human need, but really you're doing it to make yourself look more attractive, thus fulfilling a greater need, that which rests in narcissism and the need to be liked. However, you can fool everyone by wearing a sign around your neck saying 'HUNGER STRIKE TO PROTEST POVERTY IN AMERICA!' and get a rep as a politically righteous person. But really all you're doing is making trouble, because the food you don't eat will just rot and be thrown out by the grocery stores, because that food has been allocated to you, not some homeless person and if you think for a second you're helping to ease poverty you're dead wrong. You're only exacerbating the problem because that grocery clerk working the graveyard shift won't get that extra ten-cent share from your purchase. Only by conspicuously consuming will you allow others to prosper. Anyway, my perspective on the question you raise is realistic, not idealistic, it is human nature to serve one's self wholly and completely in every waking thought and deviation will only bring chaos."

"What about Mother Theresa?"

Tory shrugged. "Space Alien."

"But every other activist is a phony, because they only want the admiration of others…"

"That, and maybe to skim funds from charitable contributions."

"You know Lewis, you didn't use to talk this way…"

"I'm being tutored."

"Well," Courtney sighed, "I came here to talk about us but now I don't see any point. You seem very cold."

"Hey C.K., you asked…and I'm entitled to my opinions. If you feel like talking about us, let's talk."

"I don't know if I want to now. Who is this girl anyway? Why are you dumping me for her? You know, you used to be really easy to get along with. Now you've got all these opinions and philosophies but you still sleep all morning long and the first thing you do when you wake up is smoke pot. I don't get it, it all seems very contradictory. Look at me Lewis, I'm totally hot. What's this chick got that I don't?"

"A life."

Stung, Courtney looked at him hard and then got up from the bed and picked up her purse. She paused at the door. "Maybe you'll grow out of this. Call me when you do."

"Actually C.K., I'm trying to grow into it."

"Sonofabitch." She stormed away, the sounds of her anguished crying echoing off the tile floor and hard walls, audible until she slammed the heavy front door on their relationship.

Tory listened until she was gone and then picked up the framed photo she'd thrown. "I'm sorry C.K.…It's a Lewis trait."

****

When Jack Bonn finished his match Frances helped him hot walk the pony and pack away his riding gear. They skipped the post-match drink with the others players, stabled the horses, tipped the grooms, then left the Equestrian Center and drove home. They were mostly quiet until Jack asked "How's your romance going?"

Frances took her gaze from the window to smile at him. "Fine, I think."

"You don't seem particularly in love, though…"

"It's still pretty early."

"True. Is it a kind of love?"

"Do you love your horses?"

"In the way that they serve me."

Frances nodded. "I suppose that's how I feel about Tory right now."

Jack laughed. "You are so careful."

"Well love is the one thing we are under no obligation to dispense. I'm supposed to love you because you're my Dad, but I don't have to no matter how well you treat me. I might love Tory but as I said it's pretty early and I really don't know who he is. And I don't know if he loves me either. I suppose that's what I like about him."

"Have you met his family yet?"

Frances shook her head.

"I don't think you'd like 'em. The Lewis family is obvious, though Tory seems different, more promising. I hope for your sake he's not ruthless like his grandfather. There's a tough bastard."

"How do you know him?"

"He's part of the preservationists overseeing the Bridge restoration. My interests are with a steel and re-bar company. If Pliny Lewis has a grudge against them the deal's off."

"Why don't you just buy him off?"

Jack Bonn laughed. "I wish we could! Pliny Lewis doesn't take graft. He's not corrupt, just mean and connected. But he's old too, his reach isn't that long anymore. He was something in his day, though. Boy could he strongarm!"

"Tory talks about him all the time."

"He's got the kid's ear. Probably because there's no one else worth a damn in his life."

Then there's another thing we have in common, she thought. Her father pulled off the freeway and made his way west to Grand. When they arrived home Jack thanked her and again offered a dinner party, which Frances accepted. "Who will you invite?"

"Just a few people…I don't have a lot of friends. You, of course. Probably Tory, and Mom."

Jack Bonn darkened, his stare was cold and mean. "I won't come."

"Fine. But you will pay for it."

"Frannie, I think you need to get back into therapy."

"Don't change the subject." She was solid in defiance. "If you don't want to come that's alright but it's my party and I'll invite who I please."

****

The sky was a bloody rouge color with striations of clouds stretching far off into the western sunset, and Pliny Lewis felt mortal as he pitched stones from his pocket into the backyard bathtub. He sang a tune while he tossed the rocks, it was an old song but Frances knew the words and she sang with him as she and Tory came around the back gate into Pliny's yard.

Pliny stopped singing and eyed his grandson and the girl. Frances continued to croon and walked past him to glance casually into the tub before she took a seat on its edge, her song finished. She thumped the iron tub with her fist. "Almost full."

Pliny palmed the stone in his hand and regarded her with distrust that Tory saw but did not understand. "Yes," he told her.

"And it's sinking into the earth. When it's full the ground will swallow it completely."

Pliny stared at her. She turned away from him to Tory and cleared her throat. "Tory, can I have something to drink?"

"Sure," Tory told her. "Pliny, want anything?"

"No thank you," the old man replied, never taking his gaze from Frances. Tory took his leave and when he had gone inside Pliny retreated a few paces and edged into a lawn chair. He and Frances watched each other until Pliny initiated. "You're very pretty. Where did Tory find you?"

"I found him," Frances smiled. "He was lost and astray."

"Not as lost as you might think, my dear. He still has me to watch out for him. Did I mention that you are pretty?"

"You did, and as Tolstoy remarked, 'what a strange illusion it is to suppose that beauty is goodness.'"

"That has never been my error," he said, shaking a crooked finger. "You ought not be so upfront with me, I might warn him."

Frances laughed a silvery laugh and swung her legs coquettishly. "Oh well, caution away! He won't notice."

Pliny grimaced, his eyes narrowed. With all his might he threw the stone in his hand at Frances; she ducked as it whizzed past her skull and rapped hard against the back fence.

She straightened up and cocked an eyebrow. "Any more?"

"No, that's all for now." He settled back in his chair. "What's your name?"

"Frances Bonn."

"You're Jack Bonn's daughter. Yes, I know you. I've seen you riding that black horse around the Arroyo."

"That's me. And I've seen you stooped over, picking up rocks. So this is where they end up." She patted the tub again. "What is this, some kind of stopped up hourglass, this vessel of rocks? What are you measuring old man...your destiny?"

"Get out, witch!"

Frances grinned. "Moi? I'm just a girl. My my, you're a testy old goat. Look, you can do anything you want with your old rocks, it's immaterial to me. I just came over to meet Tory's cherished grandfather, not provoke him. However, now that I've done that let me apologize for my suppositions. And my youthful brass."

Pliny felt suddenly fatigued by her. "You will be the death of me, I'm sure of it."

"Oh please." She brushed his macabrity aside and stood up. "I'm just your grandson's girlfriend. Frankly I don't see what he so admires in you. You seem crazy to me." With that she headed into the house.

"Tory! Tory, where are you?" She found him in Pliny's kitchen. "Let's get out of here, your grandfather's demented."

"But I just fixed this iced tea! What's going on between you two anyway? Pliny's a little eccentric but he's sharp. I thought you'd like him."

"I find him crazy and no, I don't like him. And he hates me."

Tory set the tray he was carrying down on the counter and pulled Frances to him. "He's old and he's lonely. Look, let me talk to him a minute, and then we'll go." He kissed her and said "Okay?"

Frances murmured her assent and Tory went back out to the yard. Pliny fixed him with a stern look and leaned forward in his chair. "Tory, you'll have to break up with that girl. She's no good."

"Can't do it, Pliny."

"I'll give you two weeks. After that I cut you out of my will."

Tory folded his arms. "Pliny, this is the first time you've ever threatened me."

The old man shook his head. "I'm sorry. I do not do it lightly."

Crouching before the Lewis patriarch, Tory took Pliny's hands in his. "Pliny, I've sought your advice on a lot in the past but I'm not looking for it here. Now you made an offer regarding my inheritance and you can withdraw it if you want but you shouldn't worry about Frances. She's just a girl I'm dating, she's cool."

Pliny looked at him gravely. "Two weeks."

Tory stood up and went back inside Pliny's house to fetch Frances. After they left Pliny stayed seated in his lawn chair until darkness fell around him. Finally he lifted himself from the chair and slowly, painfully, found his way to his small studio. He set up a clean canvas on his easel, fixed it tight, and when his pallet was ready spread a broad stroke of alizarin crimson across the canvas face. He stepped back to view the stroke, found it to his liking, and continued on. He painted for a time until he tired, then he settled on a cot in the corner and fell asleep, muttering "my family is gone" over and over.

24

Full Moon and Jim's 'a Singin'

It was Saturday evening the week hence before Pietro could see out
of his left eye. His double vision funneled into a respectable focus early in
the afternoon, then rapidly cleared; by nine p.m. he felt capable of driving
and headed to Gus's for a celebratory drink. There a young blond divorcee
remarked that it was quieter than most Saturday nights and that she would
buy Pietro a drink if he'd shoot a game of pool with her. So he did and hit off
a draft when he felt like it, and everything was fine until Jim Coulter came in
yelling.

The divorcee fled; Pietro ducked out the back door and crouched behind
the dumpster. Jim followed in hot pursuit and stood stupidly outside the bar
yelling "You can run but you can't hide!" into the dark, until that wore thin
and he went back inside to see what was what.

"Cook! Cook! Where's my hasenpfeffer?!" The restaurant fell silent, the
bartender warned Jim to shut up. Things were heating up inside but out back
in the parking lot Pietro Bertolucci stayed cool and sorted out his feelings on
the matter; he had two solids left (not counting the 8-ball) and they were easy
shots. On the other hand he owed Jim one for the chain-whipping and there,
by the fragrance of the dumpster, Pietro wavered upon letting Jim run his
course or intervening and saving him from certain jail. But when Jim's song
drifted out to him Pietro said "fuck it" and went inside.

For Jim Coulter in all his madness sang "Mack The Knife" better than
any man alive. He knew all the Beatle's major drug songs and watched old
musicals for the show-stoppers (favoring "Show Boat" and "Porgy & Bess
over all). But "Mack The Knife" lived in Jim and tonight he was possessed,
gracing Gus's with a rendition that would have put Bobby Darin to shame; it
was this talent that reprieved him and neutralized the oft-volatile situations

he provoked when the moon was full.

Jim was already three-quarters of the way through the song when Pietro moved in and clapped a hand on his shoulder, tugging him along the length of the bar, away from the dining room and into the billiard alcove where he could do the least damage. Jim struggled a bit until he recognized his attacker, who he fixed with a huge grin. "…could it be our boy's done somethin' rash…"

"Two beers," Pietro ordered.

The bartender regarded them with a bad mixture of fear and suspicion and stepped back against the wall, one hand groping behind a stack of wine cases for the handle of a baseball bat hidden there. "That guy your pal?"

"No. Two beers."

"…Oh, the line forms on the right, babe…"

"Get him out or the cops take him." Here the bartender found the bat and tore his gaze away to nod down the length of the bar where two fat men, risen from their dinner and still wearing napkins splotched with barbecue sauce, awaited their cue. Pietro sighed, hating himself for his next move which involved headlocking Jim and hauling him outside through the back door. They would only be satisfied with dramatics.

He shoved Jim coughing and wheezing into the passenger seat and quickly moved around the car to get behind the wheel. In the moment of limbo between Reverse and Drive Jim bolted from the car and ran to the back door where he screamed "Look out old Macky's BACK!" into the bar. Pietro waited for him about a hundred yards down the street and when Jim dove in screeching with laughter Pietro peeled away and drove down a dark street with his lights off, not saying a word.

****

Tory eased the jeep up to the curb and killed the engine. "Are you sure you want to do this?"

186

Frances tore her gaze away from the massive lawn to regard him with slight annoyance. "Why not? It'll do her some good to get out. Besides, it might be fun."

Her look, coupled with her edginess and perfect legs made Tory sigh inwardly; outwardly he looked at the darkened home. "Every time this girl and I cross paths something bad happens. I don't understand what your interest is in her anyway."

Frances shifted in her seat and put her arms around his shoulders, planting noisy wet kisses on his neck, forehead, eyes, nose, and cheeks. "Come on baby, don't be a sourpuss…" She nuzzled him and kissed away; Tory gave up and returned her kisses. Margo could wait.

A half-hour later Antoinette Vitesse, incensed that someone would ring her doorbell unannounced on a Saturday night, put down the deck of cards from which she drew solitaire hands and strode over to the window. She flipped the latch and pulled hard, then stuck her head out into the night and looked down at the two young faces staring up. "Stop ringing that goddamn bell! What do you want?!"

Frances stepped directly forward. "Good evening Mrs. Vitesse, we were wondering if Margo is at home? We'd like to say hi."

Antoinette blanched. A tightness gripped her chest and a heady rush of blood poured into her brain; her left hand involuntarily slipped up to her throat and she staggered slightly. "Margo…?"

"Yes. This is where Margo Vitesse lives, isn't it?"

Up in the window Antoinette barely recovered from the shock of it all. Margo, having visitors…? It was almost a dream. She cleared her throat and assumed her most polite tone. "Yes, excuse me…yes, this is exactly where Margo lives. Please wait a moment, I'll be right down to let you in." She smiled and closed the window, turned and rushed from her room down the hall, cringing when she saw the closed door.

This was no time for manners, only action. Antoinette lowered her head and steadied her shoulder; she hit the door with all the force her hundred and five pounds and blue canvas espadrilles would generate, plowing through the lock like it was made of twigs; Margo screamed from her bed and pulled the covers over her head. "Margo!" Antoinette shouted, "Some of your friends are here to see you, get up now!"

"No! I don't have any friends! Tell them to go away! Wait…is it Hugh?"

"No it's not Hugh, I don't know who it is the boy looks vaguely familiar. Come on Margo, get dressed and go out with them tonight!"

Margo drew the edge of the sheet back and peeked out. "It's not that weird guy from the Ball, is it…?"

"Of course not, why would he come to see you? Come on dear, hurry up. I have to go, I left them waiting outside." Antoinette snatched a corner of the bedding and stripped it away, Margo shrieked and vainly grabbed for it to cover her nakedness, kicking loose her vibrator which clattered to the floor.

Antoinette's eyes grew wide. "Margo!!!"

Frances cackled as the poor girl's screams sounded from inside. Tory shook his head and hopped off the porch, starting out across the lawn but Frances was on him in seconds, blocking his escape. "No pussycat, let's not go…things are just starting to heat up." Before Tory could argue there was a loud click that caused both to turn; in the doorway of her home Antoinette Vitesse stood in silhouette and beckoned them to come inside. "Please come back, Margo will be right down. Come in and have some tea."

"Ten minutes," Tory hissed. "That's all we stay. Ten minutes, got it?" Frances nodded 'okay' and they returned to the porch.

Antoinette reached out to greet them as if she were welcoming long-lost relatives. She cupped each of their hands in hers and clutched them tightly, pulling them into the light of the single bulb over the doorway. A faint look of horror crossed her face as she smiled from Frances to Tory, but the look faded and she assumed a hospitable glow when Frances slid an arm around her waist and ushered her into her own house. "We've missed Margo so, wherever has she been keeping herself?"

"Up in her room with her vibrator," Antoinette blurted, and her wince at her own indiscretion caused Frances to laugh.

"Well we've all been known to indulge a little now and then, right Mrs. Vitesse? Oh my, what a lovely home!"

Antoinette approached a light switch and flicked it on, smiling meekly. "Yes, thank you, let me turn on some lights and you can see it better." They followed her through the dark house, Antoinette turning on every available bulb as she led them into the living room. Frances poked Tory when Antoinette stirred a small black Scotty dog from his slumber beneath the piano. "Shoo Maxie, shoo! Out!" She lit the last the lamps and smoothed her blouse. "There, that's more pleasant. Please, make yourself comfortable while I go and fix some refreshments. Margo will be down very soon."

Frances and Tory stood idly in the blazing living room and considered the furniture, deciding on a stiff settee. Antoinette smiled her approval.

They smiled back.

"Yes," Antoinette sighed satisfactorily.

The three continued to look and smile at each other until Frances cleared her throat. "Herb tea for me, thank you" she offered and Antoinette spanked her hips and said "oh silly me!" before bowing her head and rushing from the room to the kitchen, pausing at the foot of the staircase to shout to her daughter to get the lead out.

"See?" Frances smiled, taking Tory's hand in hers. "It's not so bad."

"It's depraved."

"Oh it is not, you'll see."

Maxie came back into the room, snuffling along the path of new smells. Frances turned away from Tory and regarded the dog with a sinister glare; the Scotty bumped his way around the Biedemeir couch and coughed on a hairball. Antoinette smashed a plate in the kitchen, cried "oh darn!" and did something with the water running. The hairy beast bumped its way beneath the legs of a cherrywood end table and rubbed its back along a pile of fabric swatches hanging down, progressively blackening the floral print of the top piece. It sniffed up a crumb from the carpet and ate it, then blindly serpentined its muzzle towards the seated couple. Frances' lip trembled, her mouth curled and she uncrossed her legs. A sweeping noise came from the kitchen.

The Scotty came into range. Frances aimed a pointed toe and sent a sharp kick. Maxie yelped and ran frantically from the room crying. "Small dogs are good for kicking." Tory shook his head and Antoinette came into the living room bearing an ornate China tray set with tea things. "Why Maxie what the heck is wrong with you?" She shook her head as the terrier raced past. "Honestly, I don't know what gets into that dog sometimes…"

She set the tray down with practiced ease. Frances recrossed her legs and folded her hands in her lap. "Oh what a lovely tea service Mrs. Vitesse! My stepmother has one just like it."

"These are English scones" Antoinette gestured, " and the pot is Earl Grey, but it's decaffeinated. I'm sorry but we don't have any herb tea at all." She poured two cups, slid one to Tory who declined and next offered it hesitatingly to Frances, who accepted graciously.

"Thank you so much."

"You're welcome…?"

"Frances. Frances Bonn." She extended her hand for Antoinette to shake, then gestured to Tory. "This is Tory Lewis."

Antoinette balked; her face assumed an expression of pure terror. She retracted her hand, glanced down the hallway to the staircase, looked back at the boy seated before her and retreated a step.

"We've met," Tory said.

"Oh grand," Frances smiled, taking a scone from the biscuit tray. "Say Mrs. Vitesse, I couldn't help but notice those fabric samples. Are you redecorating?"

Antoinette swallowed with difficulty and looked furtively over her shoulder again. "Um, yes, I am…" She inched away from the couple and grabbed at the pile of swatches. "They're the finest silks, you know…"

"They look beautiful. Would you show us, please?"

Antoinette looked from the girl to the boy and back to the girl again. "Um, I really don't think so…I've just remembered I left the iron on upstairs…"

"Oh please," Frances begged. "It won't take long and I really do love choosing fabrics…"

Stuck in the mire of Frances Bonn's well-mannered request, Antoinette cast a desperate look once more to the staircase before draping the first of the samples over her arm like a tea towel. "I really don't think this is appropriate for this room, see? Maxie's got dog hair over it already."

"Nonsense, it's lovely. Let's see another."

Antoinette complied and held up the next piece, a light cream color accented with blue fleur-de-lis. Frances shook her head regretfully. "No, I don't like that one. What's next?"

Obligingly the hostess plucked up the next selection; she dangled it high over her head, brought it down as she swept a stray lash from the corner of her eye with her sleeve, then straightened her arm. "I'm fond of this one," Antoinette remarked.

"Could you hold it a little higher?" Antoinette raised her arm above her head. "Hmm, maybe if you turn around…" Antoinette did a pirouette and looked hopeful. "No, it's rather ugly," Frances decided. "What's next?"

Antoinette was stretched out, one hand holding up a black and white pinstripe cloth against the drapes, the other stuck out as far as she could reach dangling a mauve block pattern against a chair back when her daughter came into the room. "Mother--! What's going on?!!"

Antoinette shrunk from embarrassment; Margo gave no quarter and pointed to the guests. "What's he doing here?! Who's she?!"

"Hello Margo," Frances greeted cheerfully. "You're looking sober."

Coming out from behind the furniture Antoinette made her best effort to calm her daughter's ire. "Margo dear, this is Frances Bonn and this is…"

"Tory Lewis!" Margo snapped. "This is the guy who nearly killed my boyfriend and then tried to rape me when I was out cold at the Cotillion!" She charged across the room and lunged over the tea service for his throat, stumbling over the low coffee table and scattering scones and cups everywhere. Tory sprang from the settee and moved behind it. "Margo, control yourself!" Antoinette shouted but Margo was not to be deterred and picked herself up along with a small jade lamp.

"You ruined my life!" she screamed, hurling the lamp at him with all her might. The lamp smashed against a bookcase and broke into a hundred pieces and Margo snatched up a fireplace poker.

Tory checked his watch. "Your ten minutes are up, Frannie."

"So sorry we can't stay," Frances told Antoinette. "Thank you for the tea and scones, they were lovely." She ducked a wild swing from Margo's poker and stepped behind the piano where Tory crouched, he having vaulted an easy chair to snatch up the little piano stool for a shield.

They waded through three assaults, fending off Margo's incendiary swipes with the piano stool, and after she backed away crying Frances darted out and ran to the front door. "Goodnight!" Frances called, and Tory fielded one more vituperative lick from the poker and batted it away. Swept up in the riposte, Margo sprawled across the carpet, defeated.

Tory reached the door breathing hard and paused before following Frances into the night. "I'd put her in an insane asylum," he advised, then slipped out leaving the two Vitesse women weeping together on the living room floor.

The couple reached their car in short time. "You sure have a way with people, don't you Frannie?" Tory said.

Frances smiled and slid into the passenger seat. "Some people don't know when to quit."

****

"Tory! Over here!" Cecelia waved from her corner table, relieved that her watch had ended. She had secured the table since her arrival at the Loch Ness an hour before and in that time fought off the persistent efforts of a plethora of beery bohemians desirous of it. It was a big table, the biggest in the pub, and she had guarded it like a dog in the manager ever since Angela O'Donaghue deserted her to flirt at the bar. Now with Tory and Frances pushing through she could squeeze out and leave them with the table, get herself out and away from the cramped corner and her loneliness.

"Hey Cousin," Tory greeted. Cecelia said hello and then announced that she needed some air. Frances and Tory exchanged shrugs. "Wonder what's got into her?" Frances purred.

The back door was the closest. "Excuse me!" Cecelia demanded, sidestepping a flowing stream of urine issuing from a transient. As the wino turned to see who was intruding on his pee Cecelia straight-armed him, saving her shoes and socks from a dousing. The wino was not so lucky and staggered and lost his aim, wetting his pants, and his pissed-off cursing followed Cecelia to the dark refuge of a fire escape where she sat by herself carelessly disagreeing with the fates.

She was still there fifteen minutes later when Pietro's Corvette negotiated the narrow alley and pulled up. Cecelia didn't recognize the lanky man in mechanic's overalls who popped out the passenger side, and she certainly wasn't going to call out to Pietro when <u>he</u> emerged; here was a scene that didn't involve her in the least and she wanted it to remain that way. She shifted around to watch it unfold.

And so it did. Pietro moved with force around the car and seized his companion. Even from the bleachers some sixty feet away Cecelia could see the gleam in the man's eye and know he was commissioned for trouble. He fought against Pietro's grip and strained for the entrance, once nearly breaking free until Pietro said "Whoa Jim, you can't go in there without <u>this</u>!" and belted him in the eye, sending him to the pavement like a stone.

When Jim hit the deck Pietro looked around the dark lot quickly for witnesses, then squatted down and cradled Jim's head as he came to. "Yeah, attaboy Jim, yessir you're gonna be alright. On your feet." Cecelia took her hand from her mouth; it was there to stifle a scream when the sickening crunch of bone and cement smashing together hit her ears. But Jim proved okay, he was standing and soon had his bearings, enough to curse and slap away Pietro's attempts to look at his assurgent eye. Eventually his curses gave way to a bitter cant on the undeservedness of it all and when he finally did let Pietro have a look he was calmer and indeed seemed pleased when

Pietro told him the eye was swelling shut completely and that he would have a shiner for a week or so. A minute later Jim went into the Loch Ness with a new affability and twenty bucks Pietro had given him to get drunk with, and when he was gone Pietro laughed and thumped the windshield of his Vette, generally pleased with himself.

He was still laughing when Cecelia called "Hey Rocky!" from her slightly elevated position. His sniggering stopped; he darkened and faced her as she descended the stairs, resting his hands on his hips. "So you finally knocked someone out, eh Rock?"

"You shouldn't be lurking out in the dark Cece Lewis. You might see something you're not supposed to and then, well, it's deep-six for you."

"Ha ha, you're so funny. What're you gonna do, beat me up? I don't think Tory'd take that lightly."

Pietro snorted and banished her with a wave. "You think Tory'd come out of his coma to avenge you? But you're safe anyway, I'd never hit you."

"Yeah, I guess you only hit your friends, huh?"

Pietro shrugged. "I did him a favor. He was acting like a dickhead before, now he'll go in there and buy a drink, sing a song, generally behave himself...he was determined to get arrested until I clocked him. Now he'll sleep in his own bed. A beating always cools a man down. This is a fact."

Cecelia nodded towards the entrance. "Aren't you going in with him?"

"Nah. If I wanted to be here I would have started here. What about you, what are you doing out here by yourself?"

"I'm not sure. I guess I'm just tired of Frances Bonn." She looked to Pietro for a reaction. He obliged cryptically. "She's not for everybody," he said.

Cecelia felt a sudden, inexplicable attraction to Pietro. She stole a look at him and was puzzled; any affection for the fighter, who she'd spent most of her teen life disliking for many good reasons, seemed utterly inconsistent. "What is this?" she thought. "Have I changed, or has he?" , for there did seem something shared between them...possibly some element of decency had been jarred loose during Pietro's last fight and was dominating the ones that made him berserk most of the time…on the other hand, maybe the change was with her…or maybe both.

Pietro caught her looking. "I gotta go."

He was behind the wheel firing up the ignition when Cecelia asked where he was headed. "Maybe Monahan's. Peter likes me; sometimes he'll comp me a meal. I'm kinda hungry."

"Me too!" Cecelia said quickly. Pietro recovered from his sudden surprise and leaned over to pull the handle of the passenger door; Cecelia hopped in, hoping no one was watching from some dark corner.

****

Tory returned from the bar with a second pitcher and found his seat occupied. Frances slid over and motioned for him to sit by her, then made the introductions. "Tory, this is Duke. Duke, Tory."

"Pleasure," greeted the Duke.

"Sure," replied Tory, hurriedly drying his hand (wet from the beer pitcher) to shake the Duke's dry one.

"Frances tells me you met at the June Cotillion," the Duke volunteered. "I was there too."

Tory shot Frances a look and she responded with a calming hand. "The Duke left after dinner, he didn't even see the presentations. He's a grad student at Caltech. What're you studying again, astronomy?"

"Plasma physics," the Duke corrected. "I had an experiment in the works and I had to hurry back and check on its progression."

"What were you doing at the Ball?" Tory asked, anxious to turn the subject away from Plasma Physics before the Duke could advance it further.

The Duke looked surprised. "I was Fran's date."

"Old boyfriend," Frances explained.

Tory nodded and picked up the pitcher to fill his glass. The Duke quickly offered his empty and Tory filled that up too; Frances' was still full and she knocked the table twice and excused herself to go to the ladies' room. "I'll be baa-aacckk!" she sang.

"So," grinned the Duke, when she was safely out of earshot, "what do you think of Frances?"

"She's a bully."

The Duke laughed. "Indeed she is. Her chlamydeous treasure is guarded by a cunning, hectoring virago... any intimate sampling of such is often a pyrrhic victory."

"Huh?"

"Never mind, I'm sure you'll find it so." He clapped Tory on the shoulder as he rose from the table. "The queer thing about that girl is that she can really work to your advantage or disadvantage. Of course," he added thoughtfully, "that's true of most women."

"Which was it for you?"

"Oh advantage, sure. Fran's a great girl, I like her a lot. Thanks for the beer." He raised his glass in toast and went off into the crowd.

Tory stayed alone at the table feeling disturbed. The subject of Frances's former romances had not come up, though she certainly knew all about his past liaisons...like she knew about everything else. And this Duke character, well, he was probably okay in small doses but his edge was so pronounced it made one fearful of his next thought. A Duke/Frances romance seemed hazardous, like mixing fire and gasoline. Frances/Tory was not so clearly defined, but her wicked behavior at Margo's was indicative of how far she could push the envelope if he let her.

He was brooding on the matter when Angela O'Donaghue came over with two boys. "Hi Tory, where's Cece? If you see her tell her I'll call her tomorrow."

Tory suddenly remembered his cousin. "Angela, I haven't seen Cece for over an hour. She's not with you?" He looked past her and the two boys into the bar crowd but could not see Cecelia anywhere.

"Nope, I haven't seen her since we got here. Well, gotta run!"

Frances returned. "Look, I found out where there's this dog fight in Altadena." Before Tory could respond she had her purse and jacket in hand and was moving through the crowd. Tory slid out from the table, chugged the rest of his beer standing up, and hurried after her.

He caught up with her at the jeep; she was doing a little dance step, clicking her feet and popping the door handle on every third beat. "Hey, slow down."

Frances stopped dancing.

"Christ Fran, we've only been here an hour."

That's long enough. I didn't come here to stay here, only to wait for something to happen. It did."

"You bitch!"

She stopped him at that. "God Tory, it's always the same old bull, isn't it? You get so annoyed when things get boring but you never want to do anything new."

Tory did not have any ready response and climbed in. "Do you know where we're going?"

"Yes. I'll give you directions."

"This had better be good."

25

Love

Courtney Kempner had had enough, that was plain to see. Her life since
Tory dumped her was a sludge of depression, pain and loneliness mixed
with a fair amount of bulimia that failed to purge his image from her mind,
so that when her mother ordered her to stop puking or check into a hospital
Courtney ignored her but decided on another course of action and now stood
on Cecelia Lewis's front porch ringing the doorbell until Ginny, roused from
her comfortable afternoon nap and feeling cross, flung the door open.

"Mrs. Lewis I have to speak with Cece, is she home?"

Virginia Lewis, who normally liked Courtney, folded her arms and
leaned in close. "Courtney if you ever ring my doorbell like that again I'm
going to have my gardeners drag you out back into the shed and snip your
fingers off one by one with the rose shears. Now, to answer your question,
no. Is there something I can help you with?"

Courtney looked flustered. "I'm sorry, I really am, but…but…" her face
screwed up and her eyes grew teary. "That sonofabitch Tory!"

"Oh Jesus," Ginny sighed, pulling Courtney inside. "Come on dear, let's
get us a cocktail. Anything having to do with my nephew requires one." She
led the distraught girl into the living room and sat her down, disappearing
then reappearing with two tumblers. "Courtney you shouldn't let love get
you so upset, it's so ephemeral! Here, drink this. And for God's sake don't
cry anymore. Sheesh, you'd think he was worth something, the way you're
carrying on."

Courtney sobbed into her gin & tonic while Ginny tugged at the
waistband of her pantyhose and wondered whether she should go on a diet
or buy a larger size. At last Courtney seemed capable of controlling her

emotions. Ginny took a gulp of her own drink and reclined in a nearby chair. "Now what's Tory done that's got you so upset?"

"He's going out with someone else, Mrs. Lewis! He never gave me any warning, he just dumped me!"

"Dear Courtney, you went away to a whole different continent! Did you really think he would keep his hands to himself the whole time? Come on, you know how men are!"

"Mrs. Lewis, he practically told me he loved me when I got back!"

"My dear girl, that boy is as deep as a puddle. Now if he's found someone else then you must also, that's the way love works. When Cece comes home I'll have her email you some names of some boys she knows. Then you can set your sights on some other young stud, alright?"

"Okay." Courtney swallowed the last of her drink and made a face. Ginny took her arm and led her to the door. "Good luck. And look on the bright side, at least you're not going to marry him now."

"Thank you. Goodbye Mrs. Lewis."

"Goodbye Courtney." Ginny Lewis shut the door and rolled her eyes. "Don't these girls ever read Cosmo?!"

When Cecelia came home a few hours later Ginny accosted her. "Who's Tory's new girlfriend? Spill it and hurry!"

Cecelia set her purse down and scowled. "Christ Mother, what difference does it make to you? Her name's Frances Bonn. I don't really know her, but Pliny's met her and hates her guts." She eyed her mother suspiciously. "Have you been drinking?"

"Of course Darling, it's my hobby. Why does Pliny dislike her?"

"Ask him yourself!"

"No need to be bitchy Cecelia, I'm only trying to have some parent-child communication."

"Well excuse me Mother but Tory's loves are of absolutely no interest to me, especially this one. She's brought nothing but bad luck ever since she showed up and turned Tory into a moron. Pliny's furious with him, he's furious with me for that disaster with Margo and Hugh March, and I'm ready to chuck the whole lot of you. And for God's sake, get a new hobby." She brushed past her mother and went up to her room.

Cecelia was truly angry with the world. She felt cheated, the capriciousness of youth evaded her. Her struggle was with her family and surname; an eighteen year old girl can only suffer so much humiliation, what with her father's incarceration, Pliny's agenda, her mother's alcoholism and her cousin's feckless conduct. Her escape route was some four hundred miles north where she could blend in with the forty thousand students in Berkeley and start over...if she could survive the summer. She lay on her bed and wondered why she was so alone.

Pietro Bertolucci was also alone. He had fully recovered from his injuries and except for a crooked nose and an occasional migraine he was the same as before and a few thousand dollars richer. Nevertheless, since the fight his only foray into the outside world was his adventure with Jim Coulter and subsequent encounter with Cecelia Lewis. It was this rendezvous that paralyzed him with fear, kept him in exile, the outgoing message on his voicemail stating "leave me alone." For Pietro Bertolucci had fallen in love.

She was in his mind with every song that played; her face materialized in magazine ads featuring spanky models, sensual foods or young couples in love. Fantasies of their togetherness—walking on the beach, exploring Europe, dancing-- filled his idle mind. "No," he told himself. No, no, no, no, no.

They had kissed, in front of a window display, when he pulled her to him during their post-Monahan's stroll down Lake Avenue... it was a gamble but it felt right, and when she kissed him back he knew it was good. They laughed afterwards, but kissed again when he drove her back to her car. And after that, not a word between them.

What the hell happened to him?! Their dinner was fun, the food was good, a bottle of wine courtesy of Peter Monahan lubricated the conversation...Cecelia had suddenly supernova'd; her lips, her cute nose, centered on pearlescent cheeks, tantalized him... and those eyes! Like sapphires! Her wry sense of humor, honesty and independence turned him on. So did the quiet moment of introspection he'd witnessed on a return trip from the head, when he sneaked up to their booth and saw her studying a matchbook, lost in thought…he loved her then.

So now he had to decide, was he going to be a loser or act like a man…he picked up his cell and dialed. "Cece?"

She bolted upright when she heard his voice. "Uh huh…?"

"Hey. It's Rocky."

"Hey Rock. Whadda ya know?"

"What're you doing?"

"Nothing…" In reality she was on her elbows, eyes wide, her heart pounding.

"Why don't I come over and we'll go for a drive or something?"

"I'll be waiting out front." She hung up the phone and jumped up and down on her bed like a little kid on Saturday.

****

While Pietro and Cecelia were enjoying themselves on their first official date, Tory was getting dressed in preparation for Frances Bonn's dinner party. He'd decided on navy blue linen slacks, white shirt and tie, with a seersucker sportcoat; the invitation specified no dress but declared an address which he knew to be Bistro 45, and the time, 7pm sharp. He had no clue who else had been invited and was a cauldron of ambivalence about his own presence, for he and Frances had not spoken since that Saturday night.

He was slowly comprehending the Duke's appraisal of Frances, not his exact syllogism, but a variant. She was bloodthirsty. She was savage. She was interesting and sexy and exciting, she was powerful. Her enthusiasm for passion and sex captivated him, her lust for violent fights, canine or human, disturbed him. When the brindle pit bull had bled to death, its head half-chewed off, he saw in her eyes the fire of feral sport and knew he could never please her, at least not through the normal man/woman love relationship.

For her there was a destiny of perversion and he could not, would not come along…the Margo encounter, the dog fight, Pliny's caveat…they predicted disaster if he pursued her further. Their love would become toxic, George and Martha S&M. Tory was not fool enough to partner her in such a journey; he was growing smarter every day and though this was largely due to her influence it would ultimately seal her fate.

He accepted her invitation, of course. Avoidance was easy, acting resolutely more difficult. She was beautiful and he constantly desired her… maybe he was reacting too strongly to her barbarism, maybe she was just a funster with a wild streak…he hoped that was it, for he genuinely liked Frances, even loved her for her body and spirit and always active mind that challenged him. "We'll see how it goes," he told himself. So he got in his jeep and drove to the address, the restaurant he knew it would be, and the valet took his car and a Maitre'd greeted him by name…and there was no one in the place except Frances and her mother.

They were the players in this private affair: Frances, looking beautiful in a sexy strapless black dress with gold earrings, and her mother, a woman of about a hundred, lying comatose in a hospital bed breathing through a ventilator. "Tory!" Frances smiled warmly, kissed him on the cheek, and firmly gripped his arm to prevent his exit which was his next move. The burly Maitre'd blocked his path and along with Frances made sure Tory sat down in his chair.

"What the hell is this?" Tory demanded.

"Tory, this is my mother, Marina Bonn. Mother, this is Tory Lewis." Appetizers and cocktails appeared without prompting, scotch-rocks for Tory and a martini for Frances. Marina Bonn sucked on her ventilator.

"She's brain-dead, is that right?"

Fire ignited in Frances' eyes and she leaned over and slapped him hard. "Why don't you behave yourself and be polite! You accepted this invitation now stick it out!" Tory slunk back in his chair and glared at the Maitre'd who hovered nearby. "Tory, tell Mother how we met…"

He acquiesced after gulping down his drink. Another immediately appeared. "Frances and I attended the Pasadena Guild's Cotillion. She helped me revive a young lady who'd passed out on drugs. Is that what happened to you?" To his surprise neither Frances nor her mother took umbrage. Instead Frances took her mother's thin white hand and held it gently in her own.

"Mother, Tory wants to know how you were disabled. Is it alright if I say?" Mrs. Bonn did not audibly reply, but Frances nodded anyway and then addressed Tory. "It was a swimming accident at the beach. Riptides…"

Tory nodded and drained half his glass. Frances still held the faded hand of her mother, tenderly stroking the fragile skin along the back, gliding her touch to the tip of each finger. Marina Bonn stared ahead through unblinking eyes.

They led somewhere, they were not cloudy or dead. They watched the world with pain and urgency, physically restrained by the hideous paralysis that coveted her body. Tory searched their panes for a reply to Marina's static wastefulness but their expression remained fixed and he could not tell if her gaze decried her attrition or if they held a vestige of realization, a fossilized account of her final emotions before she left the house with the lights burning.

Tory swirled his glass. "When was this?"

Frances smiled sadly. "I was not yet six."

"Where does she live?"

"Ask her yourself."

Tory cleared his throat. "Where do you live, ma'am?"

Marina inhaled and exhaled in measured breaths. Frances listened patiently then told Tory "In a condominium over near Pacific Oaks on Holly street. Pink with striped awnings…you can probably see them from your house." That was true, they were clearly visible. Tory buttered a piece of bread and looked for a menu; before he could ask Frances told him the selections. Grilled shrimp with salsa verde, swordfish with cherry tomato, cucumber and radish relish, grilled potatoes with anchovy and tomato sauce. When the food came it was remarkably beautiful; their waiter laid down three plates but Frances pushed her mother's aside and told him "She's not eating." It was removed.

Neither Tory nor Frances spoke during dinner but Tory listened to the hiss of Marina Bonn's mechanical respiration and then to the music piped over the restaurant stereo, wishing he could lean over and flip the switch on both and enjoy silence. At the conclusion of the meal Frances waved to the Maitre'd and a moment later two ambulance attendants rushed in, returned Mrs. Bonn's bed to a horizontal position, and raised the guardrails.

"Tory, my mother's leaving."

He stood up. "It was a pleasure to meet you, Mrs. Bonn."

Frances smiled at him and lovingly kissed her mother's cheek. "I'll see you next week Mother." She patted Marina's arm and watched the ambulance attendants guide the bed through the restaurant and out the door.

When Marina Bonn was gone Tory sat back down, snapped his fingers at the Maitre'd and pointed to his empty glass. The big man scowled but brought a fresh drink immediately; there was wine on the table but it went untouched. Frances had been satisfied with just the one martini and sipped Perrier after that. Mrs. Bonn did not drink.

"She tried to drown me," Frances began. Drunk on scotch, Tory did not care whether or not she explained the circumstances of Mrs. Bonn's incapacity but he did not interrupt. "She and my father were having problems. She was depressed.

"She struggled to hold me under but the sea was strong and pulled me away. Some fishermen jumped from the pier and rescued me." Frances looked agonized. "She had a lot of water in her lungs. She never really woke up."

"It would have been better if she'd died."

Frances looked down at the tablecloth. "Yes."

Tory looked at Frances, at her rich brown hair and the golden tan of her skin, at her slender fingers and toned arms. He looked at her perfect breasts shaped beneath the black dress and was sorry he would not feel them again. "Fran, I can't see you anymore."

She looked up with surprise. "Why? Because I have an invalid mother?"

"Because you're out of my league."

"Explain, please."

"You have a lot of money, you're beautiful, smart, cunning…you don't really love anything in your life and that's a great thing, because nothing can hurt you."

Frances became very emotional. "I do so love! I love a lot!" She pounded the table with her fist. "Damn you Tory how can you say that about me?!"

"Frannie, you're like so many people in my life. Your emotions are used up, you can't summon them anymore for all the tragedies of the past clogging the way, blocking your heart. You confuse care and concern for love, but they're very different feelings and I don't think you can make the journey to love. Me, that Duke guy, we're just entertaining detours, sideshows you hope might lead you to happiness somehow, someway."

"What the hell are you talking about? Are you talking about tonight? Was this a sideshow?! I invited you into my deepest, most painful secret so you could get to know me better, to see my past, to understand me more…"

"Really? Or was it to get back at your Mom? She lays there wasting while we eat delicious food in front of her, insulting her with our vitality, mocking her with our youth. Or else you set this up to invite my protests so you could slap me, teach me a lesson about empathy and the functional dysfunction of your family…well I already know about that and frankly, I've got enough weirdo's in my life. I've got a sister I never talk to, two brothers who don't give a shit about me, father and mother the same. My grandfather is the only man I trust, and even he's got designs on my life. My family is a bust; I can't have a girlfriend who plots behind my back."

Frances sighed. "This seems like a plea for attention to me."

"Dismiss it if you want to Fran. Our love affair has been great, thrilling, a total blast…but now that I know your deepest secret where do we go? Do I nod my head every time you antagonize someone and tell myself it's all your mother's fault, no don't slap me again I'll hit you back…or do I say goodbye and try to resolve my heartache by meeting some other girl who wants to love me without making me love her pain…"

"Tory, that's a lot of big talk but you've got a support system in your grandfather and cousin and I've got no one, just myself. So you can blow me off and it won't hurt you a bit, but if you were a real man you'd stick it out with me. I've only got you, Tory. And really, you were just a dumb jock until you met me. A little knowledge is a dangerous thing, and you haven't seen our relationship evolve. Instead you bolt when there is pain…" She folded her arms atop one another. "I think your grandfather is behind this. He's convinced you I'm a witch."

Tory smiled wanly, remembering Pliny's decree and thinking it ironic that his wish was coming true. He stood up. "Frannie I love you, I really do. We're not right for each other. I'll see you around." He pushed in his chair and headed for the door, snarling "get the fuck out of my way" to the Maitre'd. When he was sitting in the jeep with the engine running and the clutch in and his hand on the stick he was suddenly stricken with grief over the end of his love affair with Frances Bonn and by the time he turned up San Rafael he was bawling.

<u>26</u>

<u>A Pact With the Devil</u>

Hot wind cutting over the sill cooked the perspiration on Pliny's neck and he shifted and strained against the seat belt, trying to evaporate the damp sweat from his back and legs. "Damn you girl, couldn't you kidnap me in a better car?!"

"Sorry!" Frances laughed, drinking from a bottle of water. "Be glad I didn't rent a convertible, you'd really be heatstroked." She pressed her knee against the incurve of the wheel and capped the water, stashing it in a side pocket away from him, then reclaimed the steering wheel and floated the big car across two lanes away from the slow line of traffic.

"I'm almost glad it's ending this way. I've never killed a woman before, a point of pride for me. You would have been the first."

"Tough talk, thoroughly romanticized. You must be reading a lot of bad novels. Listen old man," and here she turned nasty, "you take your meals out of bowls. Your rants don't affect me, I'm fearless in the face of your toothless barking. But if it makes you feel honorable then go ahead, I won't pay any attention."

"You're a bitch. I don't know what Tory sees in you."

"His future. He's done with your blathering about image and Lewis epochs. I'm going to lead him to true achievement, not some soggy parochial aggrandizement."

Pliny grunted disdainfully and looked out at the desert speeding by. "You don't seem properly schooled."

"Who needs school when you've got great tits?" She laughed and punched the cigarette lighter; when it popped out glowing red hot she seized it and jabbed at him with it, chortling when she scored a direct hit. Pliny managed to slap it away out the window and sulked for a short time in pain.

"Know where I went to school? Marlborough, Mayfield, Westridge… they graduated me from one of them, I forget which one, but for me it was a dulling experience. Supremacy is not encouraged in young ladies; old grunts like you have made it a practice to keep us down. That's why you're stepping aside."

"There is a Latin phrase, '*lex talonis*.' The law of retaliation. I will see to it from beyond the grave."

Frances shrugged. "Whatever. Tory can't heed both of us. Do you find me attractive?"

"In the way that there is a beauty to a forest fire or a snake."

"Clever. Hey, want to see my breasts? Come on, I know you do." She winked and Pliny smiled slyly because he knew she would show them to him, which she did. "Pretty, right?" Frances pulled her blouse closed. "You're dying old man, and one of the last things you'll enjoy seeing are my breasts."

She was gleeful and Pliny did not disparage her for it, for he remembered his own enthusiasm for vengeance. Nor could he fault her for damning him for the sins of institutions; after all, he had built and administrated them, willfully continuing the legacy inherited from men before him.

When he looked at Frances he saw demoniac, nefarious forces allied to quest and conquer, lust and kill. They assumed her maiden's form and it took a practiced eye to see past the beauty to the harpies beneath. Her intrigue lay in her sexuality and its epicene strengths: will, passion, appetite, seduction. Merlin had succumbed to these, Pliny too, though for him it was not the hope of lusty consummation but the challenge of her adversary, and so he sweated on black vinyl seats while crossing the desert en route to his destiny. His ego had landed him in the passenger seat with his legs shackled to the firewall; he had seen through her ruse but took the bait anyway and now all he had to do was beat the odds and become his own true Superman.

And if he lost? Well, he would not be ungrateful. His ideas of death were fashioned through observation and most of his peers languished in hospital beds with their bodies decaying, reaching a terminal stage with the pace of a season's change. He was better than that, his death would not be preceded by such banality. The jagged violence of the Mojave might take him but not without a struggle, and to Pliny the odds were good he would survive the ordeal; nothing else had claimed him.

After another forty minutes of driving, some of it on secluded dirt roads leading deep into the rocks, Frances pulled the car over to the side and stopped. She unbuckled his seat belt and unlocked the shackles around his legs, and Pliny climbed out and surveyed the area. North and South and East and West, he took note of where he was relative to those. "A lot of creatures live out here. I know how to get water out of the ground. Shade's easy. Food's everywhere."

"I'm glad you feel challenged."

"Patronizing youth. When I'm back in Pasadena I'll squash you like a bug."

A small smile appeared on Frances's lips and she shifted her weight. "I don't doubt your will, Pliny. But the tub's full. Now go. See if you can discover anything along the way."

With nothing more to be said Pliny turned his weathered aged face away from her lovely young one and started out across the desert floor eastward, away from the afternoon sun, to find those answers which he was never able to uncover in his ninety years of living. He had been the Master of his own Destiny throughout his life, now he was gambling with it to solve the mysteries which had come to plague his remaining days.

Like where had his honor gone? Once feared among associates and respected by his peers, his force had dissipated with the thinning of these ranks. Retirement or death took his allies and undermined his power base, he had not the energy to fight off the youthful encroachment that wanted what he had and took it at every opportunity. He was a spectator as an old man, no longer a player and his ouster was hastened by his progeny who could conduct themselves as they saw fit without concern for his reputation or position. Ageism was not irresponsible bigotry; it took energy to control things and his had lessened as he grew older—it was just business. Now a consultant involved in only a fraction of the enterprises he had engineered, Pliny Lewis retreated and rested on his laurels. Some still feared him, but Frances had spoken the truth. He was toothless, and unless he could make it out of the desert he was dead. He walked on.

The landscape changed after awhile, there were wildflowers and cholas sprouting from the dry earth. There were more insects too, and he took note of the edible ones. Twenty minutes had passed before he looked back… Frances and the big car were a speck in the distance, still parked by the side of the road. "Goodbye Frances," Pliny whispered. A large calico tabby joined him on his trek.

"Well, well, well…bit of a tight spot, eh? I guess she got the better of you…"

Pliny ignored him and trudged across the dry sandy earth, past the chaparral and cactus. The cat stayed beside him in step. "Too bad Tory took your advice and ditched her."

"That was incidental," Pliny snapped. "I'm here because I want to be."

"Nooo," drawled the cat, "this is definitely an act of retribution. It appears you've meddled once too often in affairs of the heart."

"She is not an ordinary girl, this is not an ordinary act of revenge. This is Destiny."

"Arguable."

"Stupid animal."

"Sticks and stones…"

"You little shit," and he kicked at the big Tom, missing as the cat sallied away.

"Oh Pliny, you're so slow! Slow and myopic. You interfered once too often, your attempts to meliorate Tory's love life have earned you a capable enemy; she didn't take it lying down like James Jameson's lover and now you're on your death march. That is the plain fact. Now tell me, don't you regret having opened your big yap instead of allowing Tory and Frances the right to an unobstructed love affair?"

"No," answered Pliny. "I'll say what I want to whom I want, and no amount of cajoling from you will inspire me to repent. I never wanted an enigma for a grandson, he hasn't the brains. Tory will meet a lot more women who aren't Frances than are, my advice to him was right."

"Uh huh. And so he marches on, carrying your 'good name', your ideas bouncing around inside his big empty head like superballs. To what end? No love affair, no family, no future. You've made him into your own image, a confused man wandering around in a parched wasteland."

"I didn't…"

"Oh stop, don't deny your quixotic notions of Lewis Hegemony to me, I was there for it all! Look around you at your kingdom, Pliny!"

Pliny stopped. He and the cat glared at each other, then the cat rolled over onto its back and licked its paws. Pliny sighed and turned away, feeling at last the cat's rebuke. The sun was burning out across the Universe, turning red.

"If you walk north along the points of the long shadows you might find out where you're going," drawled the lazy feline, in between spitting a tuft of fur.

Pliny considered. "Will I get there soon?"

"No, it will take you as long as it takes you to find the answers to your questions." Then he purred cattily, "Unless you want me to tell 'em to you."

"I don't think so. I didn't like your assessment."

"Truth hurts."

"Go to hell."

"Usually that's my line," snickered the cat. "Pliny, let me say my piece, you bore me. Victory will find his own place in time, and like the solid oaks you Lewis's are (and he said this with no small sarcasm) he'll settle in and grow out. But these things take time, and it ain't time."

"What a cowardly prognosticator you are," Pliny charged, turning with hands on hips.

"It's all you deserve." The cat fanned his tail in the dirt. "You're a racist, egocentric unforgiving meddler, and a crummy painter. And you've always been so."

"I am a crummy painter," Pliny admitted.

"Well THAT'S big of you," sneered the cat. He chose this time to yawn and stretch his back and hindquarters, then said simply, "It's time for you to leave me. Go on across the shadows."

So Pliny took leave of his critic and headed north across the desert floor keeping parallel with the earth's rotation. The argument had tired him; the cat had yielded no quarter and his directions were ominous; assuredly they would not lead him to a comforting bosom or idyllic glen. To his credit his step did not falter for he did not fear death or damnation and all else seemed conquerable. He kept his head straight and his feet churning and presently a great red shape rose up from the shimmering horizon in his path.

He followed the arcing shadows towards the shape; when he neared it revealed a cluster of red canyons. All around lay nothingness, wide-open desert plain. Pliny paused. "Did the creature want me to enter these?" The wind came up just then, providing the answer, and Pliny approached the sculpted rocks a little less boldly; his fear began to stir.

The canyons provided no refuge, they served as chapel for the wind's pontification. From the scored faces of red rock appeared the anguished images of his estranged daughters, howling their pain into the roaring torrents that raked the crevasses, wearing them down. "You failed me!" Pliny shouted in his defense, but the girls wailed louder their loneliness and despair.

"Father…! Father…! Help us…!" came their cry.

"What could I do?!" Pliny shouted. "You chose your own husbands, your own paths! I warned you!"

"Father, we need your love…we need your love," sang the girls.

"Damn you, you failed me!" he shouted. "You miserable pathetic women, you failed me!"

The gale increased its violent assault, picking up loose sand and dirt from the canyon rocks and flinging the gravel into Pliny's eyes, blinding him. He staggered about, grasping for balance at rocks that crumbled at his touch. Falling to the ground, he tore at his shirt and stripped it from his body, covering his head and face. His chest ached and his back stung from the sand's bite and all around him the roar of torment sounded, suffocating him, wearing at his soul. He fought hard against it, scratching his retreat while crawling on his belly out of the canyon, spitting sand and coughing at the dust coating his lungs. With maximum effort he staggered up and away in the direction out; it occurred to him that this might be the end but still he struggled against the recriminations of his daughters with the last of his might.

His instincts were good, after a time the maelstrom of wind and sand calmed into a bitter blow and he found his way out from the red rocks into the cold night air. He fell to the ground and lay prostrate, coughing the dirt from his lungs, subdued. He had functioned his whole life indifferent to the proceeds of his most callous actions, and though the pain of his daughters wrenched at him he was not guilty; on the contrary—his ninety years of egoism had given him the tools to resist their charge of dereliction. It was not his way to be sorry. "I will get up and walk on," he told himself.

Darkness brought forth nocturnal creatures, lizards and snakes that slithered past, owls, bats and other fly-by-night predators. Coyotes trotted gracefully along the dry creek beds. The desert was alive under the half-moon light and Pliny determinedly rose and left the haunted canyon to continue his eastern journey. He was not hungry or thirsty; it occurred to him that he might be so but the sensations were absent and he congratulated himself on his asceticism. He was evolving, he was Super; the desert's hostility did not detain him.

He crossed a ridge of sand and sagebrush into a startlingly changed topography: gone were the flora and fauna of his last steps, what lay before him was a wasteland of giant volcanic rock, harsh salient edges shining like knives in the moonlight. They had been waiting for him for a thousand years, since the earth belched them up from its molten belly, hurled together with volcanic bile for mortar. Now, at his arrival, the rocks crackled as he passed by, spilling small avalanches. Pliny found their activity spooky yet invigorating and he was not afraid; the rockslides did not threaten him and there were no admonishing howls. He continued on.

Thus he was directed through a newly-opened fissure that split in a rock twenty five paces before him. This in turn led to a stairway of clefts and stones ascending and at the summit he met his third guide of his journey, a black wolf with yellow eyes. Pliny encountered him with suspicion, for it had been some time since they'd seen each other and he was surprised to find the beast so far from civilization.

The wolf greeted him first. "Hello Pliny."

"Hello Satan. I wasn't sure at first it was you."

"Nor I, you've aged since we last met."

"How've you been? Still with the old man?"

"In a manner of speaking, yes. And to answer your first question, never better." The wolf turned east. "Shall we go?"

The pair descended the rock, which was far gentler on the back slope than its greeting face, and composed mostly of soft black sand. Pliny stumbled along the way; the wolf paused while he regained his footing and allowed him a moment of rest. Remarking that Pliny seemed reluctant to continue the journey, the wolf suggested that the elder might be having second thoughts. Pliny assured him he was committed. "It's just that I didn't expect you."

Satan laughed. "That's not surprising, few do. I wonder why that is?"

"Well from my point of view my eternal reward was to be gloriously pleasant. I rather expected heaven, not hell."

"Hell is what you make of it," Satan countered. "And you're not dead yet." To this Pliny had no reply.

The path Satan beat could best be described as a tormented void, not even a beetle or ant crawled over the sands the wolf and Pliny tread and the volcanic rocks grew fewer. It was a soundless, desolate plain stretching to a blank, its nothingness stark under the cold moon. Pliny searched his feelings and decided he hoped he would not die there, for it was an area of total loneliness.

Satan read his thoughts. "You should be used to it by now."

"I loved in my time."

"You flatter yourself. Your love was incidental to your humanity, a curious predisposition of your brain function. All your actions speak to an aversion to its happiness. I cite the case of James Jameson to prove my point."

"My actions were principled. You know that."

The wolf gave a toothy grin. "That's what I like about you Pliny, your skilled extenuation. If you could see clearly the misery you have spread across your time you would at last be ashamed. As it is, you have resisted indictment and have no shame at all. Shall I show you the consequences of your actions?"

"No thanks," Pliny told him. "I never took those actions lightly. You forget that I am a man of planning and men such as myself think things through to their conclusions, then decided whether or not to initiate. I've no remorse for what I've done."

"That's a fact," growled the wolf.

"And besides, to show the misery you would have to give equal time to the good, of which there is more."

"Good is not my department," Satan said flatly.

"Nevertheless," Pliny replied, "I am allowed a fair judgment."

Satan stopped and gave a feral sigh. "Pliny, Pliny, Pliny, you are truly a man of expedience. It is not often I encounter one who so willingly does my work yet rebukes me at my claim. Did you give this much trouble to the cat?"

"More. But you needn't worry, he's an able servant. He did send me to that Canyon…that was a nasty trick. And now he's led me to you."

"That's so," agreed the wolf, adding "…though I do think you'd have found your way to me on your own, eventually."

"Well the cat was good in his own right." He cast Satan a sly glance. "You might be challenged by him one day."

"Ha! He is a quisling, easily replaced."

"I don't know about that," Pliny shrugged. "So far he impresses me more."

"That surprises me not," hissed the wolf. "Mankind is always glorifying competence, confusing dutiful execution with leadership. Then you mock your lords and tear them down in the belief that a new regime will deliver the prosperity promised in campaign slogans. And what you get is what you deserve, the rage and hatred of those long-downtrodden suddenly raised to power who eagerly turn on their supporters with viciousness so heinous even I am surprised…and their power consolidated, they fester like open sores, spreading pain throughout nations. Government is my most virulent ally, I am evil and conspiracy, stupidity and chaos. I am despair and contempt, selfishness and greed, murder and suicide.

"Intellect, free will…ha! Misused in humankind to my benefit! I take what you give me, nothing more. I have ubiquitous support."

Pliny was stunned. "You say this with no glee."

Satan's eyes narrowed and grew darker. "I am courted by your race. I take no one without their consent."

Slowly the vicissitude of Pliny's damnation became scrutable; his expression changed from puzzlement to joy as he realized Satan's final revelation, spoken in the heat of disgusted discourse, released him from the wolf's clutches. He was not damned at all, he had not resigned under the devil's excoriating remarks and confessed to being evil…his strengths had saved him from the torments of hell! He was jubilant. "I am not yours then!" he laughed, dancing around the wolf. "You can't take my soul! Whoo whoop dee doo! Ha ha!!!"

The wolf regarded him with annoyance. "I've wasted a lot of time with you, I can see that."

"Too bad for you! Hoo hoo, I've beat the devil!"

"Alright, enough of your gloating, my tongue slipped. You would never have figured it out otherwise. Do you plan on dying out here?"

His question quieted Pliny's celebration. "Um, do I have a choice?"

"Frankly, no. You've come too far already, your physical body is dying right now back at the red canyon."

"Well I'm destined for heaven then!"

"Not a chance, God won't take you. While you might not capitulate to me you've shown no remorse for your sins to Him. And don't try to weasel your way up there by doing so now," he glowered.

"Huh. What do you suggest?"

"Let me consult with the other side and see what we can work out." The wolf turned west and with a powerful coil, sprang away and disappeared. Pliny sat down in the sand to wait.

After a time Satan reappeared, leaping down from nowhere and skidding slightly in the sand. He shook himself, then trotted over to Pliny. "As I thought. You are now part of the food chain. It is the opinion of God that since I had first dibs on you, I can dispense with you. Now let me think…'"

"Why don't I get a chance to talk with God about it? How do I know this isn't one of your treacheries?"

"Be quiet, I asked you to let me think."

"No, I have a right to know!"

"First of all," said Satan with waning patience, "you've opted to take your death into your own hands and test God, a big heavenly no-no, ah ah, don't protest, you got into that car knowing full well she was going to try to snuff you." He grinned when Pliny got sulky. "And secondly," the wolf continued, "you're at my disposal. Okay wait, I think it's just come to me.

"See if this is agreeable to you. And if it isn't, who cares. I send you back, coupling your soul with another…then you take it from there. If you persist in being nasty, well then, I'll be seeing you. That's a promise. But if you can be a positive influence, you and I will not meet again."

"You can do that?" Pliny cried, somewhat astonished.

"Sure," Satan shrugged, "we do it all the time."

"Hmmm," the old man considered. "Who might this other soul be that I must guide?"

"I rather like your grandson, the one you call Tory." He grinned. "I'm sure you'll like the assignment too."

Pliny was awestruck by Satan's plan, so perfect it was to his own. "Yes! I agree to it."

"Knowing you this will probably work out well for both of us. Now listen, I'm obliged to repeat my warning—you will function as either demonic possessor or guardian angel, that's up to you. When his time comes you will be judged independent of him. He will not be responsible for your contributions, good or bad. Only you will be accountable for your influences."

"Fine"

"Then it's a pact."

<u>27</u>

<u>Pliny's Will</u>

It was a week before they found Pliny's body; by that time the carrion feeders had picked his withered frame clean and the spare rotting flesh that clung to his skeleton was left to fire ants and flies who found it an ideal nesting place for their larvae. Hardly any of him remained; even his dentures had been plucked from his open mouth and carried off by a kangaroo rat who stored them deep in his burrow. What had been figuratively accomplished by the hungry risers of business was literally claimed by the beasts of the field, and after being spotted by a low-flying plane Pliny's bones were gathered up and sent back to Pasadena for burial while his teeth were left to grin wickedly from beneath the desert floor for time eternal. Cecelia Lewis alone attended his mausoleum internment in a procedure so routine it defied mortician logic: no flowers, no minister, one mourner, no prayers or eulogy. One might have been putting a pair of shoes away in the closet.

"My condolences to your family," the mortician recited, shaking her hand goodbye. Cecelia thanked him and got into the hired limousine for the ride downtown. The morning sky was cleansing itself of cloud cover and she rolled back the sunroof to let in the light, thinking it strange that she felt no sadness at the entombment of a man she truly loved. Relief was her dominant emotion, a relaxing of the ties that bound her so tightly. While the driver merged the big car into traffic Cecelia poked around the compartments and discovered the liquor cabinet. Without hesitation she poured herself a drink, scotch straight up, then settled back to enjoy the ride.

It was Saturday again, the boulevards of the city were uncrowded and her driver immediately found a parking space on the street in front of the building housing her grandfather's lawyers. She signed in with the security guard and took the express elevator to the thirty-fifth floor, listening to the soft hum of machinery and counterweights that whisked by. She felt satisfied and empowered; she had faced a difficult task courageously. Fear had kept the others away, fear of seeing his casket slide off into the cold marble hole, fear of mortality—Pliny's and their own. Cecelia always knew Pliny would die and prepared herself for his passing by loving him while he lived. Love, the most formidable of all emotions, calling its disciples to vulnerability... Cecelia's love for her grandfather had often hurt but now it rejoiced in a job well done and took the elevator up to the law firm to be compensated.

The doors opened and Cecelia stepped out into a cloud of blue cigarette smoke. "Cece! Hey cousin!" Janelle Lewis flicked her Marlboro into the ashcan and rushed to embrace her, and Cecelia reacted in a way she thought she never would: with understanding. I know why you vanished, she thought. I do not blame you. They hugged and laughed with relief, then stepped back a pace to get a good look at each other. Janelle's blond hair was frosted and layered glamorously atop her head in a style reminiscent of a sixties movie star, her Chanel suit was alluring yet respectful. It was a new look for her, less severe, indicating a truce with the world.

"Gosh Janelle, you look great!"

"Thanks Cheetah, you do too. Kind of grown-up," and she gave a playful tug on Cecelia's arm.

"Have they started?"

The boys are in there waiting to hear what the Pliny left 'em. I just came out for a smoke. Hey, I'm sorry about gramps. I know how close you two were."

"We were all close to him at one time or another." It was true, Janelle had done time as Pliny's favorite. Teenaged rebellion distanced her from him and Janelle never sought to repair the damage in adulthood, gratefully slipping away from the family dynamic when Tory and Cecelia came of age and entered Pliny's apprenticeship.

"I gotta say, I was surprised when I got the call that I was in the will. I kind of expected him to dust us all."

"Why?"

Janelle shrugged. "I dunno. It would just seem appropriate."

Cecelia nodded, not in agreement but in avoidance. She had labored in the family mill and now wanted to be paid for her efforts. Janelle's rueful perspective was her own, Cecelia did not share her sins. Besides, it was easy for Janelle to wryly muse when she was standing in the law firm lobby holding a ticket to the catbird seat in her hand…more difficult when one's been assuredly disinherited, as their parent's were.

"Shall we go in?"

"Okay." Janelle slid an arm around Cecelia and they went through the door into a wood paneled office where Tory, Mike and Tim Lewis were seated around a large Irishman planted at his desk. Mike and Tim broke into mock applause but Tory did not join them, for which Cecelia was grateful. "Hi boys," she said, kissing each. When she reached Tory she looked for a foothold into his mind but his face was a mask of calm; he returned her kiss and asked how the burial had gone.

Cecelia slid into a chair. "He went."

"I half expected Pliny to climb out of his casket and fight to the bitter end," Tim said, pantomiming a man struggling. They all laughed and there were a few other jokes before the lawyer cleared his throat and thumbed through the documents on his blotter.

"Let's get to it, shall we?" the lawyer said. "I'm Terry McCarthy, I represented your grandfather through the drafting of several wills and I have to tell you it was an unusual process…" He looked at the faces of the family before him for a response and got none. "Your grandfather was adamant that each Will be probated properly; I can tell you with certainty that this is indeed the last Will & Testament of Pliny Lewis. It's legal to the cotton rag it's printed on. I say this to assure you of your rightful claim to properties listed herein, for there might be lawsuits arising contesting the exclusion of your parents and aunts…your grandfather was an exacting man.

"The disinheriting of Frank Lewis, Joe Lewis, Amanda Lewis Steib and Brooke Lewis Bicknell is described in this document." Terry McCarthy went on, passing copies to each of the family in front of him. "If you need extra notarized copies I'll send them to you. Needless to say, the persons listed have received the same information."

Pliny's mouthpiece continued to detail his Will and the conditions surrounding it, finally getting past the preamble to the body of appropriations. "I, Pliny Lewis, being of sound mind and body…" etcetera. When he reached the disbursement of property he looked at Cecelia. "Miss Lewis, your grandfather decided that you should have the deeds to all physical land and structures. The house at 338 Busch Gardens, Pasadena; the house in Hanalei Bay, Kauai; and the two hundred acres of ranchland in Irvine. He also left you a small parcel of ten acres in Gulfport, Mississippi. As far as I know there are no structures there, and surveys show it's swampland."

"Thank you," Cecelia said quietly.

The lawyer went on. "Appraisal of the real properties is about a hundred and fifty million dollars. Your grandfather wanted you to have a good start in life."

"Yes," she said. It was all she could manage.

"Janelle Lewis, your grandfather left you a small collection of jewelry valued at two hundred and seventy thousand dollars five years ago, and a thousand shares of stock in the Mobil Oil Corporation. He also left you a million dollars in cash. Mike Lewis and Tim Lewis, you are each awarded the same amount of money, one million dollars each, plus a portfolio of securities and bonds listed in these documents." He handed them over. Mike and Tim high-fived and took the folders. All eyes turned to Tory.

Terry McCarthy rubbed the tip of his big red nose and shifted his mouth this way and that. "Victory Lewis, I must report that recent codicils to your grandfather's will have not apportioned you the same cash gifts your siblings received. It seems Pliny thought differently when it came to securing your future—he has left you a trust of two hundred thousand dollars to use to further your education. And his principal award to you consists of his entire portfolio of preferred stock in the Arroyo Tennis and Country Club Leisure Corporation, to be transferred to you on your eighteenth birthday."

While Terry McCarthy read from the text Tory folded one leg over the other and placed his hands on the armrests of his chair. A smile crept in as he listened to the legalese. Cecelia studied him, trying to decipher the smile. What was going on inside his head? Why was he taking such a cynical consolation prize so calmly...?

Terry McCarthy concluded. "With the deeding of the forty-seven percent share Pliny has determined for you and the other four percent held in trust from your grandmother's estate, come August fifteen you will be the majority shareholder in the Arroyo Tennis and Country Club Leisure Corporation. No cash value has been indicated in the Will, but I believe the Club is valued at around forty-five million dollars. Your stock is non-transferable, meaning it can't be liquidated or sold to another party except in cases of court-ordered dissolution. I wish I could say there were options, but there are none. Pliny let his corporate term-life insurance expire last year so the Board of Directors will probably not mount any campaign to buy back the stock." He gave a conciliatory smile.

Tory grinned broadly. "Excellent."

****

"It's all in how you look at it," he said when the family had adjourned and were waiting for the elevator.

"I don't mean to be discouraging Tory, but what the hell are you going to do with a country club? That joint's never returned a single dividend in its entire existence...all it is is a piece of heritage and a bar," Janelle said.

"A very fine bar," Tim countered.

"Pool's not bad," Mike offered.

"It is Pliny's gift to me and I wholly and gratefully accept it." Tory put his hands in the pockets of his sport coat and stood tall. Cecelia felt love for Tory welling up inside her.

"I think Pliny was generous to all of us and keeping the Arroyo in the family is a great thing. At least Tory cares about the place."

The cousins looked at Cecelia as if she'd announced she was an extra-terrestrial. "The guy's seventeen years old, for crissakes," Janelle muttered. "What was Pliny thinking?!"

"At any rate, I've certainly got my membership back," Tory stated. The elevator car came and they filed in.

When they were outside Cecelia offered a ride to anyone who wanted one but all had driven separately and were discussing a plan to drink the rest of the day away to celebrate their new wealth. "Come with us Tory," they encouraged, and he told them he would, then took Cecelia aside.

"Cece, what are you going to do with Pliny's paintings?"

"I don't know. My head's still spinning from the idea that I own his house."

"Can I have 'em?"

"Sure…I guess…" She regarded him suspiciously. "Why?"

"I like 'em."

"Okay. But you're not coming over today to get them, are you?"

"No, I'm gonna go get hammered with Mike and Tim."

"Tory, why did Pliny go out to the desert to die?"

"I don't know."

"Do you think he was sick?"

"Maybe. He once told me he wouldn't die in front of the television. He was a motivated man."

Cecelia pondered this idea. After a beat she said, "Okay, I'll buy that. So what did you tell the police?"

"That he liked to walk."

"That's weird. Tory, hasn't it crossed your mind that maybe somebody snuffed him? Don't you care about solving this mystery?"

"I care a lot. Pliny was a huge presence in my life and part of me is gone. But he was not one for living in the past and now that he's dead I think he wants us to get on with our lives. That's why he stipulated we read the Will on his burial day, so we could assuage our grief with money and find comfort in the future."

"Well, I'm hesitant to say I agree with you about the money part, but for some reason I'm feeling okay about his death and it surprises me…I wonder if this feeling isn't some kind of conditioned response—that he trained us to cope with difficulty, to have no crippling sorrow over his passing. He was always a man who said 'get on with it.'"

"Right."

He and Cecelia stood for a moment out by the curb and were quiet. Cecelia wanted to say more but it suddenly felt like the end of something, like she would be saying goodbye to Tory for a long time. All the events of the past year had involved the three of them: her, Tory, and Pliny, and the latter's death seemed to signal that the game was over and they could all now go home and rest.

"Well, see you." She stepped towards the car and the chauffeur took his cue and opened the door for her, then skittled around to the front and took his position from behind the wheel. Cecelia rolled down the window. "Be careful out there," she said, nodding toward the other Lewis children.

"Okay, thanks. What are you doing tonight?"

Cecelia smiled. "Rocky's cooking for me tonight. Some kind of chicken thing."

Tory grinned and shook his head in bewilderment. "That's gotta be the strangest thing in the world, you and him…"

"I know. We're the weirdest people on the planet."

"Not quite." He leaned in and kissed her, then waved and walked over to where his brothers and sister were waiting.

<u>28</u>

<u>The Last of Frances Bonn</u>

When the doorbell rang that next morning it was incessant, urging, a mean-spirited alarm that jostled Tory out of bed, not in the best of moods. There was a thundering in his head unlike any before and it required relief, maybe a handful of tranquilizers and a beer. First? Second? The doorbell rang again upstairs and down with a belligerent shriek. Tory moaned and shielded his ears with his hands, cursing steadily as he crossed the solarium en route to the front hall, squinting as the first daylight assaulted.

"Oh shit," he groaned. "Fran, go away."

"Hello Tory."

Tory leaned his weight against the door for support, feeling dizzy and nauseous and incapable of speaking an appropriate phrase, quote, rebuff, or cabalistic cant that would make the girl disappear and magically return him to his hangover bed. "Just a minute, I have to throw up," he said and hurried away.

There was a guest bathroom a few doors down from the disused dining room and he crashed through with a hard shoulder, letting his stomach heave freely. Hot bile erupted from his sour belly and splashed into the bowl…he wretched for a second time and spasms shook his body, vomit surging with each until all of it had emptied. Afterward he felt capable of standing at the sink to splash water on his face and brush his teeth with a toothbrush he found in the cabinet; it tasted vaguely of cleanser and had probably been used to clean the toilet bowl but at this stage Tory was devoid of hygienic fantasy and didn't care so long as the scum cleared from his mouth. He rinsed with water and gargled mouthwash, then toweled off and went out to face Frances Bonn.

This latter chore (for everything this morning seemed a chore, even breathing) was conducted in the front hallway where he returned to beckon her to follow him into the kitchen where he offered her a beer and had one himself (inviting Frances's laughing comment on his mask of death), proceeding from there to his bedroom where he peeled the unit dose wrapper from a Xanax and climbed between the sheets of his bed to pop the pill into his mouth and wash it down with beer. Only then did he lower his hand and permit her to speak.

"You know Tory, you and I were a wild, sexy pair, but the wildest boy I ever went out with was that guy called Duke. I was kind of quiet around him most of the time, he was crazy enough for both of us and super smart. We would have killed each other totally by accident if we'd stayed together… you and I might have worked…Tory you were the best relationship I ever had, not once did I not like you."

Frances dipped slightly forward to see if the ex-boyfriend in the bed was listening, but his face was hidden beneath the sheets and only his hair showed. "I know I drove you crazy at the end," she sighed. "But you drove me crazy; I was under a spell or something when you were around, I wanted to tear things up. I certainly felt your energy, and it provoked me…turned me into an alley cat, I wanted to fight or fuck all the time."

"I liked the fucking," grunted the voice under the sheet.

Frances nodded and paced the floor. "So did I. It prevented me from damaging a lot of things when we fucked. That's why I couldn't help myself after you broke up with me, I had to kill your grandfather." She stopped her tour of Tory's room and waited for him to bolt upright, but he registered nothing. "Tory, I picked him up outside his house, telling him I was taking him to lunch to make amends for our volatile introduction…" She moved over and sat down at the edge of the bed, hands on her knees. "…Then I drove him out to the desert and dumped him off…half of me thought he'd crawl out of there, chastened, unwilling to meddle in your life any further now that I had usurped his power and had your full attention. I was kind of surprised when I learned he'd died."

Tory peeked out at her. "He was ninety years old. It was a hundred and twelve degrees out there."

"I know," Frances sighed. "Pliny was old, but he had his moments. He threatened me as he marched off. Still, I feel terribly guilty about it. I want to know what you want to do…"

"I want to kill you," Tory said without hesitation.

"I thought as much. I'm glad you didn't say 'call the police' or something unsatisfactory."

"I'm not like that," Tory told her.

"Good. Well, if you don't mind, let's get it over with. I don't think I can stand any more of this living."

So Tory got up and dressed while Frances waited patiently in a nearby chair. "I think by killing me you'll finally understand me. I've been alone all my life and when I'm gone you'll be alone too, and you'll stop feeling anything because all the people that matter will be gone."

Tory found his keys and jerked his head towards the door. "Let's go."

They drove down the hill past the intersection where Hugh March ran the red light and Tory parked his jeep near the bridge and got out. "Perfect," Frances smiled, agreeing with Tory's plan. "I'll die in full view of my mother's condo. Who knows, it might jolt her out of her coma. See, that's her window over there—third one from the left." Tory looked out across the Arroyo to the pink condominiums on the other side, their striped awnings playing lightly in the breeze. Marina Bonn's window looked out over the entire gulch. "I want her to hate what she did, I want her to try to fix herself, come out of that coma and save me!" She stamped her foot against the ground. "Damn her! Damn her!" Tory held out his hand and Frances cast one more look at Marina Bonn's window before joining him. Together they slipped through an opening in the fence that blocked entry to the disabled Colorado Street Bridge.

The going was tough on the Bridge, construction had eviscerated the pavement to allow for reinforcement and foundation work, and Tory and Frances had to carefully pick their way through the beams and supports along the southern edge. They reached the middle and stood in the morning sun.

"Well Frances, here we are…I'll never forget you."

"Of course you won't Tory," she said, rushing at him hard and giving him a mighty shove. Tory stumbled backward and thrashed wildly, bouncing off the open edge and tumbling over the side. He fell hard against a portion of exposed beam, banked off it and dropped away. A shaft of re-bar flashed by and he grabbed for it, made the catch and closed his fingers around the ribbed iron rod, holding on for dear life two hundred and fifty feet over the concrete wash below.

Frances screamed and clawed at her hair in anguish, then leapt out over the side.

She fell a short way, fifteen feet or so, before a stiff breeze blowing down from the mountains caught her in its stream and she billowed up like a sail unfurling. Tory kicked for a foothold and found one, swinging his legs onto an abutment and pulling himself up to a ledge. Frances stayed out over the Arroyo blowing lightly in the wind looking sad. "I was afraid of this," she sighed.

Tory clung to the ledge trying not to look down or lose his balance. He looked at the witch drifting out in front of him, who had killed his grandfather and tried to kill him. "Frannie, I'll see you around," he said. Then he huffed and puffed and blew her away.

Frances Bonn grew smaller and smaller as she drifted out over the city, westward towards the sea and away. "Goodbye Tory!" she called, her voice thin and faint in the air. When he reached safety at the top of the bridge he stood and watched her disappear into the haze. "Goodbye Frances," he whispered. When she was gone he turned away and traversed through the skeletoned Bridge, back to his jeep and the rest of his life.

29

Epilogue

On the night of August fourteen Jim Coulter fulfilled his ruinous ambitions and became the Wreck of the Week. Paramedics pulled him from the mayor's totaled car at around eleven thirty p.m. and by four a.m. the coroner's report was issued, listing severe internal injury and head trauma as probably cause of death. By virtue of Jim's high blood-alcohol content the crumpled wreck that was once a car was eligible for prominent display at the Mobil station on Arroyo Boulevard, a testament to the dangers of DUI. Passing citizens recoiled in horror at the violence exhibited so unabashedly, until they noticed the license plate stamped "HIZZONR" still clinging to the bumper, which made many hopeful that the mayor had perished inside.

Despite Jim's death the next day dawned bright and sunny and Cecelia Lewis wrestled the last large suitcase into her car, then rested a moment drinking in the calm summer morning and the sunlight sparkling through the trees. She was at last leaving for school, driving north to Berkeley to begin her college education and adulthood. She couldn't wait.

There were still a couple of goodbye's to make and she attended to the first of them, pausing outside her mother's bedroom door to knock softly. "Mother, are you awake?"

There was no answer. Cecelia hesitated, then slipped in and crept over to the sleeping form. Ginny was breathing softly between two pillows, looking calm and sweet. Cecelia gently shook her shoulder. "'Bye Mom."

"Ooohh." Ginny sat up and slipped off her satin sleep mask. "Oh Cece, are you leaving already?" She held out her arms to embrace her daughter and Cecelia fell into them. "Oh, I'll miss you so!"

Cecelia hugged her tightly. "You take care, Mother. I'll call you when I get in."

"Okay honey. Drive safely. Is Pietro making the trip with you?"

"No, we said goodbye last night. I'm alone."

"No honey, I'm always with you."

"Me too you, Mom."

"Okay. I love you." She kissed Cecelia twice and then let her go; Cecelia backed out of the room and gently shut the door behind her.

Outside she started her car, wiped the windshield and backed down the drive. She drove through town and got on the freeway but instead of heading directly north she pulled off at the San Rafael exit and drove up into the hills. As she turned up Tory's driveway she passed a realtor's sign proudly declaring "SOLD" and knew her aunt had triumphed, excising the last vestige of Lewis family life. When she reached the top of the hill she saw Tory's jeep was not there but Bonnie's Jaguar was, so she got out with present in hand and rang the doorbell.

Bonnie answered the door looking like a train wreck, her face swathed in bandages. "Oh hi Cece."

"Hi." She hesitated. "What happened?"

"Oh this?" Bonnie touched her face lightly. "Just a nip and tuck. You'll get one too someday." She smiled at her niece. They had never been close.

"Is Tory home?"

"No, he was up and out early. He said he was going to the Club. Did you bring him a birthday present? How thoughtful."

"Yes," Cecelia nodded. "Would you give it to him?"

"Sure." Bonnie took the package. "Are you leaving now?"

"Yes."

"Good for you. Well, I hope college is everything you want it to be. I'm sure it will be better than here."

Cecelia smiled at her aunt's cynicism and reached out, gave her a small hug, then turned to go. "Tell Tory I'm sorry I missed him and wish him a happy birthday!" she called over her shoulder. "See you at Christmas!"

"I doubt it! Goodbye Cece!" Bonnie shut the door and went back inside to convalesce. Cecelia wondered if she would ever see her aunt again and suspected not. She started her car and drove down the hill and away.

****

Tory crossed the foyer of the Arroyo Tennis and Country Club with two hired security guards following. He pointed at a passing maintenance worker. "You. You're fired." Without waiting for the man's reaction he proceeded through the grand dining hall and pushed past the steel kitchen doors. Three cooks were standing idly by their stoves waiting for their pots of water to boil. "You're all fired," Tory announced. "Be sure to leave your aprons and hats in the laundry, along with your time cards." The cooks were speechless, glancing at one another to see if they'd heard correctly. Finally one of them ventured to dispute him.

"But I've been here fifteen years!" the man protested.

Tory stopped and turned to glare at him. "For that you should be grateful. Now get lost!" He looked sternly at one of the two guards and exited with the other, leaving the enforcer behind to see to his wish.

His juggernaut continued through the Clubhouse, up the marble staircase and into the administrative section housing the Club's offices. He revoked memberships at whim, selectively jabbing his finger at men and women cowering in the nooks and crannies of the building, once even poking his head into the bar where he advised a gentleman to drink up, he was off the Club's roster. "Why?!" cried the man. "You're trash," Tory replied. "And you once tossed me off the courts when I was little." En route to the Chairman's office he was able to purge two others, the member who had invited Peter Albright to the Club and an ugly woman.

The Chairman's secretary picked up her purse when Tory came through the door. "That's all for today," Tory told her. "Take the rest of your life off too." Then he barged through the large oak doors like he owned the place and told the Chairman to get out.

He sat in the dark office for the rest of the day, summoning workers from the rolls and dismissing half of them. The others he briefed on his expectations for improved performance and devotion. When the bartender acknowledged his gratitude to Tory for sparing his job Tory told him matter-of-factly that the day he poured a bad drink was the day he was unemployed. Then he gave the bartender a raise and excused him.

By six-thirty p.m. he had reviewed the staff's full rotations and presided over the revocation of fifty-some memberships. The cleansing was complete, at least for the day. Some of his actions were vindictive, some good business (especially the firing of the kitchen staff, who cooked badly). What was to become of the revered and stately Club was known only to him. "I am the Boss," he declared to an assemblage of workers allowed to stay. "What I say goes."

He closed the Arroyo a short time later, chaining the doors with heavy links and new padlocks. When he arrived home he found his mother smoking a cigarette in a chaise out by the pool. "Hi Mom."

"Hi Tory. Did you have a good birthday?"

"No. It was a bloodbath. Want to go to dinner?"

"Not looking like this, thanks anyway. By the way, Cece came by with a present for you. It's on the dining room table. Also your father called to wish you a happy birthday."

"Oh." Tory nodded and walked away. His father needn't have bothered. He had not come home for Pliny's funeral or any other reason; there was no sense pretending they had a relationship. I am alone, he thought as he entered the dining room. Frances was right.

Cecelia's package shone in the darkness, it's shiny wrapping contesting the dust and staleness of the room. Tory turned on a light and carefully freed the box from its colored paper. When he opened it he found a key and a note.

Happy Birthday Tory!
Thanks for being my buddy. The key opens Pliny's house.
Use it whenever you like, or move in if you need to, I know
your accommodations are uncertain these days.
Love, Cece

Tory pocketed the key and folded the note into a neat square. He heard his dog barking furiously outside, then the ring of the phone a few rooms away. He did not answer it but waited to see if the caller would give up or if his mother would get it. When he heard Bonnie call his name he left the dining room, shutting it away.

"I'm out in the hall Mom. Who is it?"

"The USC tennis coach."

"Okay. I'm picking it up in the kitchen."

A minute later: "Hello Coach."

"Hi Tory. Sorry to call you so late but the registration deadline is tomorrow and I wanted to know if you'd decided where you're going to school this year?"

"I'll come to 'SC if I can play first team singles."

"Absolutely."

"Good. I'm a Trojan then."

"Yes! Congratulations Tory, welcome to the University of Southern California. Can you come to Heritage Hall tomorrow to meet with the Athletic Director at eleven a.m.?"

"I'll be there. Goodbye Coach." He hung up. Everything was going according to plan.

****

The same paramedics called to extract Jim Coulter from the Wreck of the Week were also summoned by the 911 operator to the home of Joseph Vitesse the following night. When they arrived they found a middle-aged woman stuck in the thigh with a scissors, all the way to the bone, and a young woman of about eighteen screaming at the top of her lungs. Police cars arrived on the scene shortly after the Paramedics but there were no arrests; the matter was handled as delicately as possible with appropriate denial. A private ambulance drew up to the house to take the injured woman to the hospital and another drove up to attend to the maniacal girl, who was soon wrapped up in a straightjacket and dispatched to the Patton State Hospital for the Criminally Insane.

Margo sobbed hysterically, fighting hard against her restraints. Her chest ached from constriction, her arms were numb from the straps that pinned them to herself and the gurney. She lay on her back heaving and bubbling snot, wondering what she was doing in the back of an ambulance.

She could see the yellow glow of freeway halogen lamps splay across the sky through the back windows; all else was dark night and freeway bridges. Traffic hissed around all sides. She was afraid and alone, kidnapped by men in white who were taking her away from her home; if she could see more of the passing landscape she could plan an escape! Navigate her way home! She stopped struggling and concentrated. Portions of freeway signs, a giant panda balloon floating next to the top of a blue sign…it was not enough. And then she recognized something, a huge glowing red butterfly-shaped sign, twisting on its standard…the ambulance drove past and the sign turned its beacon towards her.

"Yes! That's it!" The words to the song came easily and she swallowed the bolus of mucous in her throat and began to sing: "John Jacob Astor, shoulda spent it faster 'cause he ended up in the drink! Hail, hail, everybody bail! The ship is sinking and we're all thinking just one more dance before we go! Just one more dance before we go…"

She sang and sang and kept her eyes on the twisting sign as long as she could, until the ambulance was past. And Margo lay confined to the gurney in the rear of the van, singing Cecelia's song all the way to the insane asylum while the sign stayed where it was, turning back and forth in the night, advertising beer.

The End.